ANGEL OF DARKNESS

1953. Anna Fehrbach, now happily married, is enjoying her Bahamian hideaway. It's been three years since the Russians last attempted to arrest her for her attempt on the life of Joseph Stalin, and she's beginning to believe that her arch-enemy, Lavrenty Beria, has abandoned the chase. But when Anna is lured into 'one last job' for the CIA, she is plunged back into the Russian orbit...

ANGEL OF DARKNESS

An Anna Fehrbach Thriller

Christopher Nicole

Severn House Large Print
London & New York

This first large print edition published 2012
in Great Britain and the USA by
SEVERN HOUSE PUBLISHERS LTD of
9-15 High Street, Sutton, Surrey, SM1 1DF.
First world regular print edition published 2009 by
Severn House Publishers Ltd., London and New York.

British Library Cataloguing in Publication Data

Nicole, Christopher.
  Angel of darkness. -- (An Anna Fehrbach thriller)
  1. Fehrbach, Anna (Fictitious character)--Fiction.
  2. Women spies--Fiction. 3. United States. Central
  Intelligence Agency--Fiction. 4. Suspense fiction.
  5. Large type books.
  I. Title II. Series
  823.9'14-dc23

  ISBN-13: 978-0-7278-9930-9

Severn House Publishers support The Forest Stewardship Council
[FSC], the leading international forest certification organisation. All
our titles that are printed on Greenpeace-approved FSC-certified paper
carry the FSC logo.

MIX
Paper from
responsible sources
FSC
www.fsc.org   FSC® C018575

Printed and bound in Great Britain by the
MPG Books Group, Bodmin, Cornwall.

So the darkness shall be the light and the stillness the dancing.

T. S. Eliot

PROLOGUE

'On a day like today,' Anna said, 'It is good to be alive.'

We lay together on two sun beds, shaded by enormous beach umbrellas, listening to the soughing of the wind in the pine trees higher up the slopes of Montgo, the mountain that over-looks the resort town of Javea, on the Costa Blanca. Anna Bartley, née Fehrbach, once in-famous as the Countess von Widerstand, the most feared woman in the world, loved to feel the breeze caressing her naked body, although she took great care to protect her skin from excessive sun. Even at the age of eighty-nine, it retained much of the creamy texture of her youth; any freckles, and there were a few, had been the result of the exigencies of her pro-fessional life, now long behind her.

That a matriarch of so great an age should still enjoy displaying herself, if only in carefully selected company, might have struck some as distasteful, perhaps even obscene. But words such as taste or obscenity were puerile where Anna Fehrbach was concerned. In her youth she had been called the most beautiful – as well as the most deadly – woman in the world. Her

7

beauty, indeed, had always been one of her most formidable weapons, filling just as important a part in her armoury as her lightning speed of thought and reaction, her unerring accuracy with a pistol or a knife, the amazing power that could be projected through those slender arms, those exquisite hands. Too many men, and women, had hesitated for just a moment when confronted by such a vision – and to hesitate for just a moment when confronted by Anna Fehrbach was to die, if that was her purpose.

And age, accompanied by years of constant exercise and careful diet, had done no more than nibble at the superb whole. True, her hair was now white and cut short, whereas once it had seemed a shawl of golden silk that brushed her thighs. But the flawless, slightly aquiline bone structure of her face was unchanged, even if the skin was perhaps nowadays a little taut and there were crows' feet at the corners of her eyes. But those eyes, so blue, so deep, so utterly compelling, whether smiling or – even more compellingly – turned, as they could so suddenly be, into the coldest of sapphires, had, I surmised, changed not a jot, despite all the traumatic events on which they had looked over the years.

As for her figure, Anna was five foot eleven inches tall – certainly in her heyday, in the 1940s, a considerable height for a woman. Always carefully slender – with legs to die for, as so many had, and breasts on which to rest

8

one's head was to enter paradise – her body remained as compelling as it had ever been, with hardly a sag to be discerned. I had never enjoyed that paradise, had indeed only felt it against me during the odd embrace. And yet I lay here, naked beside her, content to look at her and listen to that soft, caressing voice, which, like her eyes, could so suddenly turn to steel. There was no way I was ever going to risk offending Anna.

That I should be with her at all still retained the quality of a dream. It had begun as a job of work, a personal quest for something that had for so long been so tantalizingly just beyond my grasp. I had come across her name while researching a book on the German secret services during the Hitler war. Even in memoirs published some years after 1945, the references to her had been nebulous, written almost in fear, because no one knew for sure if she had died, as she was supposed to have done, in the collapse of the Third Reich. Or, indeed, whether she had actually ever lived at all, or had just been a shadowy phantom conjured up by Heinrich Himmler and his demonic henchman Reinhard Heydrich and enhanced by Josef Goebbels' propaganda machine. Or if she was actually alive, still treading the path of deadly vengeance.

And I had rapidly discovered that she had certainly existed. There had been a reference to her marriage in 1938 – on Himmler's orders – to the British diplomat, Ballantine Bordman.

9

The wedding had taken place in Germany and any trace of it had vanished, along with so many town hall records destroyed by Allied bombing. Their marriage had also been a short-lived affair, before the fact that she was a German spy had been discovered and she was forced to flee England to avoid arrest. But, accepting that it had happened, hunting through back issues of glossy magazines for 1938 and 1939, I had come across a copy of The Tatler, featuring photographs of various celebrities attending the Cheltenham Festival. And there was one of the Honourable Ballantine Bordman accompanied by his 'beautiful new wife', chatting with a couple of other racing enthusiasts. The print was, of course, very old. Also, the photograph had been taken from a distance, in black and white, and Anna had been half turned away from the camera. Yet the image was unforgettable – the tall slender body, the long straight golden hair dropping down her back from beneath the sable hat, the sable coat that had been her stock in trade, the endlessly promising ankles, the classic profile.

Thus armed, and aware that after seventy years the photo might be meaningless, I had begun my quest and pursued it in almost every moment I could spare from earning a living. And at last my search had brought me to this lonely villa perched high on the slopes of Montgo, with magnificent views of the Jalon Valley to my right, and of Javea and the

Mediterranean in front of me.

When I pressed the bell on the wrought-iron gates, I had known that I could well be taking my life in my hands. For by the time I arrived at those gates I had pieced together sufficient of Anna's background to know that she had been, and no doubt still was, the most highly trained and lethal assassin who had ever walked this earth. The SS had come across this remarkable seventeen-year-old schoolgirl, half-Austrian and half-Irish (she still spoke English with a soft brogue) when Nazi Germany invaded Austria in March 1938 – and their senior officers had immediately recognized that if such an unusual talent could be harnessed and put to use, the benefits for her employers would be potentially enormous. Apart from her looks, which were already striking, she had been head girl at her convent, was a superb athlete, and possessed an IQ of 173.

That she had also been utterly innocent had been irrelevant; they had soon changed that. The Schutzstaffel themselves did not employ women agents, but they had presented her to their senior and even more sinister organization, the SD, the Sicherheitsdienst, the most secret inner circle of all the many secret circles that composed the Third Reich. The SD had converted her – or so they supposed – into an amoral killer whose loyalty had been secured by the simple expedient of arresting her parents and her sister, placing them in secure but not too rigorous captivity and making her under-

stand that as long as she served the Reich faithfully and well she and they would survive, and even prosper; if she did not, or failed in her various assignments, then they would perish most miserably.

Anna told me of the utter horror with which she had contemplated her fate. But the SD, with typical Nazi insensitivity, entirely failed to understand the nature of the beast they had captured and thought they now controlled. It never occurred to them that a brain as acute as Anna's, allied to such physical assets, would necessarily operate at its own level, far beyond the reach, or indeed the comprehension, of ordinary humans. All they had actually done was to create a monster of destruction, whose prime aim was their own destruction, provided it could be accomplished without endangering her family. Anna's three prime characteristics – and perhaps her greatest strengths apart from her physical abilities – had been an unwavering, almost careless, courage and determination, a deadly patience that enabled her to wait and endure anything to achieve her goal, and an equally unwavering pragmatism that allowed her to employ any and all means, regardless of moral or ethical considerations, to carry her to that goal.

Thus, within a year of going to work for the SD she had defected to MI6 and become a double agent, without arousing the slightest suspicion in her masters. And only two years later, while rising to become Himmler's most

12

trusted associate and Adolf Hitler's occasional mistress, she was also working for the OSS, the predecessor of the CIA, to carve a bloodstained swathe across three continents. But, unlike Cardinal Richelieu on his death bed, she could not say for certain that she no longer had any enemies because she had killed them all. Anna's enemies were legion, many of them people she had never laid eyes on, employed by those with long memories. Particularly in Moscow, where again nothing had been known of her true activities and the salient fact was that, acting for the SD and in her own defence, she had once attempted the life of Josef Stalin and since disposed of a considerable number of NKVD agents, so that she was regarded as the greatest of the war criminals who had somehow managed to slip through the net of Allied vengeance. She could claim that in all probability she had outlived them all; but she couldn't even be certain of that, and so even in this remote hideaway she regarded humanity with suspicion and was prepared to confront any sinister intruder with consummate force, as evidenced by the little pistol that lay on the table beside her, and literally never left her side – for when she was dressed, she wore it next to her skin.

Beside the gun, on the table, there waited her jewellery – a perpetual reminder of her overwhelming femininity – which she also put on whenever she got dressed. It was dominated by small gold bar earrings, attached by clips, for she had never had her ears pierced, and the huge ruby solitaire that she wore on the fore-finger of her right hand. Oddly, although I knew that she had been married twice, she no longer wore a wedding ring. This jewellery had been part of her equipment as an SD agent – so, strictly, was on loan from her employers – and she would reflect with a girlish glee that her erstwhile masters were now all dead ... but she still had the jewellery.

The gold chain with a crucifix suspended from it, nestling between her breasts, never left her neck, and was a reminder of her Catholic youth and upbringing, just as the gold Rolex on her left wrist was indicative of her present wealth.

But, offsetting these splendours, there was the blue stain that remained on her so-white skin, over her lower right rib cage, still reminding her, after seventy years, how close Hannah Gehrig's bullet had brought her to death, and indeed of the ever-present dangers that had always accompanied her profession.

And yet, despite all these memories of past glories and perhaps present dangers, I had been welcomed. This was partly because it had taken her only a few minutes to evaluate me as what I was – a writer who had not the slightest firsthand acquaintance with any of the events of her youth (which in any event had happened before he was born) and who was also deeply in love with the image he had created of her in his mind ... and who was prepared to be equally in love with the reality. And Anna was, above all else, a woman.

Besides, for all her continued remarkable health, she had been aware that the days were drawing in. However shadowy her role, she had played an important part in some enormous historical events. The thought of disappearing for ever and leaving not the slightest trace behind her, or being viewed as just a shadow, an illusion, a might-have-been, had been becoming almost an obsession. And here was a writer suddenly appearing, desperate to tell her story.

Out of that first meeting had grown this remarkable intimacy, this admission of me into the embracing warmth of a unique personality, whether one looked on her as a monster or, as she preferred to picture herself, as an outstanding fighter pilot who had been scrambled into action on numerous occasions and had always destroyed her adversary. As she would point out, with a twinkle in her eye, had she been flying for the RAF in the War and had been able to paint more than a hundred enemy kills on the fuselage of her aircraft, she would no doubt have been awarded the Victoria Cross.

But now her tale was surely told – except for the ending. So I asked her, 'After the hurricane, and the destruction of the Mafiosi hired to finish you off, did it all seem sort of flat?'

Anna glanced at me. 'Flat? I was about to be married.'

'Of course. That was unforgivable of me.'

She blew me a kiss. 'I know. Things like marriage sort of get lost in the vortex of my life.'

'But you did get married. And I assume lived

15

happily ever after, as in all the best fairy tales?'

She brooded on this suggestion. 'Have you ever known a fairy tale that bore the slightest resemblance to reality?'

'Oh, my God! Don't tell me...'

'Clive and I were very happy together,' she said carefully. 'After all, we had been lovers for a long time, through the entire War, whenever we could get together. But there were problems. We were both still working. Oh, he managed to spend as much time as possible with me, but MI6 still had a job for him to do and he was very loyal to them ... at least, as long as they allowed him to be. He also felt that as one of their senior operatives he could protect his wife from any adverse reaction to my continued existence on the part of the ever-changing British governments, veering as they did wildly between left and right. This was important at the time because I had to remain committed to the CIA, at least for a while. Quite apart from the interest Moscow had in me. But of course, his protection counted for nothing when the chips really went down.'

'But I don't understand how Moscow could still hope to find you. When that boat sank, Beria lost all trace of you, didn't he?'

'Lavrenty Beria,' Anna said, 'never lost all trace of anyone. And that went for his boss, Josef Stalin, as well. Those two gentlemen hated me more than the rest of the world put together. At least...' She brooded again.

'But still, after that boat was destroyed, with

16

everyone on board, they had no idea where you were, surely?'

'They knew I used the Bahamas. But you know, they still would never have found me. Until I did a very silly thing.'

'You, Anna? I find that hard to believe.'

Anna actually blushed. 'I was careless. Really, for the first time in my life. I had just completed an exhausting and, as it turned out, highly dangerous assignment.'

'Weren't all your assignments highly dangerous?'

She made one of her enchanting moues. 'This was more so than usual. So, as I said, I was exhausted, and feeling the delicious relaxation of being nearly home. And there were, well, circumstances. I will tell you of them. The important thing is that I failed to take a potential enemy seriously. In fact, I was attracted to him. Never seriously, and in fact with some suspicion, but as it turned out not enough. It was the very last time in my life that I allowed myself to be attracted to any man save my husband.' She reached across to squeeze my hand, an unforgettable gesture. 'Until you, Christopher.'

'And this person...?'

'Well, I am still alive. Although it was the nearest damn thing in my life,' she added as an afterthought.

'And Beria and Stalin are both dead. Tell me, did you actually ever meet Beria?'

Anna Fehrbach smiled.

THE ENCOUNTER

Mark Hamilton thought there could be no more pleasant way to spend an hour before lunch than to sit on the terrace of the Royal Victoria Hotel in Nassau, sipping a Planter's Punch, enjoying the breeze that alleviated the heat and savouring the view over the famous gardens surrounding the swimming pool nestling beneath the swaying trees – which was currently filled with young people, several of them extremely attractive girls – and then out past the gardens and the ancient prison (now the library) to the scintillating blue waters of the harbour, beyond Bay Street, and the docks at the foot of the hill. His relaxed mood was only occasionally distracted, but enjoyably so, by the arrival of a taxi in the forecourt immediately beneath him, discharging happy tourists, come to enjoy the luxury and freedom of the Bahamas. February was the height of the tourist season

It was difficult to reconcile this ambience with work. But it was even more difficult to accept that he *was* working, and that this assignment was about to come to an end. After three months, his employers had concluded that

18

his mission had been a failure.

Actually, they had themselves warned him that the assignment might take time, because the one thing he must not do was act hastily or be obvious. Too many people had made that mistake over the past dozen years, and none of them were still around. His brief was to observe, locate and inform. Nothing more. Certainly he must not ask any questions or reveal any interest in his quarry until she had wandered into his sights. But neither they nor he had supposed the assignment could take three months, with still no result.

He had been told that everyone who was anyone in the Bahamas eventually turned up at the Royal Victoria Hotel, whether to stay or for lunch in such delightful surroundings, or for the starlit dinner dances out here on the terrace, or merely for a drink on a hot day. Thus he had taken up residence and spent an hour or two every day with various real estate agents, looking at property, apparently without yet finding exactly what he wanted. He could do nothing more than this, because his employers did not know what name she was currently using; they were only certain that it would not be Fehrbach.

Three months, with nothing to show for it. So now the plug was being pulled. The Royal Vic was not exactly a cheap establishment. But he felt quite cheated. He had been told so much about her, thought so much about her, wondered so often if she could possibly be as beautiful or as deadly as they had described her...

He watched another taxi draw up at the foot of the steps, still idly, and then slowly sat up, the hair on the nape of his neck prickling, as the back door opened and the passenger got out. He looked first of all at high-heeled sandals on exquisitely shaped bare feet, then at the longest and most perfectly formed legs he had ever seen, exposed for a moment before she completed her exit and straightened her knee-length skirt. It belonged to a pink summer frock, with a flaring hem immediately seized and fluttered by the breeze.

The bodice was full, the décolletage modest, but it granted a tantalizing glimpse of curving white flesh. The short sleeves revealed slender arms and hands with long fingers and pink painted nails, as she pulled off her white gloves to open her somewhat large shoulder bag in order to pay the driver. Then the face. This was shaded by a broad-brimmed straw hat with pink ribbon, which she was holding on her head with her left hand. As she turned away from him, her face was hidden – but the turn exposed her hair, a sheet of long golden silk, partially restrained by a tortoiseshell clasp at the nape of her neck, cascading down her back to nestle against her thighs.

Hamilton felt quite sick. His heart pounded almost uncontrollably. After three months! And she was everything he had been told, everything he had dreamed. Here! And intending to stay, although she had only a small valise as luggage. The doorman had hurried down the steps to take it from the driver, and was greeting her as an old friend.

They came up the steps together, and now he could see her face. Another sharp intake of breath: the slightly aquiline features were flawlessly carved. He found himself hating the huge sunglasses that had obscured her eyes, though she took them off on entering the shade. Then she disappeared into the doorway on Hamilton's left. He found that he was panting. His every instinct was to hurry into the lobby and see her at close quarters. But that would be crazy, and could even be fatal. Find, identify, and establish location. Those were his orders.

He finished his drink, and a waiter hurried forward. 'Another, sir?'

Hamilton ostentatiously looked at his watch. 'No. I need to freshen up before lunch.' He got up, strolled into the lobby, moving with studied carelessness, and approached the reception desk, where the maître d' was talking with the clerk. He had come to know them quite well over the preceding three months. The woman had disappeared into the elevator, but the faint tang of her perfume lingered; something of a connoisseur in these matters, he reckoned it was 'Adoration'.

The maître d' looked up as he reached the desk. 'Good morning, Mr Hamilton. You with us for lunch?'

'Could I possibly lunch anywhere else, Charles? May I ask you a question?'

'Of course, sir.'

'That lady who was just here. Was she checking in?'

'Mrs Bartley? Oh, indeed, sir. She is probably our most regular customer.'

'Is she? How interesting. Mrs Bartley. Therefore I assume that there is a Mr Bartley?'

'Oh, indeed, sir.'

'But he is not here.'

'No, sir. Mr and Mrs Bartley seldom travel together.'

'I see. But you say that Mrs Bartley is a regular customer. As a tourist, or does she have business interests in Nassau?'

'No, no, sir. I do not think she has any business interests in the Bahamas. She lives here.'

'She lives in Nassau?' He couldn't believe his ears, that he had spent three months here and not encountered her.

'No, no, sir. She lives on her island.'

'An island? You said "her island". You mean, she owns an island?'

'Yes, sir.'

'Good lord! She must be very wealthy.'

'I believe she is, sir, yes.'

'You must forgive me asking these questions, Charles. It's just that I have a feeling I have met her before.'

'She is a most striking lady, sir,' Charles replied.

'This island ... is it far?'

'Not very, sir.'

'And presumably there is a ferry, or some form of public transport. I mean, how does she come and go?'

'There is no public transport, sir. Mrs Bartley is a very private person. When she has been away, she stays here until she is picked up by her boat.'

'You mean she has her own boat as well as her own island?'

'Well, of course, sir. You can't live on an island without having a boat.'

'I'm afraid I have never owned an island. I suppose it has a name? This island?'

'Indeed, sir.'

'And?'

Charles looked embarrassed. 'I think you should ask Mrs Bartley that, sir. As I said, she is a very private person. But if you are an old acquaintance of hers, I am sure she'd be happy to meet you again.'

'I shouldn't think she remembers me, as I am not the least striking.'

'Well, sir,' Charles said, deprecatingly. Hamilton was in fact quite a striking man – tall, his substantial physique enhanced by the open-necked flowered sports shirt and hip-hugging white pants that went so well with his untidy but handsome features and wavy dark hair.

'But you say she's here for the night?'

'Actually, sir, she's here for two nights. I believe she's being joined by a friend this evening.'

'I see. Thank you, Charles, you've been very helpful.'

'Would you like me to mention to Mrs Bartley

that you may be an old friend, sir?'

'Ah ... no, thank you, Charles. If I have an opportunity, I may do so myself.'

Meeting a friend, he thought, as he went up to his room. But not her husband. It all fitted with what he had been told: that in addition to her looks and her many and lethal skills, Anna Fehrbach was also a consummate lover, of both men and women, as the mood or the necessity arose. Could it be possible that her mood might encompass him, even if only briefly? And as he had not yet found out where this island home of hers was situated, he would have to approach her, sometime over today or tomorrow. Legitimately, as far as she could possibly know. He realized that he was desperately excited.

The bellhop placed the valise on the rack. 'Thank you, William,' Anna said, tipping him, then closed the bedroom door behind him. She threw her hat on to a chair, dropped her shoulder bag beside it, kicked off her shoes, and took off her somewhat crumpled dress; she had been wearing it for thirty-six hours now. Her only underclothes were her knickers – she never used a brassière, with her muscular development there was no need – and these she also removed, along with the slender gun belt in which was holstered the .22 Walther PPK automatic pistol. Then she threw herself on the bed, on her stomach, her body nestling sensually on the cool sheets, her chin resting on her hands. She was nearly home!

As always when returning from an assignment, her emotions were a jumbled kaleidoscope. Relief that it was over, certainly. Exhilaration that she should have survived yet another close brush with death. But equally, the inevitable twinge of guilt she always felt after taking life, no matter how often she had done it, and how much she knew her victims deserved it; the count was now a hundred and thirty-three (if she had not killed them all personally, she was undoubtedly responsible for their deaths). Plus anxiety – a constant going over in her mind to reassure herself that she had made no mistake, that she had both carried out the operation and covered her tracks with her invariable attention to detail. Indeed, that was the only reason she was still alive herself. She had carried out so many of these assignments successfully that her confidence on going in was always of the highest. And yet, because – despite the opinion held by a great many people – she was a human being, the conclusion of each operation was always accompanied by this inevitable reaction.

And today the reaction was greater than ever before – because, although she was only three hours away from the sanctuary of the cay, there was something she had to do before she got there. Tonight, perhaps. And it promised to be no less traumatic than what had gone before.

The telephone rang. Anna raised her head, stretched out her arm and picked it up. 'Yes?'

'I'm sorry to bother you, ma'am.'

'Charles! Of course you didn't bother me, Charles. Is there a problem?' She spoke English with the faint Irish brogue she had inherited from her mother.

'I don't know, Mrs Bartley. But I thought you would like to know that there is a gentleman asking after you.'

Anna drew a long, slow breath, while the tension flooded her muscles. Joe? He really must be agitated; he wasn't due until tonight. She had hoped to have a rest before having to face him.

But if it wasn't Joe...? Nassau, the Bahamas, the cay, had always been her ultimate refuge. The cay had only once been invaded, three years before, by a Mafia 'family' acting for the Russian MGB. That had cost twenty-two lives – which had very nearly included her own. But for the past three years there had been no other unwanted intruders, so she had almost come to believe that the Kremlin had at last given up their quest for the woman who had once attempted to take the life of Josef Stalin, and, perhaps even more heinously, become the only person ever to escape from the Lubianka Prison, leaving behind her a trail of blood.

'This gentleman,' she said, 'you're quite sure that he is a gentleman?'

'Oh, yes, ma'am. He is a resident in the hotel. He's been here for three months.'

'Three *months*? Good lord! You mean he's not a tourist?'

'I wouldn't say so, ma'am. I think he's in real

26

estate. He spends a lot of time looking at property. But he doesn't seem to have found what he wants yet.'

'If he has been living in the hotel for three months, he must be fairly well heeled.'

'Oh, indeed, ma'am. When he arrived he asked for his bill to be presented every week. And it is paid, every week.'

'Hmm. I assume this paragon has a name?'

'Yes, ma'am. Hamilton. Mark Hamilton.'

'English or American?'

'Definitely English, ma'am.'

'And this is the first time he has asked after me?'

'Well, ma'am, this is the first time you have been to see us since he was here.' His tone was faintly reproachful. 'I think he must have seen you coming in, just now, and he asked who you were.'

'You said he claimed an acquaintance with me?'

'Yes, ma'am. That is what he said.'

'And he didn't know my name?'

'No, ma'am.'

'But he knew my face?'

'Well, he didn't seem sure about that, either. He just said that you looked familiar, like someone he had once met, and wanted to know who you were. He thought maybe you were a visitor, like him.'

'And you told him...?'

'That you were a Bahamian resident.'

'And you also told him where I lived?'

27

'Oh, no, ma'am. I wouldn't do that.'

'You are a treasure, Charles. But didn't he ask?'

'Yes, ma'am. He asked if you lived here in Nassau, and I told him no, you lived on one of the Out Islands.'

'And he asked which one?'

'Yes, ma'am, But I told him I felt he should ask you that.'

'Thank you, Charles.'

'Did I do wrong, ma'am?'

'Of course you did not. You were asked a question, and you answered it as discreetly as you could. Do you think this Mr Hamilton will be lunching in today?'

'Oh, yes, ma'am. He lunches here every day.'

'Perhaps, when I come down, you could point him out to me. His face may be familiar.'

'Of course I will, ma'am.'

'Discreetly, Charles.'

'Oh, yes, ma'am. I'll certainly be discreet!'

Anna hung up, sat up, and considered. Having been travelling for the past forty-eight hours, she felt desperately in need of a bath and had intended to have one before lunch. But there wasn't time, if she was going to catch this character for the meal. And equally, as always in times of potential crisis, the adrenalin was flowing. The only problem was that, although MI6 had given her the right to defend herself, she still regarded it as important to keep a low profile in the Bahamas, which meant not

28

making headlines or ever getting into trouble with the law. That business three years ago could have been disastrous, but for that fortuitous hurricane which wiped out all trace of the gun battle and conveniently removed the corpses, at least from her vicinity. That was not likely to happen again.

But why should it have to happen again? This man had done nothing more suspicious than enquire about a possibly familiar face. Or, more likely, reveal an interest in a beautiful woman; the 'possible acquaintance' ploy was the oldest trick in the game. Anna had no false modesty about her looks; they had in fact, over the years, proved as valuable assets as any of her lethal skills. But he would have to be sorted out, immediately. Hopefully without a fuss.

She got up, pulled on her knickers, and considered the gun belt. The gun could be reached by a zipped side panel in her dresses. Its one drawback was that it only had a five-shot magazine. Not that she normally needed more than one bullet to destroy any immediate enemy; but in any event, designed to fit equally snugly into her left groin, there was another holster containing a spare magazine. As she had just disposed of four opponents together with a rather vicious bystander, this was now empty.

But, even though she was about to encounter a possible adversary, as she could not see herself ever needing the pistol in the civilized ambience of the Royal Vic, surrounded by staff who all knew her and who she counted her friends, she packed the belt away in her shoulder bag. Then she sat at the dressing table and applied make-up and some fresh perfume before putting her dress back on – she had intended to send it to the hotel laundry before wearing it again, but that also would have to wait – and her shoes. Then she brushed her hair, before adding her jewellery. She had not worn this for her recent assignment, save for the gold crucifix that never left her neck (the other pieces always travelled with her, in her shoulder bag). And now she was home, virtually. She clipped the tiny gold bar earrings in place, slipped the huge ruby solitaire on to the forefinger of her right hand, then unstrapped the cheap watch she wore for business travel and replaced it with her solid gold Junghans, before adding her platinum wedding band. Then she surveyed herself in the mirror.

Satisfied, she went downstairs, and was shown immediately to her table by Charles, who knew she always wished to be placed at the edge of the room with her back to a blank wall (where or why she had developed this idiosyncrasy he had no idea). Then, as she seated herself and he handed her the menus and unfolded her napkin to lay it across her lap, he whispered, 'The gentleman is exactly opposite you, ma'am. The fourth table.'

'Thank you, Charles.' Anna did not look up. 'I will have the avocado, the fillet – medium, with carrots and beans – and a bottle of Batailley.'

'Of course, ma'am.' His favourite diner seldom varied her luncheon choice of either food or wine.

Anna closed the menus and surveyed the room. Mark Hamilton had been gazing at her, and now he hastily looked away. Perhaps he only wished to identify her. But she had to discover exactly what he was about. As she had started her meal a course behind him, she kept a careful eye on his table, and had just reached her coconut ice cream when he ordered coffee,

Charles was hovering, and hurried forward as she raised her finger. 'Charles,' she said, slightly raising her voice, 'would you invite Mr Hamilton to have coffee with me, in the lounge. Or perhaps he would like a glass of wine first.'

'Of course, ma'am.' Charles hurried across the room, and she watched Hamilton start and turn towards her. She raised her glass to him. Even from a distance she could see that he was utterly taken aback by her unexpected advance. Then he came towards her.

'Mrs Bartley.'

'Mr Hamilton. I am just finishing my dessert. But sit down, please.'

Charles provided a chair from the next table.

'And a glass, please, Charles. You'll take some wine, Mr Hamilton? It's my favourite claret – not *grand cru*, but it tastes like liquid velvet.'

'I...'

Charles poured, and left.

'Well,' Hamilton said, eyeing her rings and watch. 'Thank you very much.' He sipped. 'Exquisite. But your glass is empty.' He reached for the bottle.

Anna finished her ice cream. 'My dear Mr Hamilton, one cannot possibly drink claret after eating ice cream.'

'Oh. Ah. Of course.' He replaced the bottle in embarrassment.

'I am told we're old acquaintances,' said Anna. 'I'm afraid I will have to beg your forgiveness, but I do not recall ever having met you.'

'I don't blame you. It was a long time ago. At a cocktail party in London.'

Anna raised her eyebrows.

'When you were the Honourable Mrs Bordman,' he added.

Alarm bells immediately began to jangle in Anna's brain: this definitely needed sorting out, immediately. But her expression never changed, beyond mild interest. 'My dear Mr Hamilton, that was all but fourteen years ago.'

'As I said, it was a long time. 1939.'

'And you have remembered me for fourteen years? After one meeting? We *did* meet? Where?'

'Yes, we did. At Lady Pennworthy's. And I ... ah ... well ... you were the most beautiful woman I had ever seen. Or have ever seen. You are still the most beautiful woman I have ever seen.'

Anna considered. Unlike just about every other man she had known who had paid her such an extravagant compliment, there had

32

been no change in his colouring, not the slightest trace of embarrassment at being so fulsome. He was either a consummate and experienced woman-chaser, or the speech had been carefully rehearsed. She smiled at him. 'You say the sweetest things. Shall we have coffee?'

She rose and led the way into the lounge, sat in a leather armchair. The tray of coffee was immediately placed on the low table in front of her. Hamilton sat opposite. 'Brandy?' she asked.

'Ah...'

'Or perhaps you have a business meeting this afternoon? I am going to bed. I have had a long and exhausting trip to get here.'

'I'd love a brandy.'

'Two Hine Antique, Charles.'

'Yes, ma'am.' He hurried off.

'That fellow seems to be very fond of you,' Hamilton remarked.

'We've known each other a long time.'

'You mean, you have lived in the Bahamas a long time?'

'Is there anywhere else to live?' She leaned forward. 'Black or white?'

'Oh, black, please.'

'And sugar?'

'Three lumps.'

Anna served. 'I can see that you are a connoisseur. Of coffee,' she added.

'What makes you say that?'

'Simply that you know how to drink it. What do the Brazilians say? Coffee should be as

33

black as night, as hot as hell, and as sweet as sin. And they should know, as they grow it. Thank you, Charles.'

The brandies were placed before them, and she raised her glass. 'Your good health.' She leaned back and crossed her knees, to his obvious gratification. 'So, you're in real estate.'

'You seem to know a great deal about me.'

'I always like to know something about people I have known in my past.'

'And I know so little about you.'

'Oh, please, Mr Hamilton. If there is one thing that puts me off people, it is prevarication. You wouldn't want to put me off you, would you?'

Now he did flush. 'I...'

'If you know that I was once married to Ballantine Bordman then you will know that I found it convenient to leave England in a hurry in April 1940. It was, as I recall, a considerable scandal.'

'Well, I...'

'I left England hours before being arrested by Special Branch, as a German spy.'

He finished his brandy. 'You can say that, so calmly?'

'It happened. So why not tell me what you are really doing here?'

He had regained control of himself. 'As you appear to know, I am looking for real estate which might interest the firm I represent.'

She sipped coffee while she studied him. 'Is that the truth?'

34

'I am not accustomed to lying,' he said with dignity. 'I must apologize for just now. I could not believe my eyes when I saw you. Even after fourteen years. And to see that you had not changed at all! You could still be eighteen years old. Of course I knew about the scandal. But I didn't know, nobody knew, how it had turned out. And to see you here, in a British colony ... I mean, aren't you wanted by the police? As a war criminal or something?'

He seemed genuinely upset. 'Not any more,' she said. 'I was able to do the British Government a favour...' More like two dozen favours, she reflected. 'And they agreed to drop all charges against me.'

'You mean you turned State's evidence?'

'That sounds so condemnatory. I helped them bring down the Nazi regime.' Mainly, she thought, by killing as many of them as possible ... including the arch-demon, Reinhard Heydrich. 'Would you like another brandy?'

'I would. But I don't think it would be a good idea. So, you married a wealthy man and retired into private life?'

'That is one way of putting it.'

'With your own private island?'

'They call them cays around here. But the accent is on the word private. I would hate to have that privacy interrupted by some ambitious reporter or journalist in search of a reputation-making story, which by definition would also have to be a reputation-destroying story.'

'And your husband would like it even less, I

suppose. I am assuming he knows about your past.'

'Yes, he does, and yes, he would. And he is a very large and violent man.' Which was a bit rough on poor Clive – who, having been an MI6 field agent for so much of his life, was just as capable of extreme and sometimes lethal violence as herself (although he would never claim to be quite in her class), but who was also, in his private life, the soul of good manners and polite behaviour. Which was all she had ever wanted to be, she thought sadly.

'Well, don't look at me,' Hamilton protested. 'I was just overwhelmed to see you again. I would never dream of revealing your secret to anyone.'

'Thank you, Mr Hamilton. I truly appreciate that.'

'On two conditions.'

She raised her eyebrows.

'One is that you call me Mark.'

'Mark. I like that. Very well, Mark. And the other?'

'That you have dinner with me tonight, and perhaps show me some of the night life here in Nassau.'

'I would love to do that, Mark. But I'm afraid I can't.'

His turn to raise his eyebrows.

'I have a previous engagement for dinner tonight. One which I'm afraid cannot be broken. It is a business matter.'

'Oh!' He looked quite upset.

Anna smiled. 'But I should be free tomorrow.'

'I got the impression that you were on your way back to your island. Cay.'

'I am. But the cay will still be there in twenty-four hours.' She finished her brandy and stood up. 'Now I'm off to have my siesta; I need to be on the ball tonight. We'll do something together tomorrow night, I promise.'

THE LAST ASSIGNMENT

Anna went upstairs, poured herself the bath she had wanted all day, while she undressed, and rang down for the laundry maid. Was she any further ahead?

There was a lot about Hamilton that was suspicious. And yet he could have been telling the truth. She did recall attending a cocktail party at Lady Pennworthy's in 1939. But as there had been no one there of the slightest interest to her – professionally, that is, as a possible provider of information for Heydrich – her recollection was of colossal boredom.

The problem was, she *wanted* him to be telling the truth. It was a long time since she had encountered so attractive a man. Perhaps never. Indeed, she recalled that her initial reaction to Clive had been distinctly hostile – because he, as an MI6 agent who had instinctively sensed an enemy, had projected considerable hostility towards her, as he desperately tried to prevent her seducing his immediate charge, the Honourable Ballantine Bordman.

Her bath was ready just as the laundry maid arrived. Anna turned off the taps, wrapped herself in a hotel dressing gown, handed over the dress, and was promised that it would be returned by six. She closed and locked the door, took off the dressing gown and her jewellery, and sank into the water with a sigh of pleasure. She leaned back with her eyes closed, then soaped herself, slowly and luxuriously.

Clive had failed to achieve his objective. After all, she had been acting on Heydrich's orders. But the initial hostility had grown as Clive had, even more desperately, tried to prevent Bordman from committing the ultimate folly of marrying her. At the time, she would have been more than happy had he succeeded; marriage to that fat over-sexed slob had been the last thing she wished to experience. But, having been lured to her bed and in the throes of passion given her the information she had been told to obtain, Bordman had discovered that she was a virgin – the reason she had been selected for the assignment – and had insisted on acting the gentleman and proposing marriage. He had, in any event, fallen madly in love, if not with her, then certainly with her body and her SS-taught sexual capabilities. She was appalled. But Heydrich and his boss, Himmler, had been over the moon. If they had hoped that she could cause him to be indiscreet about his mission, as he had, they had never anticipated such a bonanza. Bordman had been not only a high-ranking diplomat but a prominent member of the British establishment. To have their tame agent installed at the very heart of that community, rubbing shoulders with all the top people in the land, had been beyond their wildest dreams.

Clive, as he later confessed, had been no less appalled, from the other side of the fence. He had tried to have her arrested on her arrival in England, and then to have her placed under round-the-clock surveillance. He had failed. The SD had given her a spurious title, Countess von Widerstand, a ridiculous choice because *Widerstand* means resistance, but her apparently aristocratic background had been painted in with meticulous and unarguable detail; and now, in addition, she was married into the British aristocracy.

Thus all his efforts to bring her down had been in vain, until that March day in 1939 when, as she was paying a private visit to Berlin, she had taken with her, in her handbag, the microfilm of secret documents she had stolen from Ballantine's safe and photographed, instead of sending it through the spy network in London, as she was required to do. Heydrich had been furious – less, she thought, at the breach of security, than at the evidence that she would, when she felt like it, break his rule of absolute, immediate and unquestioning obedience to orders. It gave her immense satisfaction to know that in losing his temper and commanding her to be humiliated – strapped naked to a bar to be caned like a delinquent schoolgirl, then having electrodes attached to her genitals to make her suffer exquisite pain – he had been signing his own death warrant.

She shampooed her hair as she considered how a life can be changed, irrevocably and for ever by a single incident. Because three days later, when she had at last been able to leave her bed, she had gone for a walk ... and encountered Clive, also on a visit to Berlin. As he had not known she was there, he had been equally taken aback; but when, in a mood of outraged defiance of the Reich and all it stood for, she had invited him into her apartment for a cup of coffee, it had seemed to him a golden opportunity to probe further, in the hope of discovering something that could be used against her to convince his superiors how dangerous she might be.

Half an hour later they had been in bed, and he had been halfway down the route she had led Ballantine, without any clear idea of where she wanted it to lead. But when they were interrupted by her SD minder and she disposed of the intruder with a single blow to the neck, he realized that to have her eliminated, or even arrested and deported, would have been a waste of a singular talent ... if she could be 'turned' to work for Britain. To his delight, she had proved amenable – but he had no idea that her brain had been working in the reverse direction, calculating that by secretly working for the British she might be able to revenge herself on the Reich, without at the same time endangering her parents.

There had been no love involved in the transaction. However mutually satisfying they may have found each other, both of them had been working, in their different ways. It was only over the next few years of working together that mutual trust had developed into mutual respect, and then mutual admiration, and eventually (on her side, at least) love. Clive had been slower to reach that goal. She knew he had found it difficult to give his all, without reservation, to a woman with such lethal talents – and even more, to a woman who, although he had come to know her so well as a person, had, he always felt, had a part of her personality closed to all outsiders.

Well, he was not wrong there. If he respected, and indeed admired, the way in which she could apparently, at a moment's notice, transform herself from a gentle and intensely feminine woman into an angel of destruction, he had no idea, no concept, of what that transformation involved. But then neither did she. She knew it had something to do with her SS training; but it had lurked in her subconscious before then, first surfacing early in her days at the training camp, long before she had known that she would be taught to kill and use her hands in unarmed combat, when one of the other girls had attempted to rape her, and in a moment of irresistible, concentrated but always cold fury she had broken her tormentor's arm in two places. That incident had, in fact, alerted her instructors that they possessed something even more out of the ordinary than they had first supposed – which had led her, by the most remarkable route imaginable, to this bath in this hotel and would tomorrow take her back to her private paradise. By which time, she was resolved, it would all be history.

Unless Mark Hamilton got in the way – and she desperately hoped that he would not.

Hamilton sat on his bed. His entire body was tingling. Although he had not actually been able to touch her, he had sat within touching distance of her, inhaled her scent, listened to the soft melody of her voice, watched the movement of her hair, the sheer sheen of her legs, and, above all, gazed into the most compelling eyes he had ever seen.

If only it could be possible to stay here for ever, getting to know her, without ever having to think of her destruction. And that was an unthinkable thought – that if he did his job, all of that vibrant beauty would be reduced to dust. He wondered if, assuming the figures given him were correct, all of the apparent dozens of men who had got too close to her and perished for their temerity, had thought, with their last breath, that it had been worth it?

Botten had been the last, and had seemed to have been within reach of his goal. He had apparently never even seen the countess, but had employed a Mafia family to find her and carry out the job. He had told Moscow that he had succeeded, and that the hit would be completed in a week. Then both he and the family had simply disappeared off the face of the earth. Unfortunately, he had given Moscow no information as to how the plan was to be carried out, or the location of the victim's home. Some victim!

Hamilton had found that hard to believe. He found it even harder to believe now, having met her. And yet, there had been something about her. She had not conveyed menace, or anything sinister. Simply an overwhelming confidence, the confidence of a woman who had no fear, because she had had a life of unbroken success, proved herself superior to any adversary time and again. And now he had joined the ranks of those adversaries. If she ever penetrated his cover, he wondered, how she would do it? And what would it feel like, to find himself looking into those huge blue eyes above the barrel of gun, knowing that he was living his last few seconds on earth? Suddenly he felt quite cold.

But the job had to be done; he had no desire to be reduced to dust himself. He sighed, and picked up the telephone. 'I'd like to make a person-to-person call,' he told the operator. 'Long distance. It's to a Mr John Smith, in London,

England.' He read the number from the note in his wallet.

'Very good, sir. If you will hang up, I will call you back when the connection is made.'

'Thank you.' Hamilton replaced the receiver, looked at his watch. Two o'clock. That meant seven o'clock in England. They'd be having a pre-dinner drink.

He kicked off his shoes, lay back. Was she suspicious? He could think of no reason for her to mistrust him; but in any event he had to continue to allay her suspicions, hopefully gain an invitation to her cay. And he was going to enjoy that.

He had almost dozed off when the phone rang. 'I have your connection, sir,' the woman said.

'Thank you.' He sat up.

'Yes?' the familiar voice said.

'I have made contact.'

'At last. Give me the name and address, and then you may return.'

'The name is Anna Bartley. I do not have the address.'

'What?'

'Yet. I will get it. The approach must be made with caution. Thus I may require another few days.'

'Just get the address,' the voice said. 'We are waiting.'

The phone went dead.

The jangling seemed to come from another

planet, only slowly penetrating Anna's subconscious. Having not slept for thirty-six hours, even though her body and her mind were trained to such extreme exercises in stamina, she had been more exhausted than she had realized. I am getting old, she thought. Another reason for calling a halt, before that treasured stamina gave out.

She reached for the phone and picked it up. 'Yes?'

'I'm sorry to bother you, Mrs Bartley,' Charles said. 'But there is a gentleman who wishes to see you.'

'Another one?' Then she realized who this one had to be; he was, after all, early. She wasn't in the proper mood for what had to be done. But actually, she was in the best possible physical position to carry out her plan. 'I assume this one's name is Andrews?'

Charles was surprised. 'Why, yes, ma'am. So it is.'

'And he has checked in?'

'No, ma'am. He has not done so.' He sounded even more surprised. 'He does not have any luggage.'

'Thank you, Charles. Will you ask him to come up to my room?'

'Ah ... yes, ma'am.'

Anna replaced the phone, then got out of bed, went to the bathroom to wash her face and clean her teeth, and brushed her hair. Then she took the Walther from her shoulder bag, unlocked the bedroom door, and got back into bed

– sitting up with the sheet arranged across her lap, her hair shrouding the pillow, and her right hand, holding the pistol, resting on her groin and thus concealed by the sheet. She did not suppose she was going to have to use it here in the Royal Vic, or anywhere else in Nassau; she certainly hoped she would not have to, even if she had the legal right to do so, but the sudden appearance of the gun could have a devastating effect on an adversary's ability to concentrate.

A few minutes later there was a tap on the door.

'It's not locked,' she called.

It swung open, and she gazed at the man, who was gazing at her. But, unlike Hamilton, he had looked at her often enough before, and in the nude. 'Every time I see you,' he remarked, 'you are naked and in bed, with someone or other.' He spoke with a soft southern drawl.

'I am always naked when I am in bed,' she pointed out. 'I do not own any nightclothes. And as you can see, at this moment I am sharing my all only with myself. Sometimes it makes a pleasant change. I think you should close the door.'

He obeyed and turned back to face her. Joseph Andrews was six foot three inches tall, a physical characteristic that always appealed to Anna. He was also very thin, and now that he was past fifty his hatchet face was taking on an almost cadaverous appearance. But he was, Clive apart, her oldest living friend, even though from time to time he had also been her bitterest enemy.

For all that, she could never forget that he was the man who had helped her escape from the Lubianka in 1941, thus saving her life. Shortly afterwards, as a senior officer in the then OSS, and now in the CIA, he had become her employer, sharing her with MI6. He had watched her at work on more than one occasion and knew her every capability.

And he had also fallen in love with her. But they had only once ever shared a bed. Circumstances had led to their separation immediately afterwards – principally her kidnapping by the NKVD (as the MGB was then known) on leaving his apartment. That had led to the sudden deaths of the six Russian agents involved, which had left both the State Department and MI6 in a state of frantic disarray as they tried to get her out of America before she could be charged with murder.

They had not been entirely convinced by her invariable explanation: 'What was I to do? Let them take me back to Moscow for a show trial and public execution?' In fact, over the following four years, although they found her invaluable time and again, they had also become increasingly concerned at their inability to predict or control just what she might do next – so at last they had determined that she simply had to be eliminated, if possible without a fuss.

They still had not grasped exactly what they were dealing with, had wound up with one of their best men in the morgue, but at the same

47

time left her with the unhappy realization that both Moscow and Washington were now out for her blood. MI6, Clive, had rescued her from that predicament, broadcasting that the infamous Countess von Widerstand had died in the flaming ruins of Berlin in April 1945, and giving her a new identity to start a new life, with her parents.

Of course it had not worked. Both the Russians and the Americans had traced her, and the bankrupt post-war British Government had been unable to protect her adequately. So, four more dead Russians, and flight. But this time with Joe, who had turned up at the same time as the Reds and watched spellbound as she dealt with the immediate problem. He had then offered her, in the name of his government, immunity from prosecution for all past crimes – as most people categorized the events of her sanguinary life – if she would come back and resume work for the CIA.

That had been a gamble she might not have been prepared to take but for two connected facts. One was that at that moment she had been a penniless fugitive, uncertain that the British Government, in the interests of international relations, might not hand her over to the Russians, if they were able to catch up with her. The other was that Joe had promised her American help in retrieving the ten million dollars in Nazi gold that she had secreted at the end of the War, and which had been buried inside what was to become Russian-controlled Germany. This they had done. It had cost another twenty-odd Soviet lives, making her in Russian eyes the most wanted criminal ever and converting her into Washington's private nemesis.

That had been six years ago. For those six years, she had served the State Department faithfully and well. Always at considerable risk to her own life, but always successfully – just as she had been successful in creating her own little private world here in the Bahamas, and even marrying the only man she had ever truly loved ... although the fact that he still worked for MI6 continued to make that life entirely clandestine. But now...

'So,' he commented, 'what's the problem? Peterson said you seemed a bit agitated when he saw you, and your message – that it was most urgent you see me immediately – also sounded agitated. What went wrong?'

'Nothing went wrong. Schmettow is dead.'

'That's my girl.' He pulled up a chair and sat beside the bed. 'And you're here, as large as life and twice as beautiful, and in the pink. So tell me what's on your mind? And would you mind very much covering up those tits? Sitting here looking at them is very distracting, as I'm not allowed to touch them.'

'You're welcome.'

He studied her for several seconds. 'So there *is* a problem. Was it very close?'

'A bit. Schmettow and his bodyguards were not difficult. They looked at me for a few seconds too long. But the bastard had a pet.'

'Don't tell me! You mean a Rottweiler or something? I thought you loved dogs, and always got on with them?'

'I do. This was a king cobra. About which I had not been informed,' she added coldly.

'Holy shit! It didn't...'

'No, it did not. Or I wouldn't be here now, would I? But I hate killing living creatures. Except humans who deserve it. Animals never deserve it. They are always either defending themselves or obeying instructions.'

'Still, it must have been a shattering experience, especially if you didn't know it was there. Do you dye your hair?'

'Not yet.'

'But you're shaken. Or you wouldn't have insisted on seeing me in person.'

'I am not the least bit shaken, Joe. I wanted to see you, in person, because I have something to say to you, in person.'

'Oh, yes?' His tone had become watchful.

'I want out.'

He frowned. 'You said you weren't shaken.'

'I said that I am not the least bit shaken. I want to have a child.'

'What?!'

'As it seems to have escaped your notice, I *am* a woman. I am also thirty-two years old, and in three months I am going to be thirty-three. The sands are running out, in that direction. Besides, I want to be young enough to enjoy my daughter's adolescence.'

'Suppose it's a boy?'

50

'Then it will be his adolescence. Anyway, I intend to have more than one. I'm very happy that you are accepting this, Joe.'

'Well, I am not happy at all. Frankly, the idea of you sitting in a rocking chair with an infant tugging at those tits is beyond my powers of imagination.'

'You'll get used to it.'

He leaned forward, his hand resting on the sheet beside her thigh. 'Anna, we need you.'

'And you've had the best of me, for six years. Now it's time to give something back.'

He leaned back. 'You're serious, aren't you?'

'Joe, surely we've been friends long enough for you to know that I am always serious, even if I see life as one huge macabre joke. If I did not see it that way, I'd have blown out my brains long ago.'

'Which humour applies even when you're about to kill someone.'

Anna gazed at him. 'Yes, Joe. Even when I'm about to kill someone. I just told you, it preserves my sanity.'

'And that's why you've taken all of your money out of Stattler's hands.'

'We, Clive and I, are quite capable of handling our investments.'

He gazed at her for several seconds, then sighed. 'OK. If you're hell bent on this crazy scheme, we won't stand in your way.'

'That's very reassuring. And thank you.'

'So, give me some dates. When do you reckon you'll need to commence your maternity leave?

And then I suppose you'll want maybe ... twelve months away? Fifteen?'

'Joe,' Anna said, 'I am not asking for leave. I am quitting.'

'Now, Anna, be serious.'

'I am very serious. I'm going to be a mum. I have no intention of coming home one day and being asked by my daughter, or son, or both, Mummy, what did you do today? And having to reply, oh, killed four or five people. Those days are done.'

His eyes narrowed. 'You think you can just walk away from the CIA?'

'I am simply retiring from the business. Everyone is entitled to retire.'

'And if we refuse to accept your retirement?'

Anna's eyes were cold. 'What exactly would you do about it?'

'Well...'

'I think,' she said, 'that there are two things you need to remember. The first is that Moscow has been trying to nail me for eleven years. And I'm still here, and there are a hundred and thirty-three heavies who are not.

'Of course,' she added modestly, 'only about half of those were Russians. But it is still something you need to bear in mind.'

'You know what you suffer from?'

'You've told me, often enough. Hubris. The important thing is that I *am* still here, and they are not. And if you think you can apply pressure in other directions, there is the second point you need to bear in mind, of which you may not be aware. Three years ago I carried out a last job for MI6.'

Joe's frown was back. 'You never told me about that!'

Anna shrugged – which she knew could be devastating. 'Every girl has her secrets. The point is, Billy Baxter ... You remember Billy?'

'I remember Baxter very well,' Joe said, somewhat sourly.

'Well, of course, he set it up.'

'And Clive went along with it? Some husband!'

'We weren't married then. And he was not happy about it. But neither was I. To sweeten the pot, Billy offered me a quid pro quo. Apart from the fee, of course. He said that if I did this job for him, and for Britain, he would obtain for me perpetual immunity from arrest for anything I might have to do in self-defence here in the Bahamas.'

'And you believed him? You may be the most deadly woman in the world, but you are also the most naïve.'

'I did believe him, Joe. And you're right, he couldn't swing it then. I was quite upset. But he kept working at it; and when a couple of years ago the government switched from left to right, he was able to push it through. You must remember that I was once commanded by Heydrich to assassinate Churchill. These things make a bond.'

'I would have thought it'd make him intensely pleased to see you biting the dust.'

'Ah, but you see, I didn't do it. I changed sides instead, and began working for him. By the end of the War, I was just about his favourite woman. Although,' she said reminiscently, 'that didn't stop him cheerfully being prepared to sacrifice me on one occasion. But as I said, I'm still here, and I now have that *carte blanche*, enabling me to take out any heavy who comes gunning for me or mine in the Bahamas. And I will, Joe, if I have to.'

'I have no doubt of it,' he said. But the rancour had gone from his voice, which had become thoughtful. Alarm bells began to jangle in Anna's mind. 'However,' he said, 'do you really want to spend the rest of your life locked away on your island, gun in hand? And do you really want to take on both us and the Reds?'

'Can you offer me an alternative?'

'I can offer you the same deal as Billy, only better. In fact, that's why I came down the moment I got Petersen's message. I needed to see you just as badly as you seem to have wanted to see me.'

'Try being explicit.'

'So you want out. OK. We'll hate to lose you, but we can do a deal. Do one last job for us, and we'll not only call it a day but we'll give you perpetual immunity throughout the United States. Providing, of course, you confine your destructive impulses to Red agents or members of the criminal fraternity who may be employed by Moscow.'

'You can do that?'

'I can obtain it for you.'

'You must want this job done pretty badly.'

'We do.'

'And you reckon I'm the only one who can do it?'

'Yes, we do.'

Now she gazed at him for several moments. She had trusted him in 1946, when her world had been collapsing. And he had not let her down, then or since. And for all her brave words, she knew that life confined to the Bahamas, and hopefully with a couple of kids to bring up and educate and protect, not to mention Clive and her parents, and all the other inhabitants of her cay who trusted her absolutely and for whom she was responsible, would be very difficult if she had to spend her time looking over her shoulder. And if it *was* one last job ... She drew a long breath. 'Tell me what it is.'

'Does the name Kola el Fahri mean anything to you?'

'Only that he sounds a Middle Eastern gentleman.'

'Actually, we think he is from Libya.'

'You think?'

'His origins are a bit vague. He fought for the British in North Africa during the War, having developed a considerable enmity for the Italians. He was, apparently, a very loyal and very successful saboteur. In fact, he showed such courage and determination on so many occasions that had he been a regular he could well have picked up a string of medals, including even the Victoria Cross.'

'And you want him taken out? You are going to have to do an awful lot of convincing, Joe.'

He sat down again. 'As I suggested, he is apparently a man who forms quite savage dislikes. Since the end of the War he has formed a violent antipathy for all things Western, particularly the United States. Seems we refused him citizenship when he applied for it in 1946.'

'Why?'

'He has a criminal record. OK, maybe he earned some of that record while working for the Brits, so maybe it was rampant bureaucracy and a pedantic approach, but the laws are there.'

'Couldn't he appeal, citing his war record?'

'You or I might have taken that road, but appeals against governments are apparently not his scene. He believes in direct action.'

'Such as what?'

'He's a demolitions expert, taught by the Brits during the War. Over the past two years he has indulged in a systematic bombing campaign against US targets, all over the world. OK, in the beginning one or two were physical targets. But now he's broadening his horizons. You must have heard about that Pan Am clipper that went down last year.'

'That was unexplained engine failure, wasn't it?'

'It was a bomb, in the cargo hold. Seems the

56

bag was sorted through legitimately, but the passenger who checked it in never boarded the aircraft. As the plane went down in the sea it has taken some time for us to locate the wreckage and start recovering what we can. Apart from seventy-five dead bodies. We haven't made this public, because we don't want to start a panic, but we have conclusive proof that a man named Khouri, who is a known and close associate of Fahri's, was seen amongst the passengers before the aircraft left Lisbon, and he certainly checked a bag. But he never boarded. He was called, as a missing passenger, several times, before they got fed up and took off without him.'

'That's a bit coincidental.'

'It's also a bit careless on the part of the ground staff. We're trying to get all the airlines to install some kind of checking system to at least make sure no unaccompanied luggage gets on board in future. We'd also like to have a system for screening luggage; and, if necessary, passengers too, to make sure they aren't carrying weapons or explosives. But whether we'll ever get that off the ground is another matter. The airlines say such a procedure would require the installation of expensive equipment, not to mention specially trained personnel to operate it. Even more important, it would mean fare increases and cause flight delays and disruption to schedules, and they say the flying public would not accept that. We don't happen to agree. We feel the travelling public, who increasingly seem to want to travel by air, will put up with anything to do so – certainly if the reasons for the fare hikes and the delays are explained to them. But the airline executives feel it will just mean a crippling fall in custom and therefore revenue.'

'Well,' Anna said. 'I suppose the odds on travelling on a plane targeted by this character are still astronomical.'

'They are shortening every minute. Last month there was another US airliner brought down, out of Manila. A hundred and twenty-eight people, mostly Americans. Fahri himself has been identified as being among the passengers, and again the flight took off one passenger short. That was too much. The matter has been handed to us.'

'So? Why can't you simply arrest him?'

'For two reasons. He is not a US citizen, or resident in the States, and we have no proof. At least, no proof that would stand up in court.'

'Why is that?'

'Apart from our knowledge of his character and background and capabilities, all we have is identification of him or Khouri at all the sites where a bomb either went off or was planted. There have now been seven of these incidents. That can't be coincidence. Oh, we might make the charges stick in our courts. But other people feel we may be intending some railroading.'

'And the government where he is living won't extradite him. Where is this uncooperative place situated?'

'Fahri has a house in Surrey, about an hour's drive from central London.'

'What!' Anna threw back the sheet so violently that she was totally uncovered.

Joe stared at her in consternation. 'Have you been pointing that thing at me all the time we've been talking?'

'It's an idiosyncrasy of mine when entertaining people I don't know very well.'

'And you don't know me very well?'

'It also applies to people I know too well. Anyway, this conversation is now terminated.'

There was a knock on the door. Anna looked at her watch. 'Good lord, six o'clock!' She got out of bed, watched askance by Joe, pulled on her dressing gown, pocketed the pistol, took a £5 note from her shoulder bag, and opened the door to receive her dress from the laundry maid. 'Thank you.' She tipped her, closed the door again, and carefully laid the dress on the bed. 'Surely, if he's a killer, and the British know this, they'll cooperate?'

'They can't right now, much as I suspect they'd like to. At the end of the War, presumably looking for increased Arab support, they lauded him as a war hero, gave him British citizenship, and let him get on with it. As a war hero he has been prominent ever since, making public appearances, opening fêtes, that sort of thing. They feel that suddenly to announce they are handing him over to us, and almost certain execution, without adequate proof of his crimes

– and as you pointed out, right now our evidence is entirely circumstantial – would be a PR catastrophe. You know the sort of thing, "British Government kowtows to US" etc. We are not all that popular in the UK right now, anyway.'

'Then you have a problem. Until you get the proof you need. Now I must dress for dinner. I assume you're joining me?'

'Anna, we haven't reached a decision.'

'I have. It's not on.'

'Now, Anna. You are the only one we have who can do this.'

'Oh, yes?' She took off the dressing gown, pulled on a clean pair of knickers taken from her valise, sat at her dressing table, laid down the pistol – she could watch him in the mirror – and applied make-up. 'What I didn't tell you is that by the terms of my agreement with the British Government, I am never again to set foot in the UK.'

'Who's to know? We'd give you a false identity.'

'Big deal. Don't you realize there are people in Britain who would recognize me on sight?'

'Such as?'

'Well, Clive, of course. I don't know that he's in England right now, but he could be. And Billy. He's always there.'

'Oh, really, Anna. I believe the population of the British Isles is currently well over forty million. Do you seriously suppose the moment you step off the plane you are going to run into

60

the only two people who can identify you? We're not suggesting that you pay MI6 a visit and say "Hello, I'm back, how about a cup of coffee?".'

Anna brushed her hair. 'I don't see why you need me. You seem to know where this character is situated. Can't you just send in an ordinary hit man?'

'Can't be done. He seems to have unlimited funds, which arouses all sorts of sinister connotations anyway. With this money he has converted the house in which he lives into a fortress, complete with a retinue of armed heavies.'

'The British have let him do this?'

'As long as they don't actually shoot anyone, save in self-defence, he has broken no laws. There are quite a few people who have a paranoid fear of assassination. Oh, we could send in a squad, but that would cause an outsize diplomatic incident. We have a new president who's been in office only a few weeks. Eisenhower wouldn't take kindly to beginning his term with a full-scale quarrel with Britain over prerogatives. Anyway, with this ongoing mess in Korea, we need all our allies on board, and Britain is number one. We simply can't afford to antagonize her.'

'With allies like you, who needs enemies? And just suppose I was crazy enough to take this on, do you suppose I can get in and out of this fortress, leaving a few dead bodies scattered about, without causing a diplomatic incident?'

'Yes.'

'Convince me.'

'Fahri has only one known weakness. Women. He cannot keep his hands off any woman who takes his fancy. In fact, he is so voracious that he has his sidekick scouring the London nightclubs looking for suitable bimbos, preferably long-haired blondes. They are bribed in the first place by a promise that he can place them in show business. He never harms them, just has sex with then, and pays them well to clear off. Incidentally, look out for this aide, Khouri. He is every bit as unpleasant as his boss; and, as I have said, he's had a share in everything Fahri has done. If he gets in your way, you have our permission to waste him as well. But remember that Fahri is more important.'

Anna put on her dress. 'In case it has slipped your notice, Joe, I am no longer a bimbo. In fact, I don't think I ever really qualified. But in any event, I am now thirty-two years old.'

'That seems to be bothering you. But you are still the most beautiful woman in the world.'

'You say the sweetest things.'

'Listen. It's all laid on. You will be escorted to all the best nightclubs. And the worst. There can be no doubt that you'll be noticed and picked up.'

'Who is going to do this escorting?'

'Ah ... we thought Jerry would suit you best.'

'Would you mind repeating that? I seem to have gone deaf.'

'Well, I mean, you've worked together be-

62

fore, and have something going for each other, and...'

'One should always make sure of one's facts before making fatuous statements.' Anna returned to the dressing table to put on her jewellery. 'Jerry and I never worked *together.* You sent him to Brazil as my back-up when I was after Martin Bormann, and yes we had a brief fling. It went with the job, and he is a handsome hunk and knows what a bed is for. But when we met a crisis, all he did was get himself shot, leaving me in a most embarrassing situation.'

'But those four heavies were after you anyway.'

'I'm not talking about the Russians. As you say, they had to go regardless. But to get Jerry to hospital before he bled to death I had to drive his car.'

'What was embarrassing about that?'

'Joe, I couldn't drive a car. I had taken four lessons, and I did not have a licence. I was run in by the police, for driving too fast and on the wrong side of the road. How was I to know which side of the road they use in Brazil? And then, I didn't have a licence and I was uninsured. It was the most humiliating moment of my life. Especially as I had virtually nothing on and I was covered in mud.'

'They didn't rough you up, did they?'

'They were the soul of politeness, and when I told them that my boyfriend had been shot by bandits they couldn't have been more helpful.

They didn't even charge me with driving without a licence. But the whole thing was still very embarrassing. I had never been arrested before, well, only once or twice. And never when virtually naked.'

'And you had just left four bodies lying in a ditch. Anna, you are a hoot!'

Anna blew a raspberry. 'As for when you sent him over here to act as a back-up when the Mafia were getting too close, when it came to the crunch he got seasick and I had to commit piracy all by myself, with Jerry lying prostrate on his bunk.'

'OK, OK. But I'm not asking you to accept him as a back-up. Just an escort, until you get picked up. Then he will disappear. But he'll be there when you come out the other side, to get you safely out of the country.'

Anna strapped on her watch, thoughtfully. She had not operated in England since 1940. Just on thirteen years, and she had been twenty years old. The odds on her meeting anyone who remembered her from those days had to be so long as to be ridiculous. Except that Mark Hamilton apparently did. Unless he was a fake, acting on information.

But to be able to do one last job, and then be out, out, out! For ever! And with *carte blanche* to travel anywhere she wished in the US – which meant virtually all of America north of the Rio Grande, as she was still wanted by the Mexican police for the Capillano job in 1949. The achievement of that goal had to be worth any risk. And there was no risk. Save for Hamilton. And the small matter of Fahri and his heavies ... and Scotland Yard, once the job was done. But those were all aspects of her profession with which she had coped time and again successfully. So it was really only Hamilton.

'Do we have your acceptance?' Joe asked.

Anna stood up, smoothed her dress, fluffed out her hair, and regarded herself in the mirror with some satisfaction; her hair was still damp, but this made it lie the more gracefully. 'The guarantee will have to be in writing, signed and sealed by the very top.'

'You will have it. A courier will come to this hotel the day after tomorrow with all the documentation you need, including your false papers and flights to and from London. I assume that, like us, you wish to have this done as quickly as possible.'

'I would certainly like to be back here before Clive gets back from wherever he is. There is just one more thing. Does the name Mark Hamilton mean anything to you?'

Joe considered. 'Can't say that it does.'

'It's probably a pseudonym anyway.'

'Is he is a problem?'

'Just an old acquaintance. Or so he claims. I'm afraid I distrust old acquaintances who I cannot remember.'

'You want something done about him?'

'No. He seems harmless enough. But perhaps you could have someone check your files and see if the name crops up anywhere.'

'Will do. What sort of timescale are we talking about?'

'Back to 1938 should cover it.'

He nodded. 'I'll send you what we turn up, if anything, with the other bumf. Now, let's get down to cases. When are you returning to the cay?'

'Get your man here by lunchtime on Thursday, and I'll wait for him.'

'He'll be here, with everything you need. That includes a new passport, but you'll need a photo. He'll bring the equipment to endorse it.'

'No problem.'

'I think you should have your hair up. And wear it up to pass through English immigration. Whenever anyone thinks of the Countess von Widerstand, they remember the hair first.'

'Good point.'

'You know, it'd be much safer for you to cut it.'

'Sorry. I am not cutting my hair. I'll wear it up.'

'Suit yourself. Anyway, wear these.'

He held out a pair of horn-rimmed spectacles.

'Just what I've always wanted.'

'Now, how long will you need before leaving?'

'I have to make sure everything is all right on the cay, and I have to pack. From what you've said, this job could take a few weeks.'

'It could. Remember it's winter over there.'

She smiled. 'It'll be a pleasure to wear my sable again.'

'You know, that's another trade mark of yours.'

'Only to one or two people. And again from what you say, this character goes for style.'

'He does. So we'll book your flights for a week on Thursday. Your return will be open, and Jerry will take care of it.'

'Big deal. You understand that as I am fairly well known around here, the flights will have to be in my real name. It would be simpler and safer for me to come up to New York as myself and change identities there.'

'Can't be done. Just in case something goes wrong, we cannot take the chance of you being traced back to us. We don't want you to set foot on US soil until the job is done, and any fuss has died down.'

'You certainly know how to make a girl feel she's wanted.'

'Listen, there need not be a problem. You will fly as Anna Bartley. Just make sure no one in the UK, apart from Jerry, gets to look at the tickets, at least until you're ready to check in for your return flight. But when you land, to go through immigration you will switch passports and assume your new identity.'

She made a face. 'It's all so simple, isn't it? To you, sitting in your office. And my fee?'

'Fifty thousand.'

'A hundred.'

'Now wait a moment. Do you need that much? Do you need anything?'

'Maybe not. But a workman is worth his, or

her, hire. This could be the most dangerous job I've ever taken on.'

He sighed. 'A hundred.'

'Plus expenses.'

'That will all be taken care of.'

'Thank you. OK, Joe, we have a deal, for the last time. Tell me about the delivery.'

'His name is Horace Spence. Short, squat and balding. Not your type.'

'Password.'

'The only place that's hotter than this is Owattamie.'

'Say that again.'

'I don't even know if it exists. So no one else is likely to know either.'

Anna sighed. 'OK. Owattamie. Now let's finish with business for tonight, go down, check you in, and have a drink and then dinner. Where's your bag?'

'I don't have a bag.' He looked at his watch. 'I'd love to have dinner with you, Anna. But I have a plane to catch.'

'At this hour? It's seven o'clock.'

'It's a private plane.'

'How the upper classes travel. Well, then...' She held out her hand.

He held it to draw her against him. 'Anna ... take care.' And kissed her. 'Hasta la vista.'

She kissed him in turn. 'Joe, darling, not if I can help it.'

She gave him ten minutes, then went downstairs. 'I shall be dining alone after all Charles.

Or maybe not.' She looked through the open doors into the bar. 'I'll let you know. But I'll eat on the terrace. Oh, and could you radio the cay and tell Tommy I'd like to be picked up the day after tomorrow, in the afternoon?'

'Will do, ma'am.'

She went into the brightly lit bar, chose a stool next to Hamilton. She was back on a high, the adrenalin flowing. To think that within a month she could be out the other side. She remembered believing that before, in 1944 and again a year later. Neither of those plans had worked out. But she was determined that this one was going to, no matter what it took to achieve. 'I'll have a champagne cocktail, George.'

'One champagne cocktail coming up, Mrs Bartley.'

'Well, hello,' Hamilton said. 'Did you have a good nap?'

'I had a very good nap, thank you. And you?'

'I'm afraid not. I found I had too much to think about.'

'Oh, dear. Thank you, George. And cheers.' She sipped. 'Nothing serious, I hope?'

'I could not stop myself thinking about you.'

'Now, that could be catastrophic.' She smiled at him. 'So stop thinking about me, and enjoy me instead. I find I'm free for dinner after all.'

'You mean your date isn't coming?'

'The bastard has stood me up.'

'I find that hard to believe. I mean, that anyone who had a date with you wouldn't show.'

'I entirely agree. But I have a more attractive

replacement. Do I not?'

'I'm flattered.'

She finished her cocktail. 'Well, then. Shall we?'

He looked at his watch. 'It's only a quarter past seven. Bit early, isn't it?'

'The earlier we eat, the more of the evening we have left after dinner. You said you wanted me to show you some Nassau night life.'

She signalled Charles to lay an extra place at her table.

INCIDENT ON A BEACH

'I'll have the grouper and a bottle of Montrachet, Charles,' Anna said. 'I've given up eating red meat or drinking red wine in the evenings,' she explained to Hamilton. 'I hate indigestion.'

'Good point. I'll join you.'

The meal was served.

'I wonder if I may ask you a question?' Hamilton asked.

'Of course you may ask me a question,' Anna agreed. 'I don't have to answer it.'

'I was wondering what your husband does for a living? I mean, whatever it is, he seems to do it very successfully. You own your own cay, you have a yacht, you clearly travel a lot, you

70

have a lavish lifestyle...'

'I suppose you could say that my husband does a bit of this and a bit of that. As for the lifestyle ... the money is mine. An inheritance.' From the Third Reich, she thought.

'I see. An heiress, and a beauty too. Your husband is a very lucky man.'

'You say the sweetest things.'

'So, where would you like to go after dinner?'

She had deduced both that he held his liquor almost as well as she did and that, if he really was fascinated by her, he was not likely to be distracted by a few exotic dancers. If she was going to get into his head, her approach would have to be more direct. 'Do you have transport?'

'I have a hire car, yes.'

'Well, then, let's take a drive. It's a beautiful moonlit night.'

They finished their meal just before nine, and went down to the car park. 'Where did you have in mind to drive?' Hamilton asked.

'Take the coast road west.'

'You mean to Cable Beach?'

'We'll go beyond Cable Beach. Do you know the island?'

'Some of it. But mainly around Nassau, looking at property.'

'There's not a lot of property for sale west of Cable Beach, unless you mean to build. There's certainly land available.'

'You mean, you own land in New Providence?'

71

'Good lord, no. I'm taking you to a beach I know. A quite stunning spot, about fourteen miles out of town. And you'll never guess what it's called.'

'Probably not. What is it called?'

'Love Beach.'

He shot her a glance.

'Actually,' she said, 'I hate to be a party pooper, but I think it's named after a person rather than an activity.'

To their right, through a fringe of casuarinas, the moon sparkled on the calm water. 'This whole island,' he commented, 'is nothing but superb beaches.'

'Some are better than others,' she promised him. 'And taken as a whole, the beaches on New Providence can't compare with some of those on the Out Islands. If only because nowadays they're so crowded. I have a beach on the cay that is superb, and empty. Save for me.'

'I'd love to see it,' he ventured. But as she made no immediate response, asked 'How long have you lived there?'

'Six years. That was well before devaluation, and the Bahamas were a bit of a backwater, certainly as regards tourists. They were just too expensive compared with Miami. But when the pound was virtually cut in half, they became cheaper and so the flood gates were opened. In Nassau, at least. But I suppose it'll spread throughout the entire archipelago.'

'Except for your island, I gather. You came here with your husband?'

'No. I wasn't married then. I came here with my parents. I was looking for somewhere to live, and I liked this best.'

'I assume this was after you had received your inheritance. But obviously not from your parents.'

'Obviously.'

'But you preferred not to settle in Nassau itself?'

'I like my privacy.'

They were now past the glowing lights of the Country Club and Cable Beach, and the houses had disappeared. The night became a kaleidoscope of bright moonlight and sudden shadows cast by the trees.

'I hope you don't think I'm being inquisitive,' Hamilton said.

'As a matter of fact, you are. But if it amuses you, keep going.' You may well eventually hang yourself, she thought.

'It's just that in addition to being incredibly beautiful, you are incredible interesting.'

'Would I be interesting if I were as ugly as sin?'

'Do you know, I think you would. There is so much about you that is tantalizingly mysterious. Hello!' He slowed the car. 'Which way?'

The road in front of them suddenly bifurcated, one arm following the coast to the right, round a low but sheer hill, the other continuing straight ahead.

'They both go in the same direction, and join up a bit further on. But I would stick with this one. The one on the right is the old road, but it became very crumbly and unsafe, so they punched this new road through the hill.'

'Ambitious. There are lights.'

'Gambier Village. Only a couple of miles, now. There. Pull down that path to the right, but take it slowly.'

They passed the lights and he changed down and turned off the surfaced road on to a track, slowly descending through a small forest of coconut trees. 'Wow!' he commented.

'Isn't it something?'

Hamilton stopped the car where the track ended in sand, and gazed at an almost perfect crescent of beach, stretching from shallow headland to shallow headland. The water lapped gently at the sand, perhaps thirty yards away; and beyond, a couple of hundred yards offshore, there was a ripple of surf on the reef. 'And your beach is better than this?'

'Oh, yes. But as I said, mainly because it's utterly private.' Anna got out of the car, took off her shoes, and stepped on to the sand. 'But this is a close second, because it's far enough out of town to make it a bit too much of an expedition for your average tourist.' She walked down the sand. 'Won't you join me?'

He got out, his shoes crunching, drew a long breath. Would she? Did he dare? 'If we had our swimsuits with us we could go for a moonlight dip. Or are there likely to be sharks or something at night?'

'Sharks seldom come inside the reef, even at

74

night. And of course we're going to have a moonlight dip. That's why I brought you here.'

Hamilton felt physically sick. She would!

Anna dropped her shoes, released her dress, and let it slide past her shoulders to the sand. Back to the laundry. But tomorrow she'd be wearing slacks. 'I don't own a swimsuit,' she explained.

Hamilton licked his lips as he realized that she was wearing nothing under the dress save her knickers, and these now also sank round her ankles. She stepped out of them and turned to face him. 'Or do you have something to hide?'

He could hardly breathe. The moonlight, streaming across the water to reach her, seemed to lift her out of the darkness in a halo of light. He wished it was coming from behind him. But even in the gloom, if her pubic hair was indistinct, nothing could hide those magnificent breasts, although the nipples were unclear, or her splendid thighs and unforgettable legs. 'I ... ah ... I have more to take off.'

'Then I think you should start doing that.'

'But what about that jewellery? It looks very expensive.'

'It is. But salt water isn't going to harm it.'

'And the watch? Is it gold?'

'It is, and it's waterproof.'

'It's a very unusual design.'

'That's probably because it's German.'

She walked down the beach and the water rippled around her ankles; it had not yet cooled off from the heat of the day, and was warmer than the night air. It reached her knees and then her thighs. When it was round her waist and starting to wet her hair, she turned back to look at the beach and watch him wading towards her. He was facing the moon, and was certainly a fine figure of a man. The sight of her naked had had a pronounced effect.

But she had no intention of having sex with him. This had nothing to do with any ethical scruple about betraying Clive, who knew that she would always do whatever she deemed necessary to stay in front of any threats to her security, but rather that Mark Hamilton, while certainly not distasteful in any way as a man, was an enigma. Thus for the moment she was using her various weapons to destroy his defences. What might happen after that would depend on just what those collapsing defences revealed.

He was close, and she ducked her head completely to soak her hair, and then swam away from him, the golden cloud drifting behind her. 'Where are you?' he called, anxiously, uncertain in the moonlight shimmering on the water.

Anna submerged, and swam beneath the surface, back to him. She came up behind him – he was now shoulder deep – and wrapped both arms round his chest and both legs round his thighs. 'Right here.'

'Anna! Oh, Anna.'

As she was taking deep breaths her breasts

inflated against his back, her hardened nipples scouring his flesh. He tried to turn, still in her embrace, but she was too strong for him and retained her position.

'Anna!' he gasped. 'Please.'

She relaxed her grip, and he did turn. She had allowed her legs to drop, but now she brought them up again, resuming their grasp on his thighs while she felt him rise between them. 'Can you do it standing up?'

'Anna!' He found her mouth with his own, kissed her parted lips. 'Are you serious?'

'Perhaps,' she said. 'If you'll tell me who you really are, and what you really want.'

'Oh, Anna...' And then he looked past her; her back was to the beach. 'Oh, my God! People!'

'What are we going to do?' he asked, his brain seething with alarm and frustration.

'Tell you what,' Anna said, now in a thoroughly mischievous mood. 'We could give them a thrill.'

'Anna, there are three men.'

Anna released him and slid down into the water, her feet touched the sand as she turned to look at the beach. The three men had come out of the trees beside the car, and were standing above their clothes.

'I thought you said no one ever comes here?' Hamilton protested.

'I said visitors seldom come here. Those are local, probably from Gambier.'

'Do you think they know we're here?'

'Of course they know we're here.'

'But if we stay out here, in the water, won't they go away?'

Two of the men were kneeling beside their clothes.

'They may,' Anna agreed. 'But if they do, they'll take our clothes with them. They'll also take the car.' She started to wade towards the beach.

'Anna ... you can't go ashore.'

'I have no intention of being stuck fourteen miles from Nassau with no transport and no clothes.'

'But there are three of them!'

The adrenalin was pumping. 'But there are two of us, one of whom is me. The odds are all in our favour.'

He gazed at her back; this view was almost as compelling as her front. What to do? He was a highly trained operative, and entirely capable of taking care of himself in a punch-up. But it was no part of his plan to let her know that. And besides, he had a sudden urge to discover just how she would handle herself, if her skills were as remarkable as her reputation. He could always pick up the pieces afterwards.

The sea was down to her thighs, water draining out of her hair. She didn't know whether or not he was following her. The men on the beach had now realized that she was approaching them. For a few seconds they watched her as she emerged, thighs and then legs uncovering: even in the semi-darkness, she knew she was an unforgettable sight. Then they muttered at each other. She couldn't hear what they were saying, but one called out. 'Hey woman, what you want?'

'I want you to put down those things you have just picked up, including the car keys, and then clear off.'

'You stupid or what?'

'Man,' said the second man. 'You seeing them tits?'

'Yeah,' said the third. 'I got to get me hands on them.'

They hadn't yet noticed the jewellery.

Anna left the water 'If you put all that stuff back, and leave now,' she said, speaking quietly, 'you won't be harmed.'

'You,' remarked the first man, 'going harm us? Man, you know what we going do with you? We going take sweetness from you. You come here.'

Anna obligingly obeyed. Now her whole body was a seethe of latent energy, as was her brain. After fourteen years she dearly, and genuinely, wanted to call a halt to her violent career, but she knew she was going to miss the blood-tingling excitement of going into action. And if these foolish layabouts wanted trouble...

'That's right,' the first man said. 'Now you get down on your hands and knees, and crawl over here. Is your ass I want first.'

The fools had not even separated, to force her to decide who to attack first. But now the leader came forward as, again obediently, she dropped to her hands and knees, digging the fingers of her left hand into the sand. The idiot was actually turning folly into suicide: by unbuckling his belt and starting to drop his pants, both occupying his hands and hindering his movements. 'You got sense,' he commented. 'You just stay so, and I ain't going hurt you. Well, only a little.'

He was standing above her, holding his pants round his knees with one hand, fondling a massive erection with the other. Anna waited as he went round her to stand behind her. 'Man,' he said. 'That is the sweetest ass I ever did see.'

Anna moved with all the lightning speed developed over her years of training and experience. She reared on to her knees, turning as she did so, and her left hand delivered the moulded ball of damp sand she had gathered into the man's face. He uttered a yell of dismay, while Anna's right arm, travelling with all her force and ending in a hand held rigid and as hard as steel, crashed into his genitals. Now he gave a scream of the purest agony, and dropped to his knees in turn, both hands clutching his injured organ.

But Anna knew too well that the only mistake one could make in a serious fight was to give an opponent a chance to recover. She rose to her feet and again swung her right arm, as usual with all of her force and this time with all of her body weight as well, into his shoulder where it joined his neck. The scream ended as if a switch had been turned off, and his body collapsed in a heap at her feet.

Anna knelt beside him, tested his pulse. Damn! she thought. The blow could have been controlled – without her full weight it need not have been fatal – but at that moment she had been consumed with hatred, for the various men, and women, who had from time to time raped her, or attempted to do so. Not one of them was still alive.

'Christ, woman,' said one of the other men. 'What you done? You done hurt him.'

'Actually,' Anna said, rising to her feet, 'I done kill him.'

They goggled at her.

'So my advice to you,' she continued, 'is to clear off before anyone else gets hurt. But first of all give me the car keys.'

'Bitch,' the man said. 'You fucking bitch! You kill Billy! I going cut them fucking tits right off.' His sexual interest in her seemed to have dwindled, but now he ran at her.

'Anna!' Hamilton shouted from behind her. 'He's got a knife!'

Anna had seen the glint of steel in the moonlight. She stood absolutely still until he reached her, and carved at her with a huge sweep of the blade. Then she skipped to one side, and in the split second before he could turn back had moved behind him and against him, throwing her left arm round his neck. He struck behind himself, but as he did so she slid her right hand down his arm to grasp his wrist, released his neck to seize his upper arm with her left, and

81

forced the arm down with all her strength, at the same time bringing her right knee up, equally with all her force.

The crack sounded almost like a pistol shot, and was accompanied by another piercing scream. The knife fell to the sand and she kicked it away. The man dropped to his knees, pawing at his right arm with his left hand. 'You break me arm,' he wailed. 'You break me arm.'

'Oh, me God!' cried the other man. 'You break he arm.'

'He should have taken my advice,' Anna said severely. 'It could easily have been his neck. Now, you...'

'I ain't done nothing,' he shouted. 'I ain't doing nothing.'

'That is a very wise decision,' Anna agreed. 'Bring those keys to me.'

'Mistress...'

'Just do it.' Her voiced cracked like a whip. 'Or would you prefer me to come to you?'

'I coming, mistress. I coming.'

He advanced cautiously, left arm extended, keys dangling from his fingers. Anna didn't know whether he was armed, but he showed no inclination to attack her. She took the keys. 'Thank you. Now help your friend to get up, and take him away. You're only a couple of miles from Gambier, as I am sure you know, and you should be able to get some help for his arm there.'

'But what we going do about Billy?'

'I don't think there is anything you can do

about Billy, save inform his family that he is deceased, and have his body collected and buried. Good night.'

The man heaved his moaning companion to his feet, and the pair disappeared into the darkness.

Hamilton finally left the water to stand beside Anna on the sand, aware of a flood of conflicting emotions. Consternation, certainly; in all his years in the field, he had never seen such immediate and total destruction of the opposition ... without the use of a weapon. Professional admiration was tinged with apprehension; the suspicion that he might fare no better were he that opposition ... except that he would know what to expect. But also a realization that, as long as he played his cards right, she was vulnerable, because she trusted him. As now. She was naked, and standing with her back to him. Were he armed with his favourite weapon, the knife, he could complete the entire operation now with a single thrust into her back followed by a pass across her throat. And there was a knife lying on the sand at her feet. If he dared. If, indeed, he could bring himself to destroy such perfection. But until he had come to a decision, it was essential to preserve the image he had created, that of a fly-by-night rendered totally out of his depths by what had happened. 'My God!' he said 'What are we going to do?'

Anna gave him the keys. 'Leave. We can

dress later. When we've dried a bit.'

'We'll have to be dressed by the time we reach the police station.'

'Mark, we are not going to the police station. When we've dried and are dressed, we'll go back to the hotel and go to bed.'

'But ... we must report what happened.'

'Why?'

'Anna...' he almost wailed. 'You have just killed a man. And probably crippled another.'

'I don't think I had too much choice. If there is one thing I abhor, it is being raped. And they would have taken my jewellery. Apart from the value, it has a considerable sentimental importance for me.'

'Well, of course it was self-defence. I'll support you.'

'It would still mean a hell of a lot of publicity, and that I can do without.'

'But you can't just walk away from a dead man. If we don't report it, those men certainly will. And they'll be telling their story first.'

'What story do you suppose they are going to tell? That they were taking a stroll along Love Beach and were suddenly attacked by a maniacal white woman who killed one of them and probably crippled another? Let's say that you're a police sergeant and a couple of lay-abouts approached you with that tale, what would your reaction be? Apart from the obvious one that they had to be drunk.'

'But when they find the body...?'

'*When* they find the body, which I shouldn't

84

think will be for some time, because our friends are not going to report it at all. Anyway, if they did make the mistake of reporting it, the police would draw the obvious conclusion. Clearly the three of them were walking on the beach, drunk, they quarrelled, had a fight, and one of them got killed. The other two panicked, and concocted this fantastic story about some murderous woman. They'd be laughed all the way to the noose. Ugh! I stink of stale sweat from that bastard. I'm just going to have a quick dip.'

She went back into the water, knelt in the shallows, watching him, just in case he was tempted to abandon her. But he seemed petrified.

Actually, he was again considering possible options. He was within six feet of the knife. But he knew she was watching him. It could no longer be a surprise thrust. And the thought of opposing that terrifying speed and strength, not to mention that unearthly beauty, face to face, was indeed paralysing. He could still hear that bone breaking. So he reminded himself that that was not his remit. Indeed, it had been specifically forbidden.

She returned out of the water, shook herself, gathered up her clothes; and Hamilton stirred. 'What about the knife?'

'That stays right there,' she said. 'The only prints on it are those of its owner. Another reason for him not to say a word. Let's move.'

He scooped up his own clothes and followed her. 'I'm surprised you didn't kill them all,' he remarked, in a feeble attempt at sarcasm.

Anna got into the car. 'I never believe in taking life unnecessarily.'

He digested this as he started the engine and made a three-point turn. Then he said, 'You know, you almost sound as if you've done this sort of thing before.'

'My life has had its ups and downs,' she conceded.

He negotiated the track in silence, and they reached the road. 'Turn right,' she commanded.

'What? Aren't we going back to town?'

'There's another road that runs down the centre of the island. I'll show you the way. If we return along the coast we'll probably run into those two again, and by now they may have met up with friends – who could then support at least part of their story, that their attacker was driving a possibly identifiable car. If we don't turn up, they have nothing at all save their fantasy.'

He turned right. 'Do you always think this quickly and clearly?'

'I'm alive.' She directed him, as they followed the road round the deserted American base at Windsor Field. 'So what does happen now?' he asked.

'I told you, we go home to bed. I'm sorry if you feel cheated, but frankly...' she looked down between his naked legs. 'I don't think you're in the right mood any more. We'll see what we can do, tomorrow.'

'You mean you'll still be here?'

'I told you that I wasn't going home till Thursday.'

'And then you will just disappear?'

He was becoming distinctly tiresome. 'I have to go back to the cay,' she explained. 'But it so happens that I will be travelling again in a week's time, so I shall be back in Nassau briefly. I'll be overnighting at the Vic, so we can have a last drink together then.'

'Last drink?'

'This time I may be away for several weeks. So, unless you're planning on spending the rest of your life here...'

'Actually, I was planning to go home next week anyway. That is always supposing we aren't both under arrest by then.'

'Oh, Mark, there is absolutely no possibility of that, even if you get drunk and start shouting. No one would believe you, any more than they'd believe those thugs. Do I look the sort of woman who goes around killing people? Stop here.'

'Eh?' He braked to the side of the road. To their right the ground rose sharply into a low escarpment, to their left the moonlight glimmered from the still waters of Lake Carmichael.

'Time to get dressed,' she explained, reaching across to remove the keys from the ignition.

'What are you doing?'

'I do apologize, Mark, but I would hate you to suffer a sudden panic and drive off leaving me standing here.' She gave a wicked chuckle. 'I could well be assaulted.' She handed him his clothes. 'Out you get.'

He obeyed and she also got out. Her body was still damp, but not sufficiently wet to soak her dress, at least obviously. Her hair was very wet, but she wasn't going to deny that she had been swimming, if not on Love Beach. It was still not yet eleven o'clock and the hotel would no doubt be thriving, but the only people they were likely to encounter sober were the hotel staff, who all valued her custom too much to ask questions. 'There,' she said, getting back in. 'Now we're all decent.'

He started the engine. 'Anna ... I think there is an awful lot you need to tell me.'

'It's very late, and I am very tired. Let's talk about it tomorrow.'

Because she had also not elicited anything about him, she thought, as she stood beneath a hot shower to wash the salt from her body, and rinsed her hair again and again. Save that on the evidence of this evening she found it very difficult to believe that he could be a field agent for any covert operation; she could not even be sure that he had ever seen a dead body before. But there was also a great deal of evidence that he knew a lot about her past. It could be entirely innocent, or...

Whereas, she thought, as she wrapped her hair in a towel, turned off the light, and slipped beneath the sheet with a sigh, she ... A hundred and thirty-four ... and one king cobra ... And for the first time her victim had not been in the line of duty. As for survival ... she could not be certain that the first man had intended to kill her, or even the second; to many people, especially women, the presentation of a knife would ensure complete and total surrender

But they had certainly intended to rob her and rape her in the most unpleasant fashion; and again, if not to her, in view of her experiences, but to most ordinary women, to be forced to surrender to brutal and perverted rape was not a lot better than to be murdered.

So, no regrets, whatever the inevitable reaction to a spoiled evening. There were more important things to think about – such as the next month or so, and what that might involve. But as she made it a golden rule never to think about what might lie ahead when getting ready to sleep, and as she was still, despite her siesta, very tired, she put it out of her mind and was asleep in seconds.

And awoke fully refreshed. She breakfasted in bed, then showered again, dressed in slacks, a shirt and sandals, brushed her still damp hair, put on her jewellery, sent her dress to the laundry yet again, telephoned Nassau's leading photographic studio for an appointment that afternoon, and then went downstairs, prepared to cope with Hamilton's fears. But he was not to be seen.

'Has Mr Hamilton come down yet?' she asked Peter on the desk.

'Yes, ma'am. He was down just now and went

for a walk.'

'Oh. Right.' She picked up a copy of the *Nassau Guardian,* and went on to the terrace to sit in a canvas armchair and read the news. Not that there was anything of importance; it was in any event far too soon for any mention of dead bodies on remote beaches to have reached the news desk.

And now she had both the time and the mood to consider her situation. It was actually six years since she had last set foot in England, or, to be pedantic, seven. When Clive had extricated her from Switzerland in 1945, he had taken her, and her parents, to England, but she had almost immediately been whisked off to a so-called safe house in the north of Scotland, and it was from there that she had fled with Joe Andrews after the house had turned out not to be safe at all.

So, as Joe had said, it was very unlikely that she could possibly meet anyone who knew her and would remember her. Note, she thought: when doing the nightclubs she had to be absolutely sure that no ambitious newshawk snapped her picture, to be studied at leisure by his readers.

So the risks were really minimal, of being identified. And Fahri? If he was stupid enough, and lecherous enough, to invite her into his house, he would be signing his own death warrant. Hubris? But she had been in the business for so long she was confident she could cope with almost every situation, always aided by her looks and the element of surprise. No one but a chronic paranoid would expect a beautiful blonde picked up at random in a nightclub to be an assassin sent specifically to target him.

As to what she might have to endure, or even perhaps suffer at the hands of an apparent satyr, in order to complete the operation ... well, it would not be the first time, which was no doubt the reason why, in her private life, to have unwanted sex forced on her could turn her into an angel from hell, as someone had once described her.

And afterwards? The only place she had ever found herself in from which she had been unable to escape on her own had been the Lubianka. There was no private house in the world that could compare with that monolithic establishment. So...

A shadow fell across her chair. 'Good morning.'

She looked up. 'Well, hi. I was just thinking of a drink. Join me?'

'Thank you.'

He pulled up a chair and she signalled the hovering waiter. 'Two frozen daiquiris, please, Lawrence.'

'Two daiquiris coming up, Mrs Bartley.'

'Do you know all the staff here by name?' Hamilton asked.

'Just about.'

'But how do you remember which is which? I mean...'

'They all look alike to you? They are people,

Mark. I like people. Unless I am forced to dislike them.'

'And then you actively hate them.'

'True.'

'May I look at your paper?'

'Certainly. But you won't find anything in it to interest you.' She glanced at her watch again. 'I doubt that anyone has visited Love Beach, as it's a working day. Thank you, Lawrence. And would you care to lunch with me, Mr Hamilton?'

'Yes, I would.'

'Splendid. Will you tell Charles that Mr Hamilton and I will be eating together, please, Lawrence?'

'Will do, ma'am.'

'So tell me how you feel today,' Hamilton suggested.

'I feel thoroughly rested, if that's what you mean.'

'You know it isn't.'

'Well, then, I would have to say that how I feel in myself is my business, and nobody else's.'

'Because last night is not the first time you have killed someone.'

Anna gazed at him, her eyes suddenly glacial. 'Perhaps it would be a good idea for you to eat on your own, after all.'

'Anna, please forgive me. It's just that every woman I have ever known, or even heard of, would be reduced to a traumatic state after what happened last night. And the way you handled those men...'

'Do you seriously suppose I bear any resemblance to any woman you have ever known, or even heard of? Save, of course, that you seem to have already heard of me.'

'Well...'

'So you know that I spied for Germany during the War. I had to be trained to do so, and I had to be trained to protect myself, and to do whatever needed to be done to protect myself. As I told you, that is all history now; and believe me, I want it to be history. But I suppose old habits, old instincts, die hard. When those men attacked me, well, I reacted as I had been taught to do.'

He put down his glass and held her hand. 'Anna! Forgive me, please. And forgive me for not coming to your support. I suppose the fact is that I was the one who was traumatized by what was happening. And no man likes to admit that he has played the coward.'

Anna squeezed his fingers. 'I understand. And you're forgiven.'

'So ... you said that we might do something today. Sort of...'

'Resume relations? Could you?'

'Well...'

'I think we had better put it on hold. Anyway, I have an appointment this afternoon.'

'And tomorrow you are leaving. Anna! Can I come with you? I would love to see your cay, meet your parents, get some idea of how you live.'

93

She considered him. He was almost desperate. To get to know her better? To get between her legs? To get out of Nassau for a few days while the body on the beach was discovered and the police inquiries died down? Or simply to discover where she lived? But in any event, taking him to the cay was out of the question.

'I'm sorry,' she said. 'I can't do that. My husband is due back any day now. He likes his privacy as much as I do; and as I told you, he is a very aggressive and jealous man. And far more capable of creating mayhem than I am. If he were to find a strange man on the cay, well...'

'Does he know, about your past?'

'You asked me that already, and I told you, yes he does. Which I suppose is why he is so possessive. However, as I told you, too, I find that I have to travel again very soon ... So I will see you next week. If you're still here, of course.'

'And your jealous husband let's you travel on your own?'

'We're in the same line of business. And besides, he trusts me.' She finished her drink and got up. 'Let's eat.'

'Well?' the voice said. 'Give me the address.'

'I do not have it,' Hamilton confessed.

'What?'

'Yet. Listen, it is possible that I might be able to complete the job myself. Then you would not have to send a squad. Your squads have not been very successful in the past.'

'Do you know what you are saying? What you would be risking?'

'I have seen her at work. She is everything they say of her.'

'And you think you can do it, alone?'

'I think she is beginning to trust me.'

'That may be. But the boss wants her alive, not in a ditch with a knife in her ribs. Even supposing you could do it, which I doubt. Listen, just get me the address.'

Next morning, having had her bath, Anna was having breakfast, sitting at the table wearing a dressing gown, when the phone rang. 'I'm sorry to bother you, Mrs Bartley,' said Peter, the reception clerk, 'but there is a gentleman here to see you.'

'Has he a name?'

'Spence, ma'am.'

She looked at her watch. It was just nine. 'Oh. Right. Send him up.'

She poured herself another cup of coffee, got up, unlocked the door, and then took the Walther from her shoulder bag and laid it on the table, behind the coffee pot. A few minutes later there was a tap on the door. 'It's open,' she called.

The door swung in cautiously, and Anna rested her hand on the pistol. But the man was certainly short and squat and balding, and carried a briefcase. 'Mrs Bartley?' He was also definitely an American, and equally definitely taken aback at the sight of her, obviously wearing only a dressing gown, with her feet bare and her hair loose.

'Mr Spence? You're very early.'

'I took the first flight. Joe said you were in a hurry.' Anna waited, and he closed the door. 'This has got to be the hottest place I've known since Owattamie.'

'Thank you, Horace. Come and sit down. I'm afraid I can't offer you a cup of coffee; there's only one cup.'

Spence advanced, still cautiously, and sat down. 'You don't keep your door locked? I could've been anybody.'

Anna used her left hand to move the coffee pot, and he gulped. 'Holy shit!'

'If you'd been anybody, Horace, at least anyone I didn't like the look of, you'd be dead.'

'Jesus! They told me you were the best.'

'And now you know they were telling the truth. Now, shall we finish the religious recitation and get to business?'

'Yes, ma'am. May I?'

'Be my guest.'

Carefully he moved various plates and pots and placed the briefcase on the table, while Anna sipped her coffee. He opened the case and delved into it. 'One passport. You were to have a photo for me.'

Anna got up and took the photo, which she had had taken the previous afternoon, from her shoulder bag, and handed it to him. With the glasses and her hair pulled right back, and pinned into a tight bun, it made her features look rather severe, but he didn't comment, produced a small tube of glue and carefully positioned the little photograph in the right square, then took out an ink pad and a stamp, which he placed across the bottom half of the photo. The stamp was the official American seal. 'There you go.' He held out the little booklet.

Anna opened it. She was an American citizen named Anna Kelly. Joe believed in sticking to her own Christian name where possible, as he had a theory that the quickest way to detect someone using a false identity was to address them by their true Christian name and watch their response. 'Well,' she commented, 'Kelly is at least an improvement on some of the names I've been stuck with in the past.'

Spence produced a BOAC ticket in the name of Anna Bartley. 'Return to London, leaving on Thursday.' He raised his head. 'That's a week today.'

'I know that, Horace.'

'The return is open. Smitten will see to that, as he is seeing to all your arrangements in England.'

'Yes,' Anna said, somewhat doubtfully. But she remembered that Jerry, despite his failings as a back-up, was quite good at organizing things.

'Well, then...'

'And?'

'Ah!' He produced a slip of paper. 'One certified cheque for a hundred thousand dollars.'

Anna took it, glanced at the date. 'The third of March. A month today.'

'Joe said you'd be back by then.'

'I see. Next?'

'Oh, yes. Joe said to give you this.'

He handed over the sealed envelope. Anna slit it and scanned the brief note on official State Department paper:

This is to certify that Mrs Anna Bartley is a retired employee of the State Department and is not to be prosecuted for any crime she may be considered to have committed within the continental United States without reference to this department.

Of course she had known that they would have to cover themselves with the right to revoke her immunity if she were to go overboard, in any direction. She simply had to trust them. And it was signed by both the Secretary of State and the Director of the CIA. She folded the letter. 'Thank you, Horace. Now, there's one more thing you should have for me.'

'Yeah. You were inquiring about a guy named Mark Hamilton.'

'That is correct.'

'Well. we don't have any name like that in our recent files, but Joe said you wanted us to go back a bit.'

'And did you?'

'Yeah. We had to tap the FBI, because you wanted us to check the period before we existed. But they go back a long way and their lists include known agitators, on both sides of the Atlantic from before the War. That's to make sure they can't get a visa to sneak into the country.'

'And?'

'Some guy with that name is listed as being a member of the Communist Party when he was at Cambridge University in 1939. Seems quite a few of those kids had leftist leanings.'

In 1939, the year Hamilton claimed to have met her. But, as she recalled, Spence was quite correct in suggesting that there had been a large number of young British pseudo-intellectuals who dabbled in Communism in the thirties, and that was no reason for him not to have been invited to a party at Lady Pennworthy's. In fact, it has been regarded as something of a cachet to have one or two of these people floating about, if only to prove one's political broad-mindedness. 'Again, thank you, Horace. Are you going to have lunch with me?'

'No. Much as I'd like to. I'm taking the next flight out.'

'Well, then.' She got up. 'Nice meeting you.'

'Maybe we'll meet again, sometime.'

'It's possible.' Anna closed the door behind him, locked it, and placed the cheque, the letter and the passport in her shoulder bag, along with the pistol. Then she got dressed in slacks and a shirt, thrust her toes into sandals, added make-up and her jewellery, picked up her straw hat, slung the bag, closed her valise, looked around the room, and went downstairs. 'Good morning, Charles. Tommy come in yet?'

'He ain't been here, ma'am.'

'Well, it's still early. Give me a shout when he turns up. And prepare my bill, will you?'

'You got it, ma'am. You with us for lunch?'

'Indeed.'

'Table for two?' He looked disapproving. He had clearly formed a dislike for Mark Hamilton. On the other hand, it might have been that he just didn't like to have someone else getting too close to his favourite customer.

She smiled. 'I imagine so, Charles. He's very persistent. Take care of these for me, will you?' She gave him the two bags. 'I'll be on the terrace.'

Where, predictably, Hamilton already was, looking distinctly unhappy.

'Good morning, Mark,' she said brightly. 'Sleep well?' They had spent the evening dinner-dancing in the hotel, as she had thought it best to keep his nerves under control, although she had had to be very firm to keep him out of her bed.

Now he thrust the newspaper at her. 'Have you seen this?'

Anna scanned the headline – MURDERED MAN FOUND ON LOVE BEACH – and the news item below:

The body of William Bonpart was yesterday afternoon found by tourists on Love Beach, the well-known beauty spot fourteen miles west of Nassau. He had been beaten about the body, and died as a result of a blow, probably a karate chop, to the neck. The body was only partially clothed. Mr Bonpart, who has a criminal record and was known to have a violent temper, was last seen alive on Tuesday night, drinking with two acquaintances. These men, one of whom has a recently broken arm, are now helping the police with their inquiries. A police spokesman has confirmed that they are not looking for any other suspects.

'Well,' she said, 'that would appear to be that.'

'You think so? Don't you realize that when they're faced with a possible death sentence they will tell the police exactly what happened?'

'And as I said, the police will laugh them to scorn. Even if they decide to believe them, they have nothing to go on. The men never got close enough to you to give a description, and in the dark my wet hair would have appeared dark, so all they have to say is that I have long hair and big tits. That is not unique. They can't even prove that we actually exist.'

'And when these characters are hanged, for a crime they didn't commit?'

'Think a moment. That second character certainly intended to cut me up, and his pal would undoubtedly have helped him. Anyway, I doubt they'll be hanged. To convict them of murder, the police would have to determine which one of them struck the fatal blow, and when the chips are down they will certainly get around to accusing each other. They would also have to be found guilty of malice aforethought, which it obviously was not. They'll go down for manslaughter.'

'But they'll go down. For God knows how many years...'

'In my opinion, they deserve to. And think of this. If I had just lain on my back with my legs apart and let them get on with it, even supposing they hadn't cut my throat afterwards, they'd have gone down for even longer.'

'You are impossible.'

'Have you just noticed? I think it's time for a drink before lunch.'

He was brooding silently on the situation while they sipped their piña coladas when Anna looked up in delight at the large black man wearing a battered yachting cap who appeared in the doorway. 'Tommy! All well?'

'Yes, ma'am. Boat's at the dock.'

'Great. Mark, this is Tommy Rawlings, my right-hand man. Tommy, this is Mark Hamilton.'

'Pleased to meet you, Mr Hamilton.'

Hamilton looked scandalized, but he shook hands.

'You going to lunch with us?' Anna asked.

'Well, Miss Anna, I got some things to do. I going be at the boat whenever you're ready.'

'Poor Tommy,' Anna said, as Tommy disappeared. 'He just cannot get it through his head

102

that this is the twentieth century, still feels that it would be improper for him to lunch with the nobs in a place like this.'

'But you'd allow him to do that?'

'Well, of course. He's my friend.'

Hamilton digested this as they ate. At last he said, 'And you're off back to your cay?'

'Soon as I've eaten.'

'I wish you'd let me come with you. Just for a day or so.'

'Now, Mark, don't start that again. I've told you that it would not be a wise thing to do. Anyway, I'll see you again in six days, remember?'

'When you'll be off to ... You never did tell me where you're going.'

'No, I didn't, did I?' Anna finished her wine. 'Now I must rush.'

'You mean you're not having coffee?'

'No. It's a three-hour journey and I want to be home by dark. It's been fun. So, I'll see you next week.'

'For the last time?'

'Well, you never know your luck. Lunch is on me.'

He didn't demur, watched her hurry to the desk, pay her bill, pick up her valise and shoulder bag, and depart for the entrance. I make my own luck, he thought.

Presumably he could keep her here for a spell, by going to the police and telling them the real story of what had happened on Love Beach. But when it came to his word against that of an obviously well-known and popular resident, would they believe him any more than the two would-be rapists? Anyway, to do that would be to get himself involved, and he did not think the boss would like that.

However, he had not exhausted all possibilities. He had deduced that Charles – who was clearly in awe of, if not actually in love with, the beautiful and glamorous Mrs Bartley (it could only have been Charles who had inspired that pre-emptive strike of hers at lunch the day before yesterday, which he had so easily deflected by turning on the charm) was going to be of no help when it came to any more information.

So he left the table and strolled on to the terrace, just in time to see Anna's door being closed by the taxi driver before she went off. Still moving nonchalantly, he sauntered down the steps and approached the next taxi in the rank. 'Good afternoon.'

'Sir!' The driver hastily got out and opened the door for him.

Hamilton fingered a £10 note. 'That lady who just left. Would you happen to know who she is?'

'Oh, yes, sir. That be Mrs Bartley.'

'Ah. Of course. I thought I knew her name. You wouldn't happen to know where she was going?'

The driver eyed the note. 'I heard she say Rawson Square.'

'Rawson Square. That's at the docks, isn't it?'

'Yes, sir.'

'Thank you.' He slipped the note into the man's hand, turned away, and then turned back, at the same time taking another note from his wallet. 'You wouldn't happen to know why she's gone to the dock?'

The driver eyed the new note in turn. 'Well, sir, I did see she boatman, Tommy Rawlings, here a little while back. So she must be going to get on she boat.'

'She has a boat?'

'Oh, yes, sir. A big job. Lovely boat.'

'How interesting. You wouldn't happen to know the name of this boat?'

'Oh, yes, sir. Everyone does know the name of Mistress Bartley's boat. *Fair Girl.*'

'*Fair Girl.* That's an odd name for a boat, isn't it?'

'Well, sir, people does call their boats by all kinds of name. But Mrs Bartley, well, she must be name it after her cay. Fair Cay.'

'That is the name of her home? Fair Cay?'

'Yes, sir.'

'Do you know where that might be?'

'Well, borse, I knowing it is in that chain of islands up towards Eleuthera.'

Fair Girl, Fair Cay ... Fehrbach. Anna's maiden name! Well, well, thought Hamilton, she may be a genius, but at heart she's a simple soul, desperate to retain some link with her past. 'How big would this island be?'

'It ain't small. Maybe a mile long. It thin,

mind. Four hundred yards across.'

'And she lives there alone?'

'Well, no, borse. She got Tommy and he wife, and Elias Bain and he nephews. They's the gardeners. Mind you, they all does go home to Eleuthera on the weekends.'

'You mean she's alone at weekends?'

'No, no, borse. She got she mummy and she daddy.'

'She lives with her parents?'

'Well, yes, borse.' He sounded surprised that anyone shouldn't live with their parents. 'And now she got she husband as well.'

'Who I gather is not always there. That's very few people for an island a mile long. Does she have a lot of visitors?'

'No, borse. Nobody don't go to Fair Cay unless Mrs Bartley tell them to come.'

'Good heavens! Is she that bad-tempered?'

'I don't think she bad-tempered, borse. Is the dogs.'

'She has dogs?'

'Oh, yes, borse. Big things. And they that fierce.'

'What are they? Alsatians? Rottweilers?'

'They bigger than that. And twice as fierce. I am hearing that only a week gone some people, tourists they was, tried to land on that beach she got, and them dogs near eat them alive. All shook up they was, when they got back here.'

'That's very interesting.' Hamilton handed over the second note. 'You've been a great help. Have a drink on me.'

'Yes, sir, borse. I going to do that.'

'Oh, there's one last thing.'

'Borse?'

'This boat, have you any idea how fast it can travel?'

'Well, borse, that boat ... it cruising around twelve knots.'

Anna had said it was a three-hour journey back to her home. What a fool he had been these past three months, in not simply approaching a taxi driver from the start. Taxi drivers knew everything, and in a place like the Bahamas they know even more than that. But of course, up to a couple of days ago he hadn't known the name she was currently masquerading under. Hamilton returned to his room and made one of his long-distance calls. 'I have what you want.'

'Yes?'

'The lady lives on a private island, called Fair Cay. It is situated about thirty-five miles northeast of Nassau, and is one of a chain of islands leading up to the large island of Eleuthera.'

'Very good, Hamilton. It took time, but you got there in the end, eh? You may come home now.'

'I think I should stay here and brief your people when they arrive. I have managed to obtain a great deal of information on the cay, and some of it could be very important.'

'Look, just leave it to us, now.'

'As you wish, sir. There is just one thing.'

'Yes?'

'How soon will your people be in position?'

'In a week or so. They will have to travel separately to avoid arousing suspicion, and then the target must be very carefully reconnoitred. There can be no mistakes this time. We have waited too long. But this is no concern of yours. In fact, you must be out of there before they arrive. We do not want any connection between you and what is going to happen.'

'A week may be too long.'

'What do you mean?'

'The lady is leaving again in six days' time.'

'To go where?'

'I don't know.'

'For how long is she going?'

'I don't know that either. But I understand that it may be a little while.'

'Find out.'

'Ah ... I can't possibly do that until she returns to Nassau, in six days' time.'

'Find out before she leaves. It is her destination that matters.'

The phone went dead.

108

LEAVING PARADISE

Anna wrapped her hair in a bandanna to go up to the flying bridge and take the helm. As always when on *Fair Girl*, she felt a great glow of utterly relaxed satisfaction.

Before coming to the Bahamas her acquaintance with the sea and boats had been limited, confined to the ocean-going variety, and she had enjoyed none of the experiences. She had crossed the Atlantic twice in 1941, working for the SD; and even though Himmler had guaranteed that all U-boat skippers would be warned which ship she was travelling on and that it was to be inviolate, had still expected momentarily to be torpedoed. Then in 1944, when travelling by Finnish ferry out of Stockholm en route back to Germany, again after carrying out a mission for the SD, she had been torpedoed, and found it a most uncomfortable experience; it had been December. She had resolved then that she would never go to sea again.

But when, after considering several places, she had – with Joe Andrews' encouragement (he liked to keep his people close at hand) – finally opted for one of the seven hundred islands that make up the Bahamas, she realized that her attitude would have to change.

'What you have to have,' said Jimmy Flynn, the CIA agent who was 'minding' her until she got settled, 'is your own boat.'

'I know absolutely nothing about boats,' she pointed out.

'I'll teach you,' he volunteered.

And he did so. He even selected the boat for her to buy, this forty-two-foot Chris-Craft, with two powerful diesel engines, six sleeping berths in three comfortable cabins, a spacious saloon-cum-galley, two steering positions, and every possible aid to navigation and communication.

She had fallen in love with it at first sight, and her love had grown as she learned to handle it in any and all conditions. Now she was as proud of her skills at helming and navigation as she was of the lethal powers instilled in her by her erstwhile masters, which had been capitalized on so often and cold-bloodedly by her more recent employers – but now for the last time. Then it would be the boat and the cay for the rest of her life. And Hamilton? As she had quickly realized, the information provided by the CIA was provocative, but not necessarily damning.

The important thing was that his behaviour the night before last ruled out any chance that he could be a Russian agent. Apart from his obvious fear at the appearance of those three men, and consternation at the way she had dealt with them, anyone hired to assassinate her would hardly have passed up the golden oppor-

110

tunity presented of being alone with her when she was naked and unarmed. Anyway, she found it hard to believe that the Soviet secret police, the MGB, would still be hunting her after eleven years of expensive failure. And now she had everything she wanted – most importantly the right to defend herself and her cay with all the considerable powers at her disposal. She wondered if Hamilton would still be there next Wednesday? But that was not very important. If he was still hanging around when she returned from this mission...

Meanwhile, she was home again, if only briefly. For her, home began the moment she set foot on her boat. And now that she had threaded her way through the harbour shipping and was out of the narrow reef-strewn eastern entrance, she could look forward to seeing the cay rising over the horizon at any moment.

She adjusted the throttles to the cruising speed of twelve knots. The sea was calm, as it usually was in the lee of the islands, unless there was a hurricane in the vicinity; and, as she was now several miles west of the chain that curved all the way from New Providence to Eleuthera, she engaged the autopilot and relaxed, while Tommy came up the ladder to sit on the bench beside her. 'So what's been happening these past couple of weeks?' she asked.

Tommy had been with her for six years. Within a couple of months of buying the cay, she had taken him and his wife on as general factotum and housekeeper respectively, built them a house, and paid them above the average Bahamian wage. This had earned their total loyalty, enhanced when soon afterwards she had turned up with *Fair Girl* and placed Tommy in charge of the boat when she was not on board it herself. He had been a fisherman in his youth (he was still only in his mid-forties) and not only knew boats and engines but, more important, the Bahamian waters, which for all their natural beauty contained innumerable dangers for the unwary. This knowledge he had passed on to her over the years.

What the pair of them thought of her, and said about her, in the privacy of their house on the cay, or to their friends when, as they did every weekend, they returned to their home in Eleuthera, she had no idea. She knew they had to have opinions of their own. That she might be extremely wealthy was not in the least unusual amongst foreign residents in the Baha-mas. But Desirée had to be aware that in her study her employer kept an arsenal of weapons – from pistols, through a Remington riot gun and two tommy-guns, to a bazooka – and that she practised regularly with all of them, save the bazooka, on the underground range she had created beneath the house. Most of them had been donated by the CIA to help her defend the cay against the Russian-employed Mafia – and they had all been used, although none of her staff had been on the island when the assault had taken place.

Certainly their almost awed respect for her had never wavered. Now Tommy replied, 'Nothing much, save for them tourists last week.'

'What tourists?' Anna was immediately alert.

'People from Nassau, I guess. They had a chartered boat, and they found their way through the north reef, mostly by luck, I reckon, and tried to land on the beach.'

'Couldn't they see the KEEP OFF sign?'

'Well, they must have done, ma'am. It's a big enough sign. But you know what these tourists are like. They see a nice empty-looking beach and don't pay no attention to signs.'

'And you had to see them off?'

'Well, no, ma'am. I didn't even know they was there; I was working on the boat at the dock. But the dogs were loose.'

'Oh, my God! What happened?'

'Well, I think them people made it in time. When I heard the barking, I left the dock and run across the island. By the time I reached the beach, they were back in their boat. Man, they was scared. Two fellows and two girls. They shout at me, a whole lot of swear words. So I tell them to watch the sign and clear off.'

'And the dogs?'

'They rushing up and down in the shallows, all excited, with they teeth bared and thing. Man, if I didn't know them, and they didn't know me, I'd have been scared white.'

Anna squeezed his hand. 'But you do know them, and they do know you.'

'Yes, ma'am. But ma'am, they ever bite somebody?'

They saved my life, Anna recalled, three years ago. By biting that Mafioso bastard, the only member of the crew of that ill-fated yacht who got ashore and had had the drop on me. But Tommy knew nothing about that, as he had not been on the island at the time; nor should he ever. So she said, 'Not to my knowledge, Tommy. But I guess there's always a first time.' She watched the island emerging over the horizon. Home, she thought.

The island-studded reef that stretched south-west from Eleuthera, almost to New Providence itself, enclosed a huge area of relatively shallow water to the east; on the north-west side it fronted the North-West Bahama Passage, a broad and very deep stretch of water that was habitually used by big ships out of Fort Lauderdale.

The several cays were separated by stretches of razor-sharp coral rock that could tear the bottom out of any boat that encountered them. Through the reef there were several narrow, mostly unmarked, passages that had to be negotiated with great care, while Fair Cay itself was surrounded by a subsidiary reef that ran some two hundred yards off the beach along the north-western shore of the island.

It had been the home of a wealthy American eccentric before the War, and now it was the home of an even wealthier Irish eccentric. Anna had done a considerable amount of improving, which included completely refurbishing the house, adding an upper storey to the original bungalow – so the roof, now almost as high as the casuarinas that surrounded it, was visible from at sea, while her HF wireless aerial rose even above the treetops – and installing her library, a suite for her parents, and a large indoor gymnasium and firing range (she had trained every day of her adult life when not actually travelling on business).

She had also doubled the size of the catchment area, very important as the cay's only source of fresh water was the fortunately abundant rainfall. But, prudently, the large swimming pool she installed next to the house was salt. While some people had questioned the need for a swimming pool on a Bahamian island with its own private beach, the beach was exposed to passing fishing boats and yachts only a few hundred yards offshore (also to the odd adventurous tourist, as had apparently happened only a week ago) and Anna did like swimming in the nude.

Now she steered the boat through the gap in the southern reef, with the confidence born of experience. Three hundred yards to the left was the narrow entrance to her dock. This small stone enclosure had been created by the previous owner, but greatly improved and strengthened by Anna. During the hurricane three years previously, *Fair Girl* had ridden the storm securely moored against the inner dock.

Alongside this Anna now expertly guided the boat, while Tommy, having put out the fenders, stepped ashore with the mooring warps.

On the far side of the little harbour there waited an open twenty-five-foot runabout. This Anna had given to Tommy, for taking Desirée and the gardeners back to the Bluff Settlement on North Eleuthera at weekends and also for quick trips to Spanish Wells, the nearest town of any size, situated at the head of the chain, just off the coast of North Eleuthera itself. Here Anna maintained a post-office box, and the town also contained two good supermarkets from which they could obtain day-to-day perishables such as fresh milk and bread. By creating a large vegetable garden on the cay – there already was all the fruit they could eat, and fish abounded all around them – they were virtually self-sufficient apart from the bulk-buying of items such as alcohol and fuel, which they obtained from Nassau.

Satisfied, Anna slid down the ladder and into the saloon, slung her shoulder bag, and stepped ashore. Tommy was already on the dock, connecting the shore supply of electricity to make sure the batteries were always fully charged and the fridge (which at sea worked off the batteries) was constantly kept at the right temperature, so the boat was ready to leave at a moment's notice.

She walked along the dock, looking up the sloping path at the small wood of casuarina trees that shrouded the island, tall and stately, their constantly rustling leaves always audible, even when the evening breeze was hardly noticeable, though always backed by the low, constant growl of the generator. And watched the two enormous white Dogos come bounding towards her. She had chosen the Argentinian hunting dogs as her pets-cum-guard dogs for their two vital qualities: unhesitating loyalty and obedience to their owner and his or her friends, and unbridled hostility to strangers. Residents on the cay were their friends; all others, unless specifically instructed otherwise by their mistress, were enemies.

Now they danced round her, panting with excitement; they seldom barked except when roused. She ruffled their great heads. 'Juno! You're putting on weight.'

The bitch gurgled happily. Anna was always commenting on her weight, but her dinner was never reduced.

'Jupiter, you old devil! I hear you've been terrorizing the natives, as always.'

Another happy gurgle – they could tell if she was pleased or displeased by her tone. Then they fell into line behind her, and paused patiently as they reached a large black lump sitting in the centre of the path. Anna scooped the cat into her arms for a hug and a kiss. 'Isis, you darling!'

Isis spent most of her time in Anna's bedroom – indeed, in Anna's bed – save when she felt like a meal or a drink. She never seemed aware when Anna was leaving, or even to notice when she was away. But with that sixth sense unique to cats she always seemed to know when her mistress was coming back, although this was partly inspired by the excitement which permeated the entire house when the message summoning the boat arrived from Nassau. Now she purred loudly as Anna carried her up the path towards the woman who waited for her at the top.

She put the cat down to embrace her mother. There were no extravagant words of greeting, just a long, intense hug; they had had to do this too often in the past. But Jane Fehrbach asked, in the soft Irish brogue she had bequeathed to her daughter, 'Is all well?'

'Now I'm home, Mama.'

Jane sighed, and held Anna's hand as they continued towards the house, with all three animals now following, the cat walking between the two dogs; they were her friends.

Jane Haggerty had been a well-known investigative journalist when she was sent by her newspaper, a London daily, to Vienna in 1919 to do some articles on the horrendous situation existing there, as the erstwhile capital of a great empire had been left, like a cut flower in a vase, to dwindle, bereft of all outside sustenance, its people dropping dead in the streets of starvation.

Tall and beautiful, like her daughter, Jane had astounded both her Irish family and her English colleagues by choosing to remain in Austria, having fallen in love with a crusading reporter named Johann Fehrbach. In May 1920, when their daughter Annaliese was born, they had married, had another child, and settled down to live as happily as they were able to in an Austria torn by economic problems and a succession of dictatorships.

All had been swept away in the Anschluss of March 1938, when Johann, author of a series of articles denouncing Fascism, and particularly its Nazi offshoot, had been among the first arrested, along with his family; and they had all seemed destined for a terminal existence in a concentration camp, when a senior SS officer recognized the potential of his eldest daughter. There followed a long seven years of imprisonment, not harsh in itself but made almost intolerable by the assumption that their favourite child had embraced the Nazi Party. It hadn't been until 1944, when Anna made an abortive attempt to rescue them, that they learned that for the previous five years she had actually been working for the Allies. The following year, with Clive's help, she had been able to get them to England, and a year later to bring them to this island paradise, where they were as safe as ever before, protected by her skills and now those of her husband – skills they had seen put into devastating practice three years before, when the Mafia mounted their catastrophic attempt to invade the island.

They had also had to get used to the fact that she was the world's most highly skilled assassin. That had taken some assimilating, but she had been able to convince them that, except when defending herself, and them, she killed only to order, and then only targets who her employers had convinced her were menaces to mankind and could not be dealt with by conventional means.

But that reassuring aspect of her profession could not disguise the fact that every time she departed on one of her mysterious ventures into the outside world she was taking her life in her hands; and that, by the laws of nature and history, one day she would not come back. So every moment they could spend together was to be treasured.

Johann's feelings were identical to his wife's, but whereas Jane retained her stature and had even regained much of her youthful sparkle, even if her hair was streaked with grey, Johann had aged. Although he was only fifty-eight, his snow-white hair and continuous tremble made him appear at least twenty years older. Now he also silently embraced his daughter.

'I'm starving,' said Anna. And looked past them at the large black woman standing in the doorway. 'Desirée!'

'Is good to have you back, Miss Anna.'

'It's good to be back. What's for dinner?'

'I got one big conch chowder.'

'That sounds tremendous.' She accompanied them into the house, and Johann hurried to the sideboard, where he had already opened a bottle of her favourite Veuve Clicquot. Anna sipped. 'Aaah. I gather you had some excitement last week?'

'Would-be trespassers,' Johann said. 'The dogs saw them off.'

The animals had followed them into the house, but while Isis had headed immediately for the stairs leading up to Anna's bedroom, the dogs were sitting together, panting. Anna stroked their heads, 'Good dogs! Well done!'

'Any mail?'

'One. From the postmark, I'd say it's from Stattler.'

He gave her the envelope, and she sat down to slit it open and study the contents, which covered several sheets of paper, most of them filled with figures, while her parents watched her somewhat anxiously. Paul Stattler was the CIA accountant who had looked after her money for the past six years. 'Problems?' Johann ventured.

'On the contrary. All the transfers have been made to the banks I designated and are now entirely in my hands, and Clive's, of course. Stattler's not happy, needless to say. None of them are. But ... it's done.'

'You don't mean they've agreed?' Jane asked.

'Yes, albeit reluctantly.'

'That has got to be the best news we've ever heard,' Johann said, and refilled their glasses.

'There is a small caveat.'

Both her parents lowered their glasses and looked at her.

'One last job,' Anna explained.

'One last pound of flesh,' Jane said bitterly.

'It's something only I can do.'

'Don't they always say that?'

'In this case, it's probably true. One last job, and then I'm out.'

'Oh, Anna! When?'

'I leave next Wednesday. I assume there's been no word from Clive?'

Johann shook his head.

'Well, if he's not back before then, you'll have to tell him.'

'Aren't you worried about him? He's been gone almost a month.'

'Of course I worry about him, Mama. But I know he can take care of himself, just as he knows I can take care of myself. I also know that were anything to happen to him, Billy would let me know immediately. So, no news is always good news.'

Jane sighed. While she understood that her daughter's totally confident, pragmatic approach to life was principally responsible for her survival, it was still terrifying.

'Now,' Anna went on, 'I may well be away for a little while this time. Entirely because the job may take a couple of weeks to set up. So don't worry about it, but...' She opened her shoulder bag and took out the cheque. 'I'll leave this in my desk. You'll see that it's dated the third of March.'

Johann frowned. 'That's a month.'

'Yes.' Anna handed it to him to study 'You'll see that it's certified, so it's quite safe. Now, I'd like you to give that to Clive, should he arrive

122

back before I do. But either way, if I'm not back, he or you must go to Nassau on the third of March and deposit it in the account.'

'A hundred thousand dollars,' Johann mused. 'This must be a very big job.'

'Call it a golden handshake.' She smiled at them, brightly. 'Let's eat.'

As always, Anna slept soundly, the more so as she was in her own bed, with Isis curled in her arms. But also, as always when at home, she was up at dawn, going down to the gym to exercise vigorously for half an hour. She would then indulge in a little firearms practice, activating the switch that had a succession of man-sized targets moving across the far wall, some twenty yards away; this wall was heavily padded, both to protect the stonework and to obviate the risk of a ricochet.

Having put on her earmuffs, Anna faced the opposite wall, counted ten, turned, and opened fire. After emptying the magazine, she took off the muffs, switched off the power, ejected the magazine, laid the empty pistol on the table, to be cleaned and oiled later, and went forward. Each target had a neat hole in the centre of the forehead. She remembered the first time she had ever fired a pistol on a range like this. Then the target had been a living man, and an SS officer had been standing beside her. She could still recall the feeling of utter sickness, both physical and mental, as she realized what she was required to do. Nor had it been the slightest

123

bit alleviated by the assurance that her victim was a condemned felon, doomed in any event to die, by slow hanging, if she did not kill him, and that he would far rather a quick and clean end.

But any temptation to refuse had been ended by the fate of the girl immediately before her – who had refused, and promptly been stripped naked to be flogged until blood was running down her legs, before being removed to spend the rest of her probably short life in an SS brothel. Even more compelling had been the knowledge that apart from what might happen to her, her parents and her sister would suffer even more horrifying fates.

She had been just eighteen years old, and in that instant she had had to make the decision that turned her from an innocent schoolgirl into ... An angel from hell? Or the devil incarnate?

But it was going to end. After fifteen blood-stained years. She went to the hollow space behind the wall to take down the used targets and replace them from the stack of cut-outs stored beside the range, reflecting as she did so that retirement was going to bring its own problems. While her speed and accuracy enabled her to be economic of ammunition in the field, the constant practice required to maintain that speed and accuracy involved a profligate expenditure of cartridges. Whenever necessary in the past, she had merely informed her employers that her stock of ammunition needed replenishment, and it was done. When she was working for the SD, replacement magazines for her Luger had been supplied by the SS armoury; more recently, those for the Walther, as well as spare targets, had been provided by Petersen, the CIA agent in Miami, with no questions asked, and picked up by *Fair Girl*. She had a fair stock of each left, just as she had more than a hundred rounds each of scatter and solid shot for the riot gun; but obviously her source was about to dry up. Even Clive, while he might be able to keep up her supply, would have difficulty importing large amounts of ammunition into the Bahamas.

And then she smiled, as she realized that she was guilty of tunnel vision. Surely, once she was retired, her expenditure of both cartridges and targets should dwindle, although she had no intention of allowing her skills to do so? And in any event, now that she had her immunity to travel in the States as she chose, she could replenish her stocks herself; few American armaments retailers had scruples about selling as much arms and ammunition as anyone wished to buy.

She closed the gymnasium and went upstairs. The dogs were waiting for her on the veranda. The gym was soundproofed, but they knew she was up, and they also knew her routine when she was home. Now they joined her in the pool, for several minutes of vigorous swimming, up and down. Next, it was to the outside shower to wash off the salt, to suffer which they stood patiently while Anna directed the jet to every part of their bodies, to make sure no potentially itchy spots were left; then they rolled on the grass beside the pool while she rinsed her hair.

Satisfied, she went back to her bedroom, put on a pair of shorts and a loose shirt, tied her wet hair in a bandanna, thrust her bare feet into flip-flops, and joined her parents for a sumptuous breakfast. She left all housekeeping details to Jane and Desirée; there was always ample cash in the house for their shopping trips to Spanish Wells.

Then it was time for her inspection. First of all she made sure all the screens were proofed; this was necessary because, while the fine mesh kept out mosquitoes and other flying insects, it was ineffective against the far more numerous sand flies, and so required regular painting over with repellent. Then, accompanied by the dogs, she walked round the flower garden that bordered the poolside lawn. Because of the sparse soil and occasionally destructive rainfall, flowers were the most difficult things to grow on the cay, but there were massed banks of colourful oleander and flamboyant, surrounded by hibiscus hedges. Although these plants' multicoloured blooms died every night, Desirée kept the house vases filled, and fresh flowers were always there next morning.

Leaving the garden she went to the power house, a hundred yards from the main building, sandals crunching on the pine needles dropped from the casuarinas – which could be murderous to bare feet, although the dogs did not seem bothered.

There were two 25 kilowatt generators in the little shed, one working, the other silent. Tommy alternated them to make sure they were both always in perfect condition, as they needed to be to sustain the island – not only the lights, but the various water pumps, both fresh and salt (all the toilets operated on salt water), and the giant freezer in the house, and they had to supply power to the other houses, and down the hill to the dock. When she acquired the island, the power had been carried by overhead cables, which had been extremely vulnerable to strong winds, and to certain failure in the event of a hurricane. So she had had Tommy and the gardeners bury them all, to render the supply invulnerable as long as the generators worked, a big task but one which had proved its worth: during the 1949 hurricane there had been no failure.

Behind the generator shed, and feeding into it, was the oil storage tank. This had a 5,000 gallon capacity, and filling it was Anna's greatest expense, as it involved getting a tanker up from Nassau and then running a supply line from the harbour up to the tank. However, this only needing doing every couple of years, and at the moment the sight gauge was showing well over half full.

Next to the tank were the fresh water filters, through which the supply from the cistern was piped to the various houses. These were very necessary, as although Tommy cleaned them out every couple of days, almost immediately green scum and algae started to gather.

From the shed, which was on the same ridge as the house, some twenty feet above sea level, she looked down through the coconut-tree fringe on to the beach, a long curve of the whitest possible sand. Beyond was the green, shading to blue, of the lagoon; and beyond that the reef, only visible because of the ripple of surf; and beyond the reef the far deeper blue of the deep-water passage, which dropped to several hundred fathoms within half a mile of the shore. Today, there was not a ship to be seen. The nearest land out there, Abaco, was more than forty miles away.

She followed the path, which led to the other side of the ridge before dividing, one branch leading down to the dock, the other through the trees. Here she came first to the Rawlings' house, empty at the moment as Desirée was up at the main house and Tommy at the dock; then the gardeners' house, again empty as they had already started work. Leaving these behind, she entered the orchard (not organized to any plan), where fruit trees grew in profusion, from huge sapodillas, laden with succulent fruit, to equally luscious mangoes, and then limes, lemons and oranges, a blaze of green and yellow. The bananas and plantains formed a separate grove, their stems drooping beneath the weight of the fruit, while the avocado plants, equally heavily laden, were no less luxurious in the number and size of their fruit. And there were always the water-melon vines littering the earth, the rugby-foot-ball-like gourds punctuating their progress, lying in wait to trip unwary feet. The island was so opulent in fruit she regularly sent the surplus to the produce centre on Eleuthera, simply to get rid of it; as most other people, whether on the mainland or the adjacent islands, were doing the same thing, there was little financial return.

The situation was different in the vegetable patch, which came next. The soil gathered in depressions in the coral rock that comprised the island, and the vegetables needed constant care to survive the ravages of the thousands of in-sects that sought to devour them. Indeed, Anna had known nothing about agriculture when she first came here, so to get the best results she had had to both learn and use her natural common sense, and persuade her gardeners to do the same. The Bahamian attitude was that as half of each crop was certain to be lost, it was a waste of time trying to prevent such acts of nature. But Anna had taught them how to support the tomato vines – their chief crop – in order to pre-vent them trailing on the ground to provide sustenance for the caterpillars, as well as to use sprays. Now they watched her approach with both pleasure and apprehension – she could be critical – and with genuine warmth at having her back.

'Man, is good to see you, boss,' said Elias, the head gardener.

'It's good to be back.' She greeted the two younger men. 'All well?'

'Oh, yes, ma'am.' He gestured around himself with considerable pride. 'We going to have one good crop.'

'I can see that. Well done.'

They glowed.

'Now, what about the cistern?'

'Oh, that nearly full, ma'am. We had plenty rain.'

'Excellent. Let's have a look.'

She led him along the path to the area where the hens were. It was not actually a run, as there was no enclosure beyond a wire fence to prevent the fowls from straying too far. When she first came to the island, it had been infested with what were known as chicken snakes, a variety of the constrictor family, growing to about six feet long. These did not necessarily live off chickens – there hadn't been any – but feasted on rats, raided birds' nests, and indeed devoured any living creature that wandered within their grasp. She and Tommy had rapidly got rid of them, and now she had a flock of some fifty hens and a cockerel, who kept her table supplied with eggs and occasionally meat, though most of their meat was bought in Spanish Wells.

The fowls fluttered and pecked and clucked over the considerable area allotted to them, paying scant attention to either the humans or the dogs, for Jupiter and Juno had been taught from their smallest puppyhood that the fowls were inviolate, and had thus formed the opinion that the fluttering creatures were somehow sinister and to be avoided. They never ventured into chicken territory unless accompanied by their mistress, and always, as now, slunk through it at her heels.

Beyond the hens, at the north-eastern end of the island, was the catchment area. This consisted of a large sheet of concrete – very nearly the size of a football pitch, sloping from north-east down to south-west and thus facing the prevailing weather – into which the rain poured and cascaded down to flow through gutters into the cistern. This was roofed to keep off bird droppings and drifting leaves, and fenced to discourage any living creatures who might be intent on inadvertent suicide.

But even so, it had to be carefully tended. Anna stood on the lip and looked down into the water. At its highest, as after one of the violent rainstorms that were not uncommon, it was six feet deep, and now was at the five-foot marker.

She inhaled the slightly acrid tang. 'Looks good and smells good. How are we off for chlorine?'

'Oh, we got plenty, boss. Tommy did bring up some drums last week.'

'Well done, Elias. Carry on.' She went down the rocks to the beach, followed by the dogs, took off her sandals, and walked home along the sand while they frolicked in the shallows. All hers. And when she came back from this last mission, all tensions would be behind her.

Hamilton got to work immediately, making the rounds of the airlines; there weren't too many. Bahamasair had flights to the mainland, so he started with them, although obviously Anna would only be using the States as a staging post to pick up an international flight. 'Mrs Bartley asked me to check and make sure her reservation for next Thursday is in order,' he explained.

The girl riffled through several sheets of paper. 'I'm sorry, sir, but we don't seem to have a booking for Mrs Bartley.'

'You know who Mrs Bartley is?'

'Oh, yes, sir. She flies with us regularly. Would you like me to make a booking? Thursday, you say. Where would she be going? Miami?'

'I wouldn't do that,' Hamilton replied. 'She must have made a mistake. I'm dining with her tonight. I'll ask her about it then.'

'Very good, sir.'

He tried Pan Am, and drew a blank there as well. There were a couple of local charter firms, but if she was using one of them he was sunk, although they too would only run to the mainland or one of the other islands in the group. That left BOAC. It was a forlorn hope, because he had been told that Anna Fehrbach was *persona non grata* in Great Britain, and the British carrier operated only on the route to London out of Nassau, at least when going north-east.

But he believed in being thorough, and was taken completely by surprise when the clerk, in this instance a man, said, 'Oh, yes, sir. Mrs Bartley's booking is in order. It's in first class.'

'Ah,' Hamilton said. 'Thank you. She wanted to confirm the time.'

'The flight departs at eighteen hundred. That is, six o'clock. She should check in by five thirty.'

'That sounds OK. And when will it land?'

'It will refuel at Gander. That's in New-foundland. Depending on weather conditions, it may also have to refuel at Shannon. But it should certainly land at Heathrow – that's the new London airport, you know – by noon on Friday.'

'Thank you. That sounds just right. I need to return next week myself. What have you got available?'

'On Thursday?' He checked his lists. 'There are some seats available. But I'm afraid first class is fully booked.'

'Actually, Friday would suit me better.' It would be too risky to travel on the same flight.

'Friday.' He checked another list. 'There are first-class seats available on Friday.'

'And I assume there is only one flight a day?'

'Yes, sir. Outgoing the route is London, Hamilton, Nassau, overnight in Kingston, then Bridgetown. Ingoing it's Bridgetown, Kingston, Nassau, overnight in flight, refuel at Gander, then London.'

'Very good. Would you book me on the Friday evening flight?'

He paid for the ticket, returned to the hotel,

went to his room, and called London. 'The lady leaves Nassau at six p.m. on Thursday, flying BOAC, touching down Heathrow around noon on Friday.'

'No, no, Hamilton. You have made a mistake. The lady is not allowed entry into the British Isles.'

'Then I presume she will be travelling under an assumed name.' Or at least, he thought, landing under one, as the ticket is booked in her real name.

There was a brief silence. 'You are sure of this?'

'I am sure she will be on that flight.'

'Very good, Hamilton. We will take it from here.'

'I shall be returning the next day.'

'Excellent. Report to the house and you will receive your fee.'

'And my expenses. These have been considerable.'

'And your expenses.' The voice sounded tired.

'When will you take action?'

'As soon as it is practical to do so.'

'I would not like it to be done before I get there.'

'Hamilton, your part in this operation is completed.'

'I would like to be there when she is taken. I think I deserve that.'

'As well as your fee? And your expenses?'

'I know what she is capable of.'

134

'So you said before. But we, also, know what she is capable of. Her record speaks for itself.'

'I have actually seen her at work. Have you, or any of our people, done that?'

'All those who have are no longer with us. I find your claim hard to believe.'

'She trusts me. Which is another reason why I can be of help.'

'You have fallen into the trap,' the voice said, 'which is apparently a usual occurrence where she is concerned, of becoming fascinated by this woman. All right, Hamilton, I will see if you can be fitted into the operation, when it takes place; as you say, you may be useful. I will expect you to report by Saturday afternoon.'

The phone went dead. Hamilton had a great sense of anticipatory excitement.

Anna said goodbye to Tommy on the Rawson Square dock, while the taxi driver loaded her two suitcases into the boot of his car; she had no idea how long she was going to be away, and was taking several changes of clothing. Her sable coat was draped over her arm.

'So. I will see you, Tommy. Maybe in a couple of weeks. I'll call you.'

'Yes, ma'am.' He retained hold of her hand a moment longer than usual. 'You take care.'

He had never said that before, and he had been unusually serious on the trip down from the cay. She wondered if Desirée had overheard anything of her conversation with her parents the previous week. 'I'll try to, Tommy,' she said, and got into the taxi.

'Good afternoon, Mrs Bartley,' Charles said brightly. 'Welcome back.'

'It's only for one night, I'm afraid.'

'Yes, ma'am. You with us for dinner?'

'Of course. Tell me, is Mr Hamilton still around?'

'No, ma'am. He checked out last Saturday.'

'Oh? He had said he was leaving this week. Have you any idea where he went?'

'Well, now, ma'am, that's a funny thing. He ain't left Nassau, just changed hotels. He ever complain to you about the food or the service?'

'Who could ever complain about your food or service, Charles? He must have run out of money. You're not the cheapest hotel in Nassau.'

Charles looked sceptical, while she went to her room for a bath before dinner. She thought she could decipher Hamilton's strange behaviour: he wanted to avoid being associated with her while there was a murder investigation going on. He had certainly been in a highly nervous state.

But as he had also seemed to be keen on getting closer to her, and knew she would be here tonight, she half expected him to turn up during the evening. He didn't, and when she was having her coffee and brandy in the lounge after dinner she asked Charles, 'Last week there was some fuss going on about a dead body being found on Love Beach. I swam on that beach,

136

with some friends, oh, must be two years ago now. The thought of finding a body there ... ugh! Has anything been found out about what happened?'

'Oh, yes ma'am. They got the boys what did it.'

'Just like that?'

'Well, they did be seen drinking with the man Bonpart that same night, and they was all drunk. And they find a knife on the beach close by the body, with one of they prints on it, so it seem they had a fight, and Bonpart got killed.'

'Have they confessed?'

'Well, ma'am, they telling some fantastic story about they was on the beach and they was attacked by a white woman.'

'What, all three of them?'

'That is exactly it, ma'am. They saying this woman beat them all up, and in the fight Bonpart get killed. One woman, mind, and three men. And the knife belong to the men.'

'So the police didn't believe them?'

'They saying the police been laughing all the way to the court.'

'So what will happen to them?'

'Well, they was obviously so drunk they can't remember what happen, so they going be charged with manslaughter.'

'Thank you, Charles. That was very interesting. Well, I'm off to bed.'

Next morning she went to the bank and changed a hundred Bahamian pounds into sterling.

She was also carrying a thousand dollars in US currency left over from her last job, as she was planning to present the picture of an American hedonist who spent her days shopping and her nights dancing and drinking; if she needed more, Jerry would have to provide it. Then she had a leisurely lunch before getting ready for her departure. She no longer possessed any warm clothing, but she would be wearing slacks on the plane, and when she landed she would have her coat. As she had no idea how tight London customs were, she strapped on her Walther and her spare clip; if she needed more ammunition, Jerry would have to find it.

In her shoulder bag she packed a very sober grey dress and low-heeled shoes for her arrival, then had a trial run, securing her hair in a tight bun before putting on the spectacles and adding a severe grey felt hat; she had left her sable hat on the cay, as it was far too conspicuous. This was, in fact, an outfit she had successfully used before, when she'd wanted to conceal her natural glamour. Then she surveyed herself in the mirror, the Kelly passport held before her. Her picture was identical, presenting someone who looked like a rather grim schoolmistress, even if there was no disguise that could diminish the essential beauty of her face – or the value of her coat.

Satisfied, she changed into slacks and a shirt, packed the hat, glasses and dress in her shoulder bag, together with her false passport, then let her hair down, put on her jewellery and dark glasses, and rang for someone to collect her luggage.

'Will we see you again soon, ma'am?' Charles asked, as he ushered her to her taxi.

'I sincerely hope so, Charles,' Anna said. And she meant it.

THE WATCHERS

Having told Hamilton she was leaving on Thursday (she wondered if that had been careless?), Anna half expected to find him at the airport. But he was not there. For all his blandishments, he had apparently decided that he no longer wished to be seen in her company – perhaps because of gutless fear of somehow being involved in the Love Beach incident. Or maybe it was due to an equally gutless terror of getting too close to a woman capable of such ruthlessly decisive action when threatened. Or, most likely, to sheer schoolboy pique at her refusal to have sex with him, especially after the way she had teased him on the beach; or annoyance at her refusal to invite him to her home. Ships that pass in the night, she thought. Which was a pity; she had found him such an attractive man.

Anyway, if he was an ambitious reporter, which she had decided was the most likely scenario, she was well rid of him.

She stowed her coat and bag in the overhead locker, and discovered that she was seated next to an elderly lady who had a passion for conversation. Anna listened politely, smiling appreciatively from time to time (at least it occupied her mind), enjoyed a half bottle of wine with her dinner and slept as heavily as she usually did – despite the constant rumbling from beside her – but, with all the other passengers, had to wake up and disembark at Gander in the middle of the night, so the aircraft could refuel.

'Beastly nuisance, isn't it?' said a man with a little moustache, sitting beside her in the transit lounge – seizing the opportunity presented by her travelling companion's departure for the toilet.

Anna decided it was time to switch accents, or he might just wonder why she joined the foreign passports line when they landed. 'Ah'm happy as long as it gets us theah,' she pointed out.

'You from the States?'

'What do you reckon?'

'Do much flying?'

'Some.'

'And this is your first visit to England?'

'Ah guess so. Ma folks come from Ireland.'

He gave up, and they were soon on board and she was asleep again, this time to be awakened by the stewardess with breakfast. 'We'll be down in half an hour,' she said.

'Oh? Didn't we stop at Shannon?'

'Wasn't necessary. We had a following wind.'

Anna looked out of the window; it was broad daylight outside, but below them was a thick layer of cloud.

'Snowing in London,' the stewardess said, helpfully.

Anna finished her breakfast and retired to the toilet with her shoulder bag. In case it was searched, when she took off her shirt and slacks and before putting on her dress, she inserted her Bartley passport inside her gun belt; the belt fitted very snugly, and the little document was held firmly against her pelvis. Then she put her hair up, added her hat and glasses, and resumed her seat just as the pilot requested all his passengers to strap in as they were beginning the descent.

Her companion blinked at her. 'My husband doesn't know I'm making this trip,' Anna explained.

'Oh, my dear!' her friend said, for the first time completely lost for words.

There was no trouble at all at Heathrow. 'Nature of visit?' asked the immigration officer.

'Ah'm on vacation,' Anna explained.

He raised his eyebrows. 'It's snowing.'

'Ah saw some from the plane while we was landing. Ah'm from Wisconsin. Say, yuh reckon if Ah go to Buck-ing-ham Palace Ah'll get to meet this new queen yuh-all have?'

'I wouldn't count on it,' the man said, and stamped the passport. 'But have a nice visit.'

As Anna left the desk, she heard him say to

141

his colleague, 'Where the hell is Wisconsin?'

'In the northern United States. Right next to Canada. It's where they had that outsize blizzard last week.'

'Ah,' the first man said. 'I could swear the last time I heard an accent like that it was someone from Alabama.'

Anna realized that she had underestimated the perspicacity of the British immigration service – but they had let her through, into Britain. She found her luggage, and a porter with a trolley, and made her way into the Arrivals Hall; and there was Jerry Smitten, waiting to fold her in his arms.

'Anna!' He kissed her on the mouth; he was some inches taller than her, which was a most desirable asset in view of their past experiences. 'How long is it?'

'Three years,' she reminded him. Actually, physically he had everything going for him, as in addition to his height and curly fair hair, he had, even in his mid-thirties, fresh college-boy features and a footballer's broad shoulders and narrow hips. He had also, as she had conceded to Joe, been very good in bed, once she had broken down his Midwestern inhibitions. She was even willing to concede that perhaps he had been unlucky on the two occasions when he had been required to act as her bodyguard – in that the Russians sent to kidnap her in Brazil six years before had been quicker on the draw (fortunately they had not been quicker than her), and when they had been confronted by those Mafiosi in the Bahamas he had been overtaken by seasickness as they were about to go into action. But as Napoleon had said, give me a lucky general before a good one.

She freed herself with an effort, grabbing her dislodged hat just before it fell right off; and discovering that her glasses were blurred, she took them off. Her hair was already coming down, and in danger of restoring her normal appearance, but as they were surrounded by people hurrying to and fro she did not suppose anyone had the time to notice her metamorphosis. 'Nice to see you too, Jerry. The first thing you need to remember is that I am now a married woman.'

'You're kidding!' He looked at her left hand, but she was wearing gloves. 'Shit. You saying...'

'Nowadays I only sleep with my husband.'

'Yeah? What about this job? You know what it involves?'

'I do. And of course I am prepared to make exceptions in the interests of my profession. But you don't come into that category! Do you have transport?'

'Yeah,' he said, glumly.

'Then take me to it.'

'Thank you,' she told the bemused porter. 'This gentleman will take care of my bags now.' She tipped him, and he touched his cap, then was immediately engaged by another customer: also a woman, in a green dress, with somewhat sharp features, who had red hair and was distinctly overweight.

Jerry grimaced, but picked up a suitcase in each hand. 'It's outside the main entrance. But I guess you know your way around here.'

'Would you believe that I have never used this airport before? When I left England in 1946, it didn't exist.'

'Well,' he said, as he ushered her though the doors of the single terminal building, 'they ain't made much progress since. Oh, they've got big plans...' He gestured at the huge scars in the ground, the bulldozers and contractors' vans parked all over the place. 'More runways, more terminal buildings, more access roads ... they're talking about making this the biggest inter-national airport in the world. But it's gonna take time. And money, supposing they can raise it.'

It was now snowing quite heavily. Jerry open-ed the rear door for her, and Anna slid across the seat while he got in beside her. The driver put her bags in the boot, then got behind the wheel and they moved off. 'It's a fifteen-mile drive to the West End,' he explained.

'And this fellow?' She moved her glove to indicate the back of the driver's head.

'Oh, he works for me. Anna, this is Paul. Paul, say hello to Miss...'

'Kelly,' Anna said.

'Pleased to meet you, Miss Kelly,' said Paul.

'My pleasure, Paul.'

'Do you trust him?' she mouthed at Jerry.

144

'Absolutely. He's my sidekick.'

'So who do you work for, given that your people seem determined not to be involved, no matter what?'

'I'm a freelance journalist, reporting on the British political scene for a New York paper.'

'Where do you live?'

'I have an apartment. What these guys call a flat. Like to have a look at it?'

'Maybe. When there's time. I assume I'm booked into a hotel?'

'Yeah, the Royal George. It's pretty up-market.'

'That's what I like to hear. So let's go there. I had a broken night, and would like to get my head down.'

He sighed. 'OK. Paul?'

'You got it, Mr Smitten.'

'But we'll have dinner tonight?' Jerry asked, anxiously.

'When do we start the operation? I'd like to get it done as soon as possible.'

'Tomorrow. It's Saturday night, and this old town gets pretty lively. So I thought we'd dine at the Coca Club.'

'The Coca Club,' Anna said thoughtfully. 'I hope that doesn't mean what it sounds as if it means.'

'Well, I guess drugs are available there. But they're available anywhere in London, if you know where to look.'

'Jerry, the last thing I need is to get involved in a drugs bust.'

'No chance of that. The guy's paying protection.'

'Are you telling me that Scotland Yard is corrupt?'

'A few of its people are. If you belong to the Vice Squad, it's difficult not to get sticky fingers. The point is it's a club where all the wide boys, as they're called over here, turn up. The décor is upmarket, the liquor isn't actually poison, and it's just a little, well, risqué.'

'You mean, it's a high-class knocking shop, as they say over here?'

'No, no. Well, not obviously, though it has bare-titted dancers and that sort of thing – but,' he hurried on, 'as I said, it's where the sort of goon who works for Fahri hangs out, looking for meat.'

'If you ever refer to me as "meat" again, Jerry, you are going to wind up in hospital, and this time you are going to take a hell of a long time coming out.'

'OK, OK. Don't get your knickers in a twist. But you're here to be picked up, right?'

'In the line of duty. Now tell me about afterwards.'

'Well, you know I can't get involved.'

'I wouldn't dream of involving you, Jerry,' she assured him. Because, she thought, I have every intention of coming out of this business alive. 'I mean, when I've finished the job and want to get out of here.'

'Telephone me as soon as you're clear, and I'll take over.'

146

'Doesn't that mean that you will, after all, become involved?'

'I have it all worked out. Trust me.'

'Well,' she said, 'it looks as if I'll have to, won't I?'

The car pulled into the forecourt of the Royal George Hotel, which certainly suggested opulence.

'Dinner?' Jerry asked again, as he opened her door for her.

'Tomorrow, Jerry. At the Coca Club,' she reminded him. 'Call for me at eight.'

'It doesn't open until nine.'

'Then we'll have time for a decent drink first.'

Hamilton took a taxi from the airport to the address in Clapham, a modest detached house with a garage and a small garden. He paid the driver and cautiously carried his suitcase up the brief concrete path to the front door. Although it was no longer snowing and the path had been swept, it remained very slippery. He rang the bell.

The door was opened by a woman with sharp features and shoulder-length red hair, wearing a green woollen dress and high heels. The only thing wrong with her figure was that there was a little too much of it, in every direction. She let him in and closed the door behind him. 'It's freezing out there,' she commented.

'And only yesterday I was basking in paradise.'

147

'Lucky for some.' She gestured at a door. 'He's waiting for you.'

Hamilton nodded, knocked, and entered the room. 'Good morning, Comrade Siemann,' he ventured.

'It is afternoon,' the heavy-set man behind the desk corrected him. 'Sit.'

Hamilton obeyed.

'The countess landed on schedule yesterday,' Siemann said.

Hamilton inclined his head, in some relief.

'She was met by a man who spoke with an American accent. Do you know about this?'

'I don't know anything about this man,' Hamilton said. 'But I do know that last week in Nassau she received two visitors, in her bedroom.'

'You mean, in addition to her other vices, she is a whore?'

'She is not a whore,' said Hamilton emphatically. 'Both these men spoke with an American accent, and we have long suspected that she has links with the US Government. I think these men were representatives of a state office.'

'And therefore you assume that she's working for the USA. That may well be. Tatiana was at the airport, with Grattan. They followed her and her companion to the Royal George Hotel – where she checked in under the name of Kelly, using an American passport. If she's working for the United States that would explain how she has managed to evade us for so long, and we know that the Americans helped her take a fortune in Nazi bullion out of Germany in 1946. At a cost of more than twenty Soviet lives,' he added acerbically. 'We have always assumed that she received that help for assisting them in recovering the complete store of Nazi bullion, the whereabouts of which were apparently known to her in her capacity as Himmler's right-hand woman. And by then, of course, she was the only survivor of that crew.'

'And at the time they were supposed to be our allies,' Hamilton commented.

'They are devils, who will stop at nothing to achieve their ends. That is why they have for the past six years been protecting such a creature. And I can tell you that it is the commissar's conviction that they have been employing her as well, and perhaps still are. What you have learned may well confirm this. But this man who met her greeted her most warmly; they kissed each other on the mouth. That seems to me to indicate that they are lovers rather than fellow agents.'

'I doubt it,' Hamilton demurred. 'The countess is now married, to a man named Bartley, to whom she is determinedly faithful. I think mainly because she is afraid of him.'

'The Countess von Widerstand is afraid of a man? You have not studied her record.'

'I have studied her record, comrade. What is more, I have seen her at work.'

'So you said. And you are here. How did you do this?'

'I was with her when we were attacked by

149

three men. There was nothing covert about it; it was what the West calls a mugging. The countess destroyed them all, with no assistance from me.'

'You mean she is armed at all times?'

'She was not armed. And one of her assailants had a knife. She broke his arm as if it was a twig, and killed another with a single blow. The third ran off, with the injured man. She did this hardly drawing a breath.'

'As I observed before, Hamilton, you have made the mistake of seeing this monster as a woman, rather than a target, and allowed yourself to become fascinated by her.'

'I saw it happen,' Hamilton said stubbornly.

Siemann regarded him for several moments, then nodded. 'So you do not think this man is a lover, nor do you think the countess needs protection. Then why is he here to receive her on what is obviously a clandestine visit to England?'

'I would say that if your reasoning is correct and she is in fact working for the Americans, she is most probably here to carry out a hit; and as this man is an American, he is an agent sent here to assist her in setting it up.'

'And his greeting?'

Hamilton shrugged. 'These people are like that, careless with displays of affection, even in public.' Although, he remembered sadly, she never showed any inclination to kiss *me*, except for that wild night on the beach. And yet he had held that fabulous body naked in his arms. That was something he was determined to repeat, at least once, before she bit the dust.

Siemann stroked his chin. 'Therefore there may be other American agents in close proximity.'

'Does this affect our plans?'

'Obviously, it must do. Our business is to remove the countess to Moscow, if possible in one piece. It is not to engage in London with the FBI or CIA, or whatever these people call themselves. We may have to rethink our strategy.'

'You mean you will wait for her to return to the Bahamas?' Which might take me back again to that sunlit warmth, Hamilton thought.

'No,' Siemann said, disappointingly. 'Having her here, under our hand, so to speak, is too good an opportunity to miss. In the Bahamas she appears to be a free agent, with American protection. But we have been assured she is no longer connected with the British Government, indeed that she is no longer acceptable in Great Britain. This is obviously why she is travelling incognito; if they discover she is here, they will arrest her and deport her. Therefore not only is she no longer under their protection, but they will not lift a finger to help her. Nor will they make a big fuss if she is kidnapped.'

Hamilton looked doubtful. 'I hope you are right.'

'We are right, because we have friends in all the right places. Now, do you still wish to be involved?'

'Yes.'

'Very good. In view of your experience you may be useful. But you must not get too close – it would be disastrous were she to see you. I am inserting our people into the hotel in various capacities, so we can keep her under surveillance while we see exactly what she is up to, and plan our tactics accordingly. Then we will include you.'

'I would like to accompany her to Moscow.'

Siemann grinned. 'You *have* got it bad. I hope you have not allowed this infatuation to affect you evaluations.'

'I wish to see her humbled as much as anyone, comrade. I merely wish to be there when it happens.'

'I cannot guarantee that you will have that privilege. But I can promise that you will accompany her to Moscow. Just bear in mind, always, that she is Commissar Beria's property. Nobody else's.'

'Would you believe,' Anna remarked, 'that before this week I had never set foot in a night-club?'

'You must be joking!' Jerry exclaimed. 'All that high life in Berlin?'

'The highest life I enjoyed in Berlin was an occasional opera or SS-controlled ball – and at all of them I was working, in one capacity or another. I met Bally,' she said reminiscently, 'at an SS ball in 1938, to which I had been taken specifically to attract and seduce him.' And at

152

which, she remembered fondly, I also first met Clive.

'And I assume you succeeded?'

'If I had ever failed, at any task,' Anna pointed out, 'I would not be here now.'

He gulped, then recovered. 'But what about when he married you and brought you to London? I gather it was fairly lively even then. He must occasionally have taken you to a nightclub.'

'No he did not. Bally did not like nightclubs.'

'Stuffy. Well, I hope you are enjoying the new experience.'

Anna surveyed the crowded dance floor, the perspiring bodies huddled close against each other. Their table was situated on its edge. 'I am not enjoying the experience.'

'Why ever not?'

'Well,' she said, 'as we have all evening. One, I don't like the ambience. Two, I don't like the clientele. Three, I don't like the noise. Four, I don't like the orchestra, to whom noise seems to be more important than melody. Five, the food is appalling. And six, I'm beginning to suspect that your statement that the drinks aren't actually poison was wildly optimistic.' Anna put down her glass of sparkling wine.

'You're a hard woman to please.'

'You managed it once.'

'Ah.' He brightened. 'I was waiting for you to say that. We could go back to your hotel.'

'Sadly, Jerry, I'm here to work, not play. Or even enjoy myself. Let's give the Coca Club another whirl.'

He raised his eyebrows. 'I thought you liked that least of all.'

'I did and I do. But last time we were there, there was a chap who was definitely interested. I almost thought he was going to make a move. He didn't. But he seemed pretty well known to the staff, so he must be a regular. And I would say that he comes from the right part of the world. I think second time around he may try his luck.'

Jerry made a face, but called for the check and escorted her into the lobby to collect her coat. She was, in fact, beginning to feel a little desperate. She had been in England for ten days, and been to a nightclub on each night save the two Sundays, always wearing one of her sheath evening gowns, either in pale blue or deep green or black, colours that showed off her complexion and figure to perfection, and each with a plunging décolletage that could leave no doubt that the various curves were genuine. She had certainly attracted a lot of attention. But she had been in the business long enough to know the difference between the 'Boy, that's worth looking at' look and the 'Boy, that's something I'd like to get my hands on' look, and, most important of all, the 'Boy, that's something I just *have* to get my hands on' look.

On the eight nights there had only been one of those and, as she had told Jerry, that had been from an olive-skinned gentleman at the Coca Club. He had been distinctly handsome, his

154

tuxedo impeccable, and the waiters deferential. He had also been seated between two extremely attractive young women. But he had been unable to keep his eyes off her, and she had felt that he was mentally stripping her naked. So it was worth giving it a whirl...

It was getting on for midnight when they arrived. Consequently, the only table they could have was towards the back of the crowded room – but from her point of view it was ideally located, as, fortuitously, an aisle between the tables enabled her to look directly at the one occupied by her admirer and his two current companions. She had virtually to brush against him as she passed; and on seating herself, turned towards him, smiled, and inclined her head. He did the same, and then pointedly looked at Jerry before again looking at her.

Jerry was oblivious to this, as he was busy reading the wine and cocktail menu, no doubt trying to find something that might be acceptable to her. 'Jerry,' she said. 'I think you should go to the toilet.'

He looked up. 'Eh? I went...'

'I'm sure you need to go again. Don't hurry back. And when you do come out, go to the bar and wait there for my signal before returning to the table.'

'What's going on?'

'Just do it. Now!'

A last hesitation, then he got up and went towards the back of the room. A waiter was hovering, and now he placed a glass in front of her. 'I think I should wait to order until my escort returns,' she said.

'But this has been sent to you, madam, by Mr Khouri.'

Anna looked at Khouri, heartbeat quickening at the name, and raised the glass. 'Then thank him for me.'

She felt a pleasant glow of excitement as she recalled Joe's briefing and the adrenalin began to flow, enhanced as she tasted her drink and realized that it was real champagne. A moment later Khouri stood beside her. 'May I join you until your husband returns, Mrs...?'

'By all means,' she said 'And he is not my husband.'

Khouri sat down 'The last time you came to this club he was also with you. Is he your lover?'

'You mean you remember that?'

'No man, seeing you, could ever forget you, Mrs...?'

'You say the sweetest things. My name is Anna Kelly. And he is not my lover, just a friend.'

'And you are Irish. The accent is unmistakable.'

'You are perceptive. And it is Miss.' When on business, she did not wear her wedding ring.

He raised his eyebrows. 'It is difficult to believe that you can never have married.'

'Oh, I've been married. Twice.'

'Ah. I like the word been. I am Alois Khouri.'

'And you are...?'

'An ardent admirer of beauty.'

It was Anna's turn to say. 'Ah. And you have sufficient wealth to indulge your hobby, I would say.'

He eyed her ruby solitaire. 'As have you – or are you receiving enormous amounts of alimony?'

'Sadly, Mr Khouri, I wish it were so. I have never been very wise when it came to organizing money. The ring is a gift from an admirer. But I'm afraid I am going to have to sell it.' She was travelling too fast; but time was running out, and she had to get him while she could.

'That is very tragic,' Khouri said. 'A beautiful woman should never be out of funds. I would very much like to help you.'

Anna regarded him for several seconds. 'I think you need to explain just what you mean by that.'

'Well...' He toyed with the stem of his glass. 'Like you, I am not as wealthy as I appear. But I work for a very wealthy man, who provides me with funds, so that I may circulate in London and search for ... talent.'

Anna drained her glass. 'I think, Mr Khouri, that it is time for you to rejoin your party. But thanks for the drink.'

'Oh, please, do not misunderstand me.' His hand crept across the table so that his fingers touched hers. 'Mr Fahri is an impresario. His business is finding and recruiting talent for the entertainment industry, where, as I am sure you know, new faces are in constant demand. So we seek, and find, budding actors and actresses, singers and dancers, musicians and magicians.'

Anna allowed her fingers to lie in his, even closing them a little. 'And this is a charitable organization?'

'Well, of course not. Mr Fahri is a businessman. He will retain ten per cent of your earnings. But I would say that you would soon be earning so much that ten per cent would be – how do you say? – water off a duck's back.'

'You paint a very exciting picture, Mr Khouri. Sadly, there is a caveat. I have no talents whatsoever.' Except for destroying slugs like you, she thought.

'My dear lady, you cannot have looked in the mirror recently. A face as strikingly beautiful as yours is all the talent most women need to get right to the top. Other talents can be built around it.'

She regarded him for some seconds, looked around the room, and felt as if she had been kicked in the stomach. 'Holy shit!'

'What?' He was completely taken aback.

Anna abruptly released his hand, grabbed her evening bag and gloves, and stood up. 'I have to go.'

'But...' He stood also. 'If it is something I have said...'

'I find what you said intensely interesting. I would like to hear more. Listen, I am at the Royal George Hotel. Call me tomorrow.'

She left the room, hurried into the lobby, and gave the check-in girl the ticket for her coat. A moment later Jerry appeared. 'What happened? I got the impression you were making progress.'

'I was, God damn it,' Anna said. 'And then my husband turned up.'

Jerry goggled at her. 'You mean Bartley is here?'

'No, Clive is not here. He wouldn't be caught dead in a place like this, unless, like me, he was working. This was my first husband, Ballantine Bordman.'

'But...'

'Look,' Anna said. 'Let's get out of here. Take me back to the hotel.'

He hailed a taxi, and she prevented him, with difficulty, from asking questions until they reached the hotel. Then she invited him up to her room. He closed the door and leaned against it while she threw her coat and purse on a chair, stripped off her gloves, and poured herself a brandy from the bottle on the table against the wall. 'You?'

'Thank you.' He came towards her, took the glass. 'You look sort of shook up.'

'I don't like unpleasant surprises, if that's what you mean.' She drank deeply.

'Let me get this straight. Some guy walked into the club who you think may have been your husband...'

'For God's sake, Jerry. I know my husband. I lived with him for two years. He looked a bit of a wreck, but it was definitely him.'

'OK, so it was your husband. You told me he

didn't like nightclubs.'

'He didn't, when he was married to me. I suppose people can change their habits in thirteen years.'

'And you think he may have seen you?'

'He looked straight at me and did a double take, if that's what you mean.'

'What do you reckon he'll do next? Can he do anything?'

'Jerry, his father is dead. So he has inherited the title. He used to have a lot of clout in the government. OK, so I understand that he had a nervous breakdown when he learned the truth about me. In fact, I believe he had to be locked up for a while. But if he's out and enjoying himself, he's obviously considered sane again. And he has friends in high places.'

'And you think he may tell them about seeing you?'

Anna poured herself a second brandy and sat in an armchair. 'I would say he may do more than that. He used to hate my guts, and there is no reason for him to have revised that opinion.'

'Shit!' He poured himself a second drink. 'I can get you on a plane out of here tomorrow.'

Anna's nerves had settled. She was such a meticulous planner, her success rate being based upon information and careful reconnaissance, that she was normally able to eliminate almost all unpleasant surprises – even that beastly, and unfortunate, cobra. True its hissing preamble had been a shock, but it had occurred in the middle of an action and, since she had a

160

gun in her hand, she had been able to blow its head off without stopping to think. Encountering Bally after all these years, and in totally unlikely circumstances, had briefly knocked her off balance. But only briefly. Now she was again capable of evaluating the situation, and all the possible dangers that could arise from it, she was able to weigh them against the overall picture and, more important, her ultimate objective. 'Jerry,' she said, 'I came here to do a job of work.'

'But...'

'Whatever wheels he manages to start turning aren't going to get moving in ten minutes. Bally only knows that I'm in the country. He doesn't know what name I'm using or where I'm staying. I reckon even if he puts the whole of Scotland Yard on my trail we still have forty-eight hours before they can get close. Now, I'm on the verge of hitting the target. Khouri, that chap I was talking to, works for Fahri; Joe told me so. Khouri confirmed it tonight, and he wants to introduce me to his boss. Would you believe it, he says they can turn me into a film star. That again is in line with what Joe told me of their approach. So I was there! Then I had to leave in a hurry, but I told him where I'm staying and suggested he call me tomorrow morning. Correction, this morning.'

'You told him where you're staying?' Jerry was aghast.

'I need to get the job done, Jerry. And where's the risk? He wants to get me into Fahri's mansion, and I want to get into Fahri's mansion. Two minds with a single thought. If all goes well, the job can be completed tomorrow night.'

Jerry shook his head, slowly. 'I have a gut feeling that this is going to turn out badly.'

'Let me do the worrying. Now, can you get me out of here on Thursday morning?'

'There's a flight to the Caribbean every morning at eleven – via Hamilton to Nassau.'

She got up, delved in her shoulder bag, and gave him her ticket. 'Book me on it. If, as I hope, Khouri calls me this morning, I'll contact you and give you a final briefing. OK?'

'Anna...'

She kissed him. 'Stop worrying. I'm doing what I do best.'

She closed the door behind him, undressed, took off her jewellery and make-up, drank a glass of water, and got into bed. She'd be home on Thursday afternoon, she thought as she closed her eyes. Exactly a fortnight. She wondered if Hamilton would still be at the Royal Vic...

'I'm sorry to bother you, Mr Baxter,' said Amy Barstow, hesitantly. Amy had worked for MI6 for fourteen years. She was now past forty and, with her short blonde haircut, somewhat blunt features and dumpy overweight figure, was the epitome of the devoted secretary. For most of those fourteen years she had worked for a boss she worshipped – even if she knew it could only

162

be from afar, in view of his long-standing affair with, and now marriage to, that long-legged, long-haired blonde monster. It was only in the last three years, since Clive had partly retired and the senior secretary in the section had done so entirely, that she had been moved upstairs to work for the boss himself; and she remained terrified of him.

However, Billy Baxter was not, in appearance, a terrifying man. He was small, sharp-featured, had a thinning head of grey hair, and was habitually untidy. His only visible vice was his pipe, which he smoked constantly and filled with careless inefficiency. As a result, he was invariably surrounded by a smoky haze, his desk was always covered in tobacco strands, and the sweater that he always wore in the office was a mass of embedded shreds. But he was the most senior member of the MI6 staff and had been in the hot seat for twenty years, though he was in fact due to retire on his next birthday. For most of that time, he had, as Amy knew, controlled field operations, moving agents around the world like pieces on a chess board, genuinely grieving when one of them was lost, but nonetheless immediately replacing them with whichever man or woman he felt was best suited for the job. The great days of the War might be over, and Britain's power to influence events largely overtaken by the Russians and the Americans, but the aura of power remained.

Now he looked up from the newspaper he was

reading. 'Yes, Miss Barstow?'

'There's a Lord Bordman here to see you.'

'Lord ... Good God!'

'He says you know him,' Amy ventured.

'I thought he was locked up.'

'Well, he's in the waiting room.'

'Then you'd better show him in.'

He stood up to greet Bordman as he entered. 'Lord Bordman! This is an unexpected pleasure. You're looking well.' Being able to lie convincingly was a part of his job, but actually Ballantine Bordman, although his hair was quite white and his always jowly face seemed to have collapsed, was looking better than the last time he had seen him, in 1940, in this office – almost literally foaming at the mouth, as he had just discovered that his wife was a Nazi spy and that the British Government did not intend to prosecute her, but required him to continue acting the husband until she could safely be returned to Germany. The effort of playing that role had brought on a nervous breakdown that had put him out of circulation for several years.

He had been released from his institution just in time to inherit his father's peerage; but, as Baxter had told Amy, MI6 had had nothing to do with him during all those years. As they had parted on the worst possible terms, he could not imagine what the bugger might want now.

'I was feeling perfectly well,' Bordman announced, 'until last night, when I encountered my wife.'

'Your wife?' Baxter inquired, buying time by

164

appearing to be dense, while he thought, oh Christ, he's been hallucinating. 'I had no idea you were married.'

'I was once,' Bordman said, 'as you well know. It is not a mistake, Baxter, I ever intend to repeat. And last night I encountered that woman. Here in England. I had been told she was dead.'

'Do sit down,' Baxter suggested, as an after-thought. He sat down himself and considered the situation. It could not be true. 'May I ask where this, ah, meeting took place?'

Bordman looked slightly embarrassed. 'Some friends of mine and I were nightclubbing. And there she was.'

'Where?'

'Sitting at a table, with her tits virtually hang-ing out, covered in expensive jewellery, and holding hands with some foreign-looking chap. Holding hands!'

Baxter got the impression that this was more unacceptable than that she had been there at all.

'I meant,' he said, 'at which establishment did this take place? Annabelle's?' Where he knew the management.

Bordman looked even more embarrassed. 'The Coca Club.'

Baxter raised his eyebrows.

'Of course,' Bordman hastily added, 'it was the first time I'd been there. Naturally, we had been to Annabelle's first, but my friends wanted to experiment and someone suggested the Coca might be fun.'

'And was it?'

'Not for me. When I saw Anna...'

'I quite understand. But your friends saw her too, I assume?'

'Well, they saw a very good-looking long-haired blonde, yes. But they didn't know who she was.'

'And you did not tell them?'

'No, I did not.'

'Quite. May I ask what the countess did when she saw you? At least, I assume she did?'

'Yes, she certainly saw me. And she got up and left, immediately.'

'With her foreign friend?'

'No. She left him sitting at the table.'

'I see. May I ask what time this was?'

'God knows. Around midnight.'

'I would like to get the facts exactly straight, my lord. Your evening began at Annabelle's. I assume you had dinner there?'

'Yes, we did.'

'And what time did you leave?'

'I don't know. I know it was early. It must have been about half-past nine.'

'And you arrived at the Coca Club around midnight? I believe the two establishments are about a quarter of a mile apart. Were you walking? Very slowly?'

'Well, we may have gone somewhere else first. Look here, are you trying to suggest that I was drunk?'

'It would be helpful to know exactly what you had had to drink, yes.'

166

'I may have had a few glasses of champagne ... But that did not affect my ability to recognize my own wife.'

'Ex-wife. The countess has married again.'

'Good God! What idiot was prepared to take on a creature like her? But *you* knew that? I was told she was dead.'

'She survived the War.'

'And you did not arrest her? Have you forgotten that she once nearly killed me?'

'As I recall the incident, my lord, you were about to beat her on finding out certain facts about her.' And, he thought, you obviously did not realize that she was being very forbearing: Anna could have easily killed him, if she'd wanted to.

'I had just found out,' Bordman said, 'that in addition to all her other vices she was an adulterous bitch. So what's her name now?'

As the question of adultery had arisen because Anna had been found in bed with her MI6 minder, and Bordman would undoubtedly remember Clive Bartley's name, Baxter decided to avoid inducing an apoplectic fit in his office. 'I don't think that is relevant.'

Bordman stared at him for several seconds. Then he got up, but remained standing before the desk, now pointing. 'Look here, Baxter, I am well aware that at one time she did some work for you, and therefore you may have some misguided feelings of loyalty towards her, but I was assured that she had died in 1945. Now I find that she is not only alive but here in

England, living the high life. I don't know what private arrangement you had with her during the War, but she is still a wanted war criminal in this country. I want her arrested and brought to trial. If I do not hear from you that this has been done within forty-eight hours, I am going to take the matter to the Home Secretary. Good day to you.'

He stamped out of the office, and a moment later Amy came in. 'Wow!' The door had been open throughout the meeting. 'Can it possibly be true?'

'The trouble with Anna,' Baxter said reminiscently, 'is that once seen she is not easy to forget. And if Bordman's friends also saw her and confirm his description...'

'But,' Amy said, 'she's not supposed to be here, is she?'

'No, she is not.'

'Then...?'

'If she is here, you can bet your last penny that she is working for the CIA. In which case, a very large scandal is liable to burst at any moment.'

'What are we going to do?'

'She is Bartley's baby. He is supposed to be keeping her out of circulation in the Bahamas.'

'But he's been in Africa for the past month.'

'That is exactly it. She must have got restless. When is he due back?'

'Actually, this afternoon.'

'Thank God for that.' He pointed. 'The moment he walks through your door, Amy, I want him in here.'

'Comrades!' Siemann surveyed the six men standing before his desk. They included Hamilton. 'We have now had the Countess von Widerstand under surveillance for ten days, and have established a pattern of behaviour. Hamilton was of the opinion that she is here to carry out some task for the Americans, but that appears to be incorrect. As I said, she has been here for ten days, and appears to be in London entirely for pleasure. She spends all morning in the shops, all afternoon in her hotel room, presumably resting, and every evening she goes to a nightclub. As she has booked her room for a fortnight and has been here for ten days, it is necessary for us to move now, as time is running out before she disappears back to the Bahamas.

'Now, she is escorted by an American man, which makes sense in view of her American connection, but they do not appear to be very close. Although she spends her evenings in his company, he has only once, last night in fact, accompanied her to her hotel room on their return; they usually say goodnight in the lobby. She does not appear to have any other friends, or even acquaintances, in England, and does not receive or make any phone calls. This is, of course, good for us. She will simply disappear from her hotel room, and it will be a nine days' wonder.

'Now, the hotel is the Royal George. It is a very expensive place, frequented by visiting millionaires. We have been able to place an agent in there, and he has established that, despite the high level of the clientele, there is not a lot of security. There are three house detectives, who share their duties. Twelve hours on, twenty-four hours off, which enables them to vary their time off. However, again owing I suppose to the quality of the clientele, they interfere as little as possible with the behaviour of the hotel guests. They do not patrol the corridors, or anything like that. And as far as we have been able to ascertain, they are not armed. There are also three doormen, who again alternate their duties, but these are elderly men who do nothing more than summon taxis and open car doors. None of these should present a problem; nor, if everyone does his duty, should any risk of a problem arise.

'The countess is occupying Room 416, which is of course on the fourth floor. I have been unable to secure a room exactly next door, but I have been able to obtain Room 410, which is three down on the same side of the corridor. I have also secured Room 433, which is considerably further down the corridor and on the opposite side. It is, in fact, virtually opposite the elevators. These rooms are both available from today. You, Fleurmann, will occupy 410 this morning, and keep a low profile. Tonight, you will entertain two friends for dinner. These will be you, Pascall, and you, Hamilton. Now,

Comrades, Hamilton is key to this operation. He not only has an acquaintance with the countess, but has personal experience of her skills and knows what she is capable of. So you will take his advice in all things.'

'Is she *that* dangerous?' Pascall asked.

'She is that dangerous. I have been told by Commissar Beria that she, personally, has been responsible for the deaths of more than fifty of our comrades.' He smiled at them as he listened to the sudden intakes of breaths. 'And Hamilton has seen her kill a man with her bare hands. So if you make a mistake, you are unlikely ever to see Russia again.'

'Isn't there a chance that I may encounter the countess in the hotel?' Hamilton asked. 'As you said, she knows me.'

'There should be no risk,' Siemann assured him. 'Until we are ready for her to do so. You, Grattan, will be on watch outside the hotel. Every night she has gone out, the countess has always left the hotel, with her escort, at eight o'clock. There is no reason for her to vary that pattern. Hamilton and Pascall will arrive at eight-thirty. If, however, she has not left by eight-fifteen, you will telephone and the attempt will be postponed for the following night.

'Hamilton, you understand that it is necessary for you to reveal yourself when she returns from her evening out. This will be the most dangerous part of the operation. But you tell me that she knows nothing of you other than that you are a tourist who she encountered in

Nassau and who revealed an interest in her. Am I correct?'

'Ye-es,', said Hamilton a trifle doubtfully.

'Therefore she will be unlikely to destroy you on sight. Even the Countess von Widerstand has only ever killed either after careful planning or when she feels herself to be endangered. There is no reason for her to feel in danger from another chance meeting with you, especially as you tell me you have established yourself as a timid man who abhors violence. Correct?'

This time Hamilton nodded with more confidence.

'Very good. We may therefore rely on the fact that she will at least engage you in conversation for a few minutes, which is all we need. The position will be improved because this will be the small hours of the morning and she will be returning from a night of dancing; she will have had a lot to drink, and will be thinking only of her bed.

'Now you, Fleurmann, will enjoy a leisurely dinner with Pascall and Hamilton, stretching it until midnight. Then the three of you will retire to Room 410 for a brandy. This is not an uncommon occurrence in these hotels, and no questions will be asked. Grattan will remain on watch outside the hotel, and the moment the countess's car arrives he will telephone your room...'

'How will I be able to do this?' Grattan asked.

'There are four call-boxes in the hotel lobby. At two o'clock in the morning they are not

172

likely to be occupied, at least not all of them. As soon as you receive Grattan's call, Fleurmann, you will open your bedroom door just a crack. The countess always spends a few minutes saying goodbye to her friend in the lobby, so you will have time to get ready.'

'You said that last night her escort accompanied her to her room,' Pascall interjected. 'What if he does so tonight?'

'That is a remote possibility in view of the previous pattern. But in a moment I will outline the procedure to be followed if that should occur. Pascall, you are in charge of the serum. Drimer, Grattan will telephone you too. You are a visiting doctor, and you will also take up residence this morning. The room you have booked is, as I have said, 433. As soon as you receive Grattan's call, you will stand by but remain in your room, again with the door slightly ajar.

'Now, the moment the elevator comes to a stop, you, Hamilton, will leave 410 and walk casually towards it, as if intending to go down to the lobby. You will obviously pass the countess in the corridor. You will stop, and greet her in amazement. Make sure you have her turn back to face the elevator. Now will be the most dangerous moment. As soon as the countess is engaged in conversation, Pascall and Fleurmann will leave 410 and approach her from behind. You will be wearing crêpe-soled shoes, and in any event the corridors are carpeted – but you must remember that if she hears you coming and turns before you get to her, all your lives will be in danger. In addition to her un-armed skills, she is invariably armed.'

'She was not armed that night in Nassau,' Hamilton said.

'So you said. However, we cannot count on such continuing good fortune. Now, having reached her, Pascall will thrust the needle into her left shoulder. Remember, it must be inserted six inches below her shoulder blade. You will still be in danger; but introduced at that point, the serum will work in five seconds. Should she turn before being injected, Hamilton will have to throw both arms round her body until the serum can be injected and take effect.'

Hamilton gulped, but nodded.

'Now,' Siemann continued. 'The serum in-duces the same external symptoms as a heart attack, and the countess will be unconscious for several hours. When she wakes up she will feel nothing more than a slight fuzziness, and of course a pain in her shoulder, but by the time she wakes we will have completed the opera-tion. The three of you will panic when the coun-tess suddenly collapses while engaging you in conversation. You will shout for help. One of you will return to the room to telephone the desk. But before any other help can arrive, you will be attended by Dr Drimer, who fortuit-ously not only happens to be occupying a room on the same floor but also happens to still be awake. You, Drimer, will examine the countess, and announce that it is a heart attack and she must immediately be removed to hospital. By

174

this time hotel staff will have arrived, and you will direct them to call an ambulance. Meanwhile, you will have the countess taken downstairs to the lobby, as there is not a moment to be lost. As she gets there, an ambulance that, again fortuitously, happens to be passing is hailed by Grattan, who has been using a phone in the lobby to telephone his wife. He hears the commotion and the staff telephoning for an ambulance, realizes there is an emergency, sees an ambulance driving by and, as any public-spirited citizen would do, flags it down. Once the countess is in the ambulance, the business is completed. Within an hour she will be on the boat.' He looked at their faces, triumphantly. 'Are there any questions?'

'A hotel like the Royal George will have its own in-house doctor,' Hamilton commented.

'That is not important. Dr Drimer will be first on the scene, and will take charge.'

'The hotel doctor may well wish to accompany the countess to the hospital, to make sure all is well.'

'If he does that, he will not be seen again. The same applies to the escort if he is with her. He will be as shocked as everyone when it happens. If he seeks to take control of the situation, Drimer will see him off as well. If he wishes to accompany her to the hospital, he is of course welcome to do so. In which case, he too will not be heard of again.' Another look at their faces, then he nodded. 'Very good, gentlemen. Make your preparations.'

175

THE ROAD TO HELL

Anna had her breakfast and bath, and got dressed, then had to decide what to do with her morning; she did not wish to go out until she had heard from Khouri.

Hanging about meant thinking about Bally. For all her confident dismissal of any possible problem to Jerry, she had been considerably upset at seeing him again; she had not laid eyes on him since April 1940, and it was now well into February 1953. If she really was going to complete the job today, and be out of the country tomorrow, she would certainly be away before he could sufficiently activate the police. Bally would probably be able to supply an out-of-date photograph of her – but, while she had the highest possible regard for Scotland Yard and Special Branch, she remained confident that even they could not possibly find her in forty-eight hours.

But the man himself! He was the very last person she would have thought it possible for her to encounter on an assignment like this. Of course people did change, over thirteen years, but Ballantine in a nightclub? And a sleazy nightclub, too?

She knew that, looked at objectively, she had treated him very badly. She had always salved her conscience by reflecting that he had enthusiastically dug his own grave, by going overboard for a teenage girl – as she had been when they first met – while he was engaged on a serious diplomatic mission for his country. But the fact remained that she had been placed there specifically to make him fall for her, and then seduce him. Having taken the initial step, he had been lost: she could reflect, this time without hubris, that when Anna Fehrbach, even at eighteen and on her first major assignment, set her sights on a man he was done for.

Of course, not even Himmler had expected Bordman to marry her; she remembered how the Reichsfuehrer had been unable to believe his, and the Party's, good fortune. And she had been a good wife. She had appeared everywhere on his arm, and shared his bed – and his often peculiar tastes – with enthusiasm, though she had not had to manage his household, as that had been the province of his butler. It was those very aspects of her revealed personality, she supposed, that had made the truth the harder to bear, the realization that every movement, every kiss, every murmured endearment, and above all every moan of ecstasy, had been faked.

She could not blame him for attempting to assault her in his frustrated rage. But she also could not blame herself for defending herself so vigorously as to hurt him, further increasing his sense of outraged manhood ... even if he had been unaware that she could easily have killed him had she wished. And he had been engaged in great international matters, with a glittering career in front of him, which had all been ended by his wife's treason, as it had been supposed.

But to see him a prematurely aged wreck of a man, seeking some sort of pleasure at the lowest possible level...

The telephone rang, breaking into her reverie and causing her to jump. She picked it up. 'Yes?'

'Miss Kelly?'

'This is she.' Her heartbeat quickened as she recognized the voice.

'This is Alois Khouri.'

'Well, hello,' Anna said. 'I thought you'd forgotten about me.'

'Could any man, having once met you, ever forget you?'

'You say the sweetest things.'

'Last night, before your so sudden departure, you suggested that you might be interested in continuing the subject we were discussing.'

'I must apologize for that. I was suddenly taken ill.'

'I am glad of that. I mean not that you were taken ill, but that you were not a Cinderella, who has to be home by midnight or be turned into a pumpkin. And you are well again, now?'

'I am very well now, thank you. It must have been something I ate or drank.'

'Indeed. The drinks they serve in that club are

178

extremely suspect. Not that I ever indulge, myself. So...?'

'Yes, I would very much like to continue our discussion.'

'Excellent. Mr Fahri was fascinated by what I had to tell him about you, and he would like you to have dinner with him tonight.'

'That sounds very nice. Where are we to meet?'

'Oh, I shall pick you up.'

'To go where?'

'To his house. It is a short distance outside London.'

'Well,' Anna said, allowing a note of doubt to enter her voice.

'Mr Fahri is, I'm afraid, housebound. His health, you understand.'

'Oh! How sad.'

'Shall we say seven thirty this evening?'

'That sounds ideal. Seven thirty.'

She hung up, and waited for her heartbeat to quieten. She was there! Well, just about. She called the number Jerry had given her; she knew that he was waiting in to hear from her. 'Hi! It's on.'

'Just like that?'

'Just like that. Seems his nibs is panting. Join me here for lunch. We have a lot to get right. But first thing, when you come bring a large empty suitcase. It must be empty, but you must carry it as if it was full. Got that?'

'Ye-es.'

'Right. I'll expect you at twelve.'

179

She ordered a room-service lunch so they would not be interrupted. 'What have you got?' she asked, as they consumed lobster bisque and a glass of champagne.

He had placed the suitcase on the rack. Now from his pocket he took her airline ticket. 'Heathrow–Oakes Field. Flight time eleven, check-in ten.'

'Good boy. Keep it, and give it to me tomorrow morning.'

'Give me an outline of future events.'

'I'm being picked up at seven thirty by that slimy toad Khouri. He's taking me to Fahri's house for dinner. From then on, I play it by ear. Joe told me the house is about an hour's drive from central London. So we should get there by eight thirty. I imagine I'll be offered a drink before dinner, which should be about nine. I can't make a move until I've checked the internal security arrangements and the layout of the house and grounds, and been escorted to bed by Fahri. But the job should be done by eleven.'

'I wish I could reconcile myself to this – I mean your being taken to bed by Fahri.'

'Oh, come now, Jerry. I've been in this business for fifteen years. It's a hell of a long time since I was a blushing bride.' Not that I ever was that, she reflected, as she got up and removed their soup plates to the heated trolley, then served their steak and salad, and poured the Chateau Batailley.

'And you're even domesticated.'

'Every woman needs to be that, however seldom she may have to use the skills. I was taught domesticity by my mother.'

'It's difficult to imagine you with a mother.'

'I know. Adolf Hitler once said I was an incarnation of Eurynome, the Pelasgian Goddess of All Things, born out of Chaos, who spent eternity dancing through the heavens, creating and destroying as she saw fit.'

He stared at her with his mouth open, and she smiled at him. 'But I do have a mother, who I love dearly.'

'And does she...?'

'Yes, she does. And no, she does not approve. But she knows why I am what I am.' She raised her glass. 'Happy days!'

'I'll say amen to that. But Anna, can't I tag along discreetly ... just in case you need me?'

Anna ate her steak. 'Jerry, if there is so much as a suspicion of your presence, you are going to get a bullet. These characters have got me sized up as a bimbo who has seen her best days and is running low on cash, so she is on the make. Nothing more than that. And that's the way it has it to stay. Savvy? Now listen. I don't know how long it will take me to get back to town, and I don't know what condition my clothes will be in when I do. But even if they're in perfect nick, I can't turn up at the airport in evening dress without attracting attention, so I'm going to have to come back here to change.'

181

'Won't that be risky?'

'How? As far as the hotel is concerned, I'm booked in for another four days.'

'Ah...' He turned his head, as there were several bumps in the corridor. 'What's that?'

'Relax, for God's sake. That's guests moving in. Midday is turnover time. The previous occupants have to be out by noon, and the new guests come in after that.'

He drank some wine.

'Now keep listening. If everything goes according to plan, I will, as I say, pick up some form of transport and come home, and hopefully go to bed for a couple of hours.'

'Hold on. Those guys will know where you're staying. That fellow Khouri certainly will, if he's picking you up.'

'Jerry, think. When I leave Fahri's house, that fellow Khouri is going to be dead. Along with any of his pals who may make themselves a nuisance.'

He gulped.

'I will then leave the hotel at nine tomorrow morning, and be at the airport at ten.'

'If you're playing it so straight, why do we need the empty suitcase?'

She sighed. 'Because as far the hotel will know, I'm just going out for my normal morning's shopping and will be back for lunch.' She opened the case and began packing her clothes, including her recent purchases. She couldn't get everything in, so had to make a selection; but that was useful, if painful, in case a maid opened her wardrobe while she was out. She then placed her jewellery in a little bag, retaining only her crucifix and watch, and put the little bag into her shoulder bag.

Jerry watched her with interest. 'I thought you never went out without that stuff?'

'I can't be certain how this evening is going to turn out, and I don't want some light-fingered mortuary attendant to get his hands on it while I'm lying on a slab in the morgue.'

'Jesus! You can contemplate that so calmly?'

'It's an occupational hazard. Not something to worry about. You need to remember that if I wind up on a slab in the morgue, I won't know anything about it. What I want you to promise is that if I don't show at the airport you'll get this bag back to my parents. The shoulder bag also contains my passport. So don't lose it.'

'Which passport?'

'The real one. I'll keep the Kelly one in my handbag, just in case Fahri wants some identification.'

'Do you ever miss a trick?'

'I'm alive, Jerry. Let's have that promise.'

'I promise,' he said fervently. 'What about the coat?'

She grimaced. 'That goes with my outfit, and I can wear it with casual gear tomorrow. If by any chance I have to abandon it, that too is an occupational hazard. This is my fifth. Now, Jerry...'

She closed the suitcase. 'See you tomorrow.'

He stood up. 'Anna...'

'Tomorrow, Jerry,' she said and kissed him.

'What appears to be the crisis?' Clive Bartley inquired, entering Baxter's office. 'I've never seen Amy so agitated.' Clive Bartley was a tall, powerfully built man with rugged features. He had graduated to MI6 from Scotland Yard's Special Branch, and had thus been in undercover work nearly all of his adult life. He had acquired a formidable reputation, both in the field and when manipulating events from behind the scenes, handling every scenario he encountered with calm assurance, including those involving his fabulous wife. The only discernible indication of his age (just past fifty), and of the various traumas that had studded his life, were the grey wings edging his lank dark hair.

Baxter, who had been his boss for most of those years, regarded him without enthusiasm. 'You'd better sit down,' he suggested.

Clive did so. 'I think you should know,' he said, 'that whatever it is, you can count me out.' He placed a folder on the desk. 'My report. I have just completed a long and very messy assignment, and I now intend to return to the Bahamas.'

Baxter began to fill his pipe, scattering tobacco. As Clive knew, from years of observation, that this meant he had an unpleasant, or at least, tricky, situation to handle, he began to tense. 'I am all in favour of you going back to the Bahamas,' Baxter said. 'Just as quickly as possible.'

184

'That is a very acceptable point of view.'

Baxter struck a match, which enabled him to concentrate on his pipe. 'Just as long as you take your wife with you.'

'You've lost me. Are you saying that Anna wants picking up? From where?'

'That is part of the problem. I don't know.'

'Billy, you must be using the wrong tobacco.'

Billy puffed. 'But I can tell you,' he said, 'that she is situated within a few miles of where we are sitting now. Probably less.'

'For God's sake. How can Anna be in Britain? In London?'

'I'd like to know that, believe me.'

'I suppose someone has reported seeing her. Billy, do you suppose she's the only long-haired blonde in the world?'

'This morning,' Baxter said, 'I had a visit from Lord Bordman. You may remember him better as the Honourable Ballantine Bordman. You were his bodyguard in Berlin in 1938.'

'He was the fat slug who managed to get his hands on Anna. Every time I think of that it makes my blood boil.'

'He got his hands on Anna,' Baxter pointed out, mildly, 'because she invited him to do so. All right, so she was acting on the orders of her Nazi bosses. But the fact remains that he did get his hands on her in a big way, and I'm sure you'll agree that any man who has enjoyed that experience is not going to forget it.'

Clive glared at him.

'Bordman,' Baxter continued equably, 'claims

185

that when he was at a nightclub last night he saw Anna, seated at a table on the far side of the room, large as life and twice as beautiful.'

'Now I know you're talking rubbish. Anna has never been to a nightclub in her life. Except perhaps when required to do so by her job.'

'Exactly.'

Clive ignored the implication. 'And you believed this twaddle? Wasn't Bordman institutionalized after his separation from her?'

'He was. But that was a long time ago. He is perfectly *compos mentis* now.'

Clive blew a raspberry. 'So he thinks he saw Anna sitting all by herself at a table in a nightclub. Does that sound like Anna to you?'

'She was not alone, Clive. She was sitting with a clearly foreign gentleman. Holding hands.'

'What?!! How is she supposed to have been dressed?'

'She was wearing a very revealing evening gown, and apparently dripping with jewellery.'

'And where did this sighting take place?'

Baxter began to knock out his pipe. 'At the Coca Club.'

'The ... that's the sleaziest club in London.'

'Quite. Bordman was embarrassed about that. It would appear that like so many middle-aged men he has started to seek new experiences.'

'And you seriously believe this story?'

'Unfortunately Bordman was not alone. His companions all saw Anna, and commented on her looks. They didn't know who she was, of

186

course, and he didn't tell them. But they apparently will be able and willing to support his description.'

'And what does he intend to do about it?'

'It's what he wants us to do that has to take priority. Because if we don't do something PDQ, he is threatening to take the matter to the Home Secretary.'

'And you are prepared to allow a pompous windbag, who is also a mental defective, frighten us?'

'Now stop blowing off steam, and listen to me. By being here at all, Anna is breaking the terms of her agreement with us, and that covers her immunity in the Bahamas. That she has that immunity, that she is actually alive at all, is known to only half a dozen people; and it has to stay that way, or heads could begin to roll. If the newspapers got hold of it, it could bring down the government.'

'Wouldn't the simplest answer be to take out Bordman?'

'I'm sorry,' Baxter said. 'I didn't hear that. And I don't want to hear it. Just keep calm. Now, if her trip is just an outbreak of loneliness at your long absence, we might be able to smooth it over, providing you manage to get her out of the country ASAP. But if, as I suspect and the evidence suggests, she is here to work – and it can only be for the CIA – we need to identify her target and stop her completing her mission before all hell breaks loose and we find ourselves up to our ears in deep shit. So your business is to drop everything, revert to being the top-class gumshoe you were twenty-odd years ago, and find her quickly.'

Clive regarded him for several seconds. 'And when I find her?'

'We'll get her out of the country – if you make it before it's too late.'

Clive stood up. 'And Bordman?'

'If I can assure the Home Secretary that we have the matter under control, we don't have to worry about Bordman.'

Clive left the office.

When Jerry left, Anna wheeled the lunch trolley into the corridor, hung out a DO NOT DISTURB notice, locked the bedroom door, and – as was her custom when about to undertake a mission, and certainly one that might take all night – retired to bed. Her mind was already fully focused on the coming job itself, and thus emptied of all worries and apprehensions, despite the as yet unknown circumstances she might encounter.

She slept soundly for two hours, rose at five, and had a leisurely bath. Then she put on her knickers, strapped on her pistol and spare magazine, and finished dressing. Despite the temperature outside, she was not wearing stockings; she had always found them a nuisance in the past, and the suspender belt was inclined to get in the way of the gun belt. Her sable would have to do the job of keeping her warm when in transit.

She chose her black evening gown as this most effectively set off her golden hair and pale complexion, and worked the side vent vigorously for some seconds to make sure that the zip was absolutely free.

Satisfied, she added perfume and make-up, brushed her hair (she was wearing it completely loose save for two small clips above her temples to hold it away from her face and forehead), strapped on her watch, and surveyed herself in the mirror. Then she checked the contents of her evening purse. Apart from her Kelly passport, she was carrying only sufficient money to pay for a taxi home; there was nothing that could possibly identify her as Anna Fehrbach or the Countess von Widerstand or, most important of all nowadays, as Anna Bartley of Fair Cay in the Bahamas. Finally, she telephoned the desk. 'This is Miss Kelly,' she said, 'Room 416. I am expecting to be picked up this evening at about half-past seven by a Mr Khouri. Will you call me when he arrives, please?'

'Of course, Miss Kelly.'

Then it was a matter of waiting, but that was a necessary part of the business. Sitting in an armchair, her arms resting to either side, her fingers spread, they and her head absolutely motionless. Already entirely concentrated, it remained only necessary, but also very necessary, to turn herself from a woman into a lethal machine which would continue towards its objective until that was achieved, regardless of the cost, to anything or anyone. And that included herself.

The phone rang at twenty past seven. 'Mr Khouri is in the lobby, Miss Kelly.'

'Thank you. I'll be right down.'

A last look around the room, a last check in the mirror, and she put on her gloves and coat and left the room. As she walked towards the elevator she realized that she had company, but she did not turn to look at him until she was in the lift, when she was joined by a heavily set man wearing a dinner jacket. She had never seen him before, so she merely smiled at him. For his part he studied her with interest, but she was used to that. His hand was hovering over the panel, so she said 'The lobby, please.'

'Me also.' He had a faintly foreign accent, but pressed the button and they went down, gazing at each other. Anna had an idea that were they both to be remaining in the hotel this evening, he would fancy his chances of making a successful advance. But the poor chap was never going to see her again.

Khouri was as flawlessly dressed and groomed as before, and bent over her hand to kiss the back of her glove. 'You are as exquisite as always.'

'As are you, Mr Khouri.'

He smiled, still holding her hand and running his finger over the glove. 'But you are no longer wearing that beautiful ring. Don't tell me you've already sold it?'

190

'It is in the hotel safe. I do not like to wear it when I go out at night, unless I know my escort very well. I mean, it's all that stands between me and bankruptcy.'

'And that gentleman you were with at the Coca?'

'I told you, he's an old friend. Quite harmless. I only allowed him to escort me because I had to have an escort.'

'Of course. Well, my dear, after tonight, I do not think you will ever have to fear bankruptcy gain.'

Anna simpered, and he escorted her to a chauffeur-driven Daimler. 'You travel in style,' she commented.

'The car is Mr Fahri's. For my own part, I have nothing.'

She was finding his obviously false humility a little tiresome, so she concentrated on watching the countryside as they left London. Noting landmarks was difficult in the darkness, but she as yet had no idea what means she would have to employ to get home. An hour out of London might mean that taxis were scarce, certainly in the middle of the night. That only left this car ... if it could be done.

The houses disappeared, and she saw trees to either side. That might be interesting. 'Where is this?' she asked.

'It is a small wood. I really cannot remember its name. Are you nervous?'

A chance to gain some information? 'Should I be?'

'There is no necessity to be nervous of Mr Fahri. He is a very charming man. But meeting him could be a great opportunity for you.'

'Will there be many people present?'

'No, no. When meeting people for the first time, Mr Fahri prefers to dine tête-à-tête.'

'But you will be there, surely?'

'My dear Miss Kelly, I am only his aide, not his equal.'

'Oh!' She filled her voice with disappointment 'Does he have many aides?'

'There is only me.'

'Good heavens! You must have been with him a long time.'

'Indeed. I served with him in the War.' His tone was proud.

'You were in the War?'

'Mr Fahri and I fought together, against the Italians.'

'And you've been fighting together ever since?'

'Eh?' His head turned, sharply.

'Oh, please forgive me,' Anna said. 'I'm Irish, you see. Isn't there a Mrs Fahri?'

'There was. But she died.'

'How sad. So you and he live alone?'

'Oh, well, no. It is a large house. There are servants, of course, and then there are the bodyguards.'

'Bodyguards!?' Now she injected a note of alarm.

'But of course. Every wealthy man needs a bodyguard.'

192

'Oooh! You said bodyguards.'

'There are four of them. But only two are on duty at a time.'

This was sounding more simple by the moment – certainly when she remembered the three heavily armed thugs who had guarded Roberto Capillano in Mexico City, or the support team surrounding Smettow only a couple of weeks ago. Not to mention that snake! Although she supposed that, when push came to shove, Khouri would also attempt to take part in the defence. She certainly hoped so. Which would leave the servants. But she could think of few servants, unless they were of the Tommy variety, who would risk their lives to defend their employer.

There remained one last matter. 'And I suppose he also has guard dogs and things?'

'Oh, yes. Two Rottweilers.'

'Gosh! How terrifying. Will they bite me?'

'Good lord, no, dear lady. They do not bite the master's guests.'

'Ah!' Anna's breath gushed in relief.

A few minutes later the car turned into a driveway, ended by wrought-iron gates. On either side of them, a seven-foot-high stone wall stretched into the darkness.

'You'll be telling me next that that wall has broken glass scattered along the top,' Anna suggested.

Khouri chuckled. 'That is hardly necessary. Not while the dogs are active.'

'Ah!' Anna commented.

The driver flashed some kind of a signal with his headlights, and the gates slowly swung inwards, closing again when the car had passed through. Then there was another drive, lined with trees and curving round an ornamental fountain to bring them in front of a very large somewhat unimaginatively four-square house, ablaze with light on all four floors.

Waiting for them was a burly man in a dinner jacket. Bodyguard number one, Anna thought. He bowed as he opened the door for her, then stood back to allow Khouri to escort her up the short flight of steps to the open front door. Somewhere in the background she could hear dogs barking, but they were not to be seen.

She entered a sumptuous high-ceilinged hall-way, where a butler was waiting to take her coat, stroking the fur reverently as he did so. She watched him hang it in a wardrobe beside the door; as it was near freezing outside, she would need it when she left. She also noted that, unlike the bodyguard or Khouri, the butler was definitely English in appearance.

Khouri gestured at the stairs climbing the right-hand wall. The other doors in the hall were closed, which was a nuisance; she was trying to gain a picture of the exact layout. She climbed the richly carpeted steps, Khouri beside her. At the top there was a deep gallery, the floor again covered in deep-pile carpeting. This was excellent, as the sound of her heels was deadened and almost inaudible, while – to add to her growing sense of certainty that this assignment was actually going to be easy – apart from the butler, who had disappeared, she had seen only the one heavy. He had remained in the hall, staring at her, certainly, but she knew that most men found watching the Countess von Widerstand a fascinating business, especially from beneath when she was climbing a flight of stairs. But nothing that she had as yet seen gave any sign of the elaborate defences that this house was supposed to contain. Was it possible that Joe's information was incorrect? She certainly had no desire or intention to execute an innocent man. Or even one who was not quite as guilty as the CIA supposed.

The gallery contained another row of closed doors. Khouri gestured her towards one of these, then stepped in front of her and gave a brief knock. Then he opened the door and ushered her in. 'Miss Anna Kelly, sir. Miss Kelly, Sheikh Kola el Fahri.'

Anna gazed at the man standing in front of her. He suggested a perfect picture of a Hollywood Arab villain: short and fat, although impeccably dressed in a dinner jacket, and wearing a fez and matching red carpet slippers. But the operative word was fat. There were rolls of flesh sagging beneath his chin, and his stomach was clearly straining both his shirt and his pants. This made him look much older than he could possibly be; if he had fought behind the Axis lines in the War, which was only a dozen years ago, she did not see how he could be even forty yet, but he looked closer to sixty. Certainly the thought of having sex with him was utterly nauseating, which made her task the more acceptable: she disliked fat men in any event. All that needed to be established for certain was that he was the man who had blown up two civilian airliners and killed more than two hundred people.

For his part, Fahri was clearly delighted. 'Miss Kelly,' he said, advancing with out-stretched hands to take hers. 'This is an honour. Alois, you have excelled yourself.' Like Khouri, his English was perfect.

'Thank you, Excellency.'

'And,' added Anna, 'it's an honour for me.'

Fahri's eyes narrowed for just a moment, then he beamed again. 'It is my business to make it so. Come.' He held her hand and led her towards a settee, beside which were two arm-chairs, while in front of it there was a coffee table. The room was large, and there were three other sitting areas, while the floor was, again, thickly carpeted. But there was not a picture to be seen, although the walls were richly panel-led.

Fahri indicated the settee, and then sat beside her. He was at least heavily perfumed. 'Alois,' he said. 'Champagne.'

There was a sideboard against the far wall, and Khouri hurried to this to return with two glasses; but he did not take one for himself. Anna was forming the impression that he might prove a far more dangerous antagonist than his master, although even her practised eye could not discern any tell-tale bulge in his clothing that might indicate a concealed weapon. But the most important thing about the evening, so far at least, was that no attempt had been made to search her, as had been the case on so many previous occasions when she had inserted herself into a target's household. Either these people were absurdly innocent, and accepted without reservation her appearance and self-established background, or ... Her initial sense of well-being was starting to dissipate.

'Your very good health,' Fahri said, sipping, and regarded her almost totally exposed breasts and the crucifix that nestled between them. 'It is not often that I have the pleasure of entertaining a truly beautiful woman.'

'You flatter me, Excellency.' Anna sipped in turn.

'That would be impossible. Tell me about yourself. Khouri says you are Irish – but of course the accent is unmistakable. And that life is not going well for you.'

'It has gone better,' Anna conceded.

She was considering her options. The moment almost seemed propitious, in that neither Fahri nor Khouri seemed to have the slightest concept that she might be anything other than the picture she presented, a handsome and rather helpless young woman who was ripe for the picking, a picture she had used with almost unbroken success for fifteen years; only that bastard of a police chief in Argentina, three years ago, had formed a more accurate opinion, and he had been assisted by outside factors.

On the other hand, she had not yet ascertained for certain whether either of the two men was armed, and they were at that moment widely separated, Khouri being indeed almost behind her. Supposing he *was* carrying a gun, while she did not doubt that she was faster and more accurate than either of them, if she killed Fahri and then turned to deal with Khouri, although he would certainly die, he would have a clear second in which to shoot; and even after thirteen years, the memory of Hannah Gehrig's bullet smashing into her ribs was not one she wished to have repeated.

Nor did she yet have any idea of what problems there might be in getting out of the house. But most important of all, she had no intention of killing Fahri, or anyone else, until she had made absolutely sure that he was the guilty man she was after; the only fear she had ever known was that of being considered, even by herself, as a murderess rather than an executioner.

And if she was right in her estimate that Fahri had invited her here to take her to bed, that would surely be a better, and safer, time for completion. So, as always, patience.

'Sadly,' he said, 'that is the course of most lives, I know. But it is often possible to alleviate, if not actually eliminate, the downs.'

'You are an optimist, Mr Fahri. But then that is the prerogative of a wealthy man.'

'You are intelligent. I like that.' He put down his glass and again held her glove, stroking it. 'I would very much like to help you, if I can.'

Anna gazed into his eyes. They were soft eyes. 'Mr Khouri did say that you might be able to find me a ... position.'

'Oh, I am certain I shall be able to do that. But for you, it must be a special position.' He drained his glass and stood up. 'Shall we eat?'

Predictably, the dining room, which was on the next floor, was another huge area – the walls lined with various sideboards, and in the centre a mahogany table designed to seat at least twenty. Fahri sat at the head of the table, with Anna next to him on his right. Now, at last, Khouri left them, but there were two butlers constantly in attendance, and through the swinging inner doors she could hear the murmur of voices, without being able to determine how many people were out there.

'I serve simple food,' Fahri explained, as dishes of scallops were set in front of them. 'These are fresh. I have them flown in from the south of France.' One of the butlers had filled their glasses. Fahri raised his. 'I hope you like Pouilly Fuissé.'

Anna had always found it a little dry for her palate, but dutifully she said, 'It's delicious.'

Certainly the shellfish was cooked to perfection; the napkins were damask, the plates Dresden, the cutlery Danish silver, the glasses Swedish crystal, and the waiters wore shell jackets and white gloves. The splendour of the appointments was leading her just where she wanted to go. 'This is a magnificent house you have here,' she remarked.

'I am pleased with it, yes.'

'I should love to see it.'

'You are seeing it, are you not?'

'Well, these rooms, yes. I meant the whole thing. The grounds.'

'Then I will show them to you. When you are here in daylight.'

Anna decided not to follow that up for the moment, and she had no intention of being there in daylight. 'But I imagine you have always lived in surroundings like this?'

'My dear lady, I grew up in abject poverty.'

'Oh! Then ... you have travelled a long way.'

'A long way,' he agreed, reflectively.

'...And Mr Khouri said you saw service in the War.'

'I was able to play my part. But then we all had to play our part, did we not?'

'Not me, Mr Fahri. I grew up in Ireland. Eire, not Ulster.'

'Ah, Ireland. A beautiful country. So I have heard. I have never been there.'

Anna gave a quick, internal, sigh of relief. Neither had she. 'I hope you will. It is, as you say, a beautiful country. But Mr Khouri said you don't go out much, nowadays?'

'I have no reason to go out, nowadays; I have everything I desire right here. And from time to time, as this evening, I am privileged to have the company of a beautiful woman.'

Anna decided to look suitably embarrassed, as their plates were removed. There followed a rack of lamb, oozing blood, and the wine was replaced by a decanted red.

'It is rather a superior Chambertin,' Fahri commented.

Anna preferred claret to burgundy and, as she had told Hamilton, it was not her habit either to eat meat or to drink red wine at night, but she again dutifully sipped, and said, 'Delicious. And of course you have your dogs. I adore dogs. What sort do you have?'

'They are Rottweilers. But they are not pets, they are strictly guard dogs. They are fed only on red meat.'

'Guard dogs? Gosh! Do you need guard dogs? The property is walled.'

'Walls do not always keep intruders out,' he demurred.

Or in, Anna reflected, considering her options.

'All wealthy men need guards,' Fahri explained. 'I also have bodyguards.'

'Good lord! You don't mean ... that man who opened my car door. Was he a bodyguard?'

'Of course.'

'Was he armed?'

'Of course.'

'Wow! I'm glad I didn't know that.'

'Would it have upset you?'

'I would probably have fainted. I've never met a man carrying a gun.' She stared at him, eyes enormous. 'Don't tell me *you* are carrying one, Mr Fahri.'

He smiled. 'There is no need for me to do so inside my own house. There are weapons readily available if I need them. But you see, in addition to my guards, the house is burglar proof. It can be sealed at the touch of a button.'

'Which is also readily available?'

'Well, there is of course more than one control panel.'

'Wow!' Anna said again. There remained only the final question. 'Will you tell me something about the War? Your experiences. What unit did you serve with?'

Fahri carved the lamb and served her. 'I was with a guerrilla unit in North Africa. You understand what I mean?'

'Oh, yes. You lurked behind the enemy lines and sniped at German and Italian soldiers.'

'Actually, I blew them up.'

'Ah!' Anna said. 'But wasn't that terribly dangerous?'

'Well, to fight in a war at all is dangerous.'

'I meant, handling explosives. Suppose you pressed the wrong button?'

'Actually, buttons didn't come into it. And yes, it was dangerous. But I became an expert.' His tone was proud.

'Of course,' Anna agreed. 'Or you wouldn't be here now.'

'That is a very good point.'

'You must find life nowadays positively boring.'

'Oh, I manage to keep amused. Now you

must tell me about yourself.'

For the rest of the meal Anna regaled him with the spurious story of her life, how she had been married twice but ill-treated by both her husbands – which at least was half true. He listened with apparent interest, but spent most of the time staring at her décolletage. The meal was completed by sorbets and coffee, and a Chateau d'Yquem. This she enjoyed. Sauterne was her favourite dessert wine, and there was nothing better than Yquem.

'That was an absolutely delicious meal,' she said, and decided it was time to move things along. She looked at her watch. 'Oh! Ten to ten. I should be going.'

'But the night has not yet begun. Tell me, that is a most interesting watch.'

'It is German. A Jung something or other.'

'May I ask how you came by it?'

'My second husband gave it to me. I think he picked it up when he was in Germany after the War.'

'How interesting. It almost looks solid gold.'

'It is.' She sighed, heavily. 'But I'm afraid it will have to go.'

'Ah! Like your ruby ring? Or has that already gone?'

She had taken off her gloves to eat, and he had duly observed her naked fingers.

'No. That is in the hotel safe. Do forgive me, Mr Fahri, but I never know what I am going to encounter when I go out in the evening to visit people I do not know very well.'

203

'Of course. You are a very sensible girl.' He got up. 'Shall we go?'

'Go where?'

'Well, we have your future to discuss. And you said you wished to see the house. We can talk as we go.' He opened an inner door to reveal another staircase, this one leading up.

'Oh,' she said. 'We start at the top?'

'No, no,' he said. 'We start in my bedroom.'

'I'm sorry, sir,' said the maître d', 'but it is a house rule that gentlemen must wear a black tie.'

'Where did you get the idea that I was a gentleman?' Clive asked, pleasantly. 'And I am not here for the evening.' He showed him his wallet.

The maître d' gulped.

Clive now showed him the photograph of Anna which he always carried in his wallet. 'I would like you to tell me if you have ever seen this lady.'

'I am sorry, sir. But it is not the policy of this club to reveal the identity of its members.'

As the Coca Club did not open its doors until nine o'clock, Clive had spent a frustrating four hours since his meeting with Billy. Coming on top of the disturbing news that Anna was risking her position, not to mention her neck, by being in England at all, this had not left him in a good humour. So he said, tensely, 'Now, you listen to me, you slimy toad. I don't give a fuck for your house rules. If you refuse to cooperate

204

with us, I am going to have you closed down, tomorrow.'

The maître d' licked his lips. 'May I have another look at the photo?'

Clive obligingly showed it to him.

'No sir, I'm afraid I cannot help you. The lady has never been in this club.'

'But you will agree that she is a most striking woman?'

'Oh, indeed, sir. A most striking woman.'

'You could say once seen, never forgotten.'

'Indeed, sir.'

'I'm glad you agree with me,' Clive said. 'Because she was at this club last night.'

Again the maître d' gulped. 'Well, sir...'

'I believe someone sent a glass of champagne over to her table.'

'Ah ... yes, sir.'

'You're doing very well,' Clive said, encouragingly. 'Now tell me, the man who sent over the champagne and then joined her at her table was, shall we say, rather obviously of foreign extraction. I would like to know who he is.'

'As I've already told you, it is against club rules to release the names of our clientele.'

'Your decision. I am going to leave now, but there are two squad cars parked outside your front door. At my signal they are going to move in here and close you down. I'm very sorry, but there may be some damage.'

'You can't do that,' the maître d' protested. 'You have to have a warrant, and a court order. And I have...' He bit his lip.

'A friend, were you going to say? I may wish to talk to you about him, later. But you obviously did not study the card I showed you. I am not a police officer. I'm in Military Intelligence, and this is a matter involving national security. I don't need a warrant or a court order to do anything in pursuance of my duty.'

This was of course quite untrue, but Clive's instinct was this man would not know that. Nor had he studied the card closely enough to gather that his interrogator was from MI6, not MI5, even supposing he was aware that the foreign branch of the Intelligence Service had no legal right to operate inside England.

The maître d' sighed. 'The man was a Mr Khouri.'

'Khouri. Thank you. And is this Khouri a regular visitor to your club?'

'Yes, sir. He is.'

'Then perhaps you know what he does for a living, when he is not nightclubbing?'

Another sigh. 'He is private secretary to Mr Fahri.'

Clive stared at him. 'Would you mind saying that again? The name?'

'Fahri, sir. Kola el Fahri, the Libyan millionaire.'

'Holy Jesus Christ!'

'Sir?'

'I need the use of a telephone.'

'There are two call boxes in the lobby, sir.'

'I want your private line.'

'Ah ... yes sir.' He showed Clive into the

206

office.

'Thank you. Now clear off and close the door. And if anyone attempts to listen in or open that door until I'm finished, he or she is going straight down to the cells on a charge of treason. I'm sure you know that that can carry the death penalty.'

'Ah ... yes, sir.' The door was closed.

INCIDENT IN SURREY

Clive dialled, and after a few rings the phone was answered by a woman, who repeated the number. 'Mildred?' he said.

'Clive! Billy said you'd just got in this afternoon. How are you?'

'I'm fine. I'm sorry to bother you, but I need to speak with Billy.'

Mildred Baxter hesitated. 'Is it important? I mean, we're in the middle of dinner.'

'Believe me, Mildred, it is very, very, urgent.'

'Oh! Well ... hang on a moment.' He heard her say, 'It's Clive Bartley. And he seems to be in a monumental flap.'

A moment later Billy was on the phone. 'Don't tell me you've found her?'

'Not exactly.'

'Oh, my God! What's happened to her?'

'Listen carefully. The gentleman Bordman

remembers seeing her with at the Coca Club last night was the private secretary of Kola el Fahri.'

'Kola ... you're not trying to tell me she's after Fahri?'

'That is exactly what I am telling you, Billy.'

'How can you be sure of that? This fellow could have just been someone she met in the club.'

'Billy, you are not listening very carefully. Anna does not go to nightclubs unless it's a part of a job. Anna does not allow herself to be picked up, unless it's part of the job. Anna does not hold hands with strange men in public – or with any men, come to think of it – unless it's part of the job. Anna would never risk returning to England, except as part of a job. Anna works for the CIA. And finally, we know that for the last six months the State Department has been trying to get its hands on Fahri for the destruction of that Pan Am flight, and they're also pretty sure he was responsible for the Manila bomb. Now, they've got fed up waiting for us to stop dragging our feet over his extradition, so they've sent they're top girl to do the job – because they know women are Fahri's only weakness, the only people who can get inside that fortress of his, if they play their cards right.'

'As Anna is so adept at doing,' Baxter said bitterly. 'Your wife!'

'Yes,' Clive said 'My wife.'

'But would Anna take the risk of coming back

here, with the possible negation of the immunity we have granted her, to take on such a high-risk project? Isn't Fahri surrounded by armed guards?'

'Anna has been dealing with armed guards all of her adult life. As to why ... who knows what pressures that bastard Andrews has brought to bear on her. Even I still don't know everything about Anna, what really makes her tick.'

'After three years of marriage ... Well, she has to be stopped. We can't have a war hero assassinated, no matter how much of a murdering bastard he may be. And if something were to go wrong and it came out that the assassin was a US agent, God knows what would happen. You had better get on the telephone and warn Fahri that his life is in danger.'

'I'm sorry, Billy, that is the one thing we cannot do. I certainly am not going to do it. And if I find anybody else trying to, I may do some shooting myself.'

'Now, look here, Clive...'

'No, Billy, you look here. If we were to do that, we could well be signing Anna's death warrant – if she is in the process of carrying out her assignment, unaware that Fahri knows who and what she is.'

'I hope you're not suggesting we just let her go ahead and do it.'

'I don't think it need come to that. Anna does not hang about when she's on a mission. If she was holding hands with Fahri's secretary or whatever last night, by now she will have achieved her objective of getting invited into his mansion. For all we know, she could be there now.'

'Clive, if Anna has managed to get into Fahri's mansion, she may well have completed the job by now.'

'I don't think so. Anna is a meticulous worker, and a meticulous planner. That's why she's survived so long. She cannot possibly have known in advance the exact layout of Fahri's house, nor the number or equipment of his guards. She will suss that out before she goes into action. Now, we know that Fahri invites women to his home to sleep with them, after entertaining them lavishly. My bet would be that if she's there tonight, Anna will check things out as best she can and then wait to be alone with him.'

'In his bedroom or whatever. You happy with that?'

'No, I'm certainly not happy with that. But there is damn all I can do about it. My business is preserving Anna's life.'

'And Fahri's, I hope.'

'If it can be done. But Anna comes first.'

'And just how do you propose to do that?'

'I want your permission to call out a squad of our people, get down to Fahri's place, throw a cordon round it so no one can get in or out, then bang on the door myself and see what turns up. It's still only nine fifteen. If we can get there by ten, I'm sure nothing will have happened yet.'

'And if you're invited in, and find yourself

face to face with her?'

'I'll play that by ear. She's certainly not going to shoot me.'

'Clive,' Billy said, earnestly, 'you do realize that we have absolutely no legal jurisdiction inside the UK? What you should do is bring in MI5, or Scotland Yard.'

'Billy, we simply do not have time to convince some stuffed shirt of an assistant commissioner than he has to do something. We have to do something now, ourselves, or the situation could get out of hand.'

Billy sighed. 'All right. go ahead. But I want it clearly understood that you're on your own. If this turns out badly and you wind up being arrested by the local bobbies, I shall deny that this conversation ever took place. It could mean the end of your career.'

'Billy, if I manage to extricate Anna from this mess in one piece, I am taking her back to the Bahamas tomorrow and you will never hear of either of us again.'

'Good luck,' Baxter said.

'Your bedroom?' Anna squeaked. 'Oh, I couldn't do that, Mr Fahri. I mean, it wouldn't be proper.'

Fahri held her arm to urge her up the stairs. 'Anna,' he said winningly, 'why did you come here tonight?'

'Well ... Mr Khouri said you might be able to get me a job.'

'That is exactly it. With your looks, your

211

poise, your elegance, the world of films is at your feet. Acting ability can be taught. Looks you are born with, and without the right looks no actress can ever get anywhere.'

'Ooh!' Anna said. 'Do you really think so?'

'I know so. But to impress movie producers there are certain other assets you need to possess, or cultivate. You need to be able to shed all inhibitions. To be a star, you will have to kiss men you have never seen before and may not like. You will have to commit acts of violence you have never dreamed of, even if they are largely simulated. If a scene demands that you have to be naked, you have to be naked. If you are required to have sex with a man, you will have to have sex with that man. All you have to remember is that it is all make-believe.'

'Oooh!' Anna squeaked again.

'Anyway, as a woman who has had two husbands, you surely are acquainted with bedroom scenes?'

'I have only been in a bedroom with my husband,' Anna protested, stretching a point.

'Believe me,' he assured her, 'the scenario never changes.' They had reached another hallway, and more doors. Fahri opened the one immediately in front of them. 'Voilà!'

Anna allowed herself to be propelled into the room. 'Gosh!' She blinked at the red-and-gold motif on the walls and even on the bed, where the sheets were blood red.

'I like colour,' Fahri explained.

Anna surveyed the bed, clearly overwhelmed.

212

'You sleep in that?'

'Every night. But I, we, are not here to sleep. What I would like you to do is undress.'

'Oh, Mr Fahri, I couldn't possibly undress in front of a strange man.'

'But I have explained that that is something you must get used to. In fact, when you take into account an entire film crew, it will have to be in front of several strange men, and women. Anyway, I must make sure your body is as good as it appears in that dress. That there are no blemishes.'

It was time. Anna pulled on her gloves and transferred her purse to her left hand.

Fahri gazed at her. 'My dear young woman, you are supposed to be taking your clothes off, not putting them on!'

Anna allowed her tone to change. 'You know, Mr Fahri, you strike me as not being a very nice man.'

'Eh?' He was taken aback. 'What?'

'In fact,' Anna said, slipping down the zip at the side of her dress, 'you strike me as being the sort of man who would plant a bomb to blow up an airliner with more than a hundred innocent people on board simply to satisfy some childish hatred for the country they come from.'

'What!?' he said again. 'Who *are* you?'

'Consider me as Nemesis,' Anna suggested. 'So come now, be a man. Tell the truth for once in your life. Did you plant that bomb in Manila?'

'What!? What's that to you?'

213

'Important. Did you, or didn't you?'

'You...'

'Did you, or didn't you plant it?' Anna withdrew her hand from inside her gown.

He goggled at the gun. 'You...'

'You are becoming terribly inarticulate,' Anna said. 'No matter. All I want from you is a simple yes or no. Did you, or one of your people acting on your orders, plant that bomb in Manila?'

'You think you can get away with this?'

'Yes.' She levelled the gun at his groin. 'Answer me, or I shall blow away what appears to be your most precious possession.'

He gaped, and clasped his hands to his crotch. 'What is it to you?' he snarled. 'They were guilty. That whole nation is guilty of trying to rule the world.'

'Thank you,' Anna said, and raised her pistol. But as she did so, a bell jangled throughout the house. Momentarily distracted, Anna half turned her head, and Fahri threw himself away from her and across the bed, revealing a remarkable agility for such a ponderous-looking man, left hand reaching for a panel on the bedhead containing several control buttons, right hand seizing a pistol that was lying on the table beside the bed; in the multicoloured gloom, she hadn't noticed it.

She recovered instantly. And, as he turned back towards her, still sprawled on the bed, lips drawn back in a wolfish snarl, she levelled the Walther and shot him in the centre of the fore-

214

head, experiencing as she did so a sense of relief; she hated having to kill unarmed opponents. But in that instant there was a series of loud thuds, and steel shutters came down over the windows.

Fuck it! she thought, and listened to the noises seeping up through the house, shouts and bangs. She went to the bed, gazed at the dead man, and the gun, which she recognized as a Browning Hi-Power 9mm pistol, with a thirteen-shot magazine. This was a weapon she had used before, and was just what she wanted, as she had no idea how many men there remained between her and freedom, supposing she could release the shutters, and the exterior doors too.

She leaned over him to take the gun from his grasp, and studied the panel. There were twelve buttons, but everything had happened so fast she couldn't be sure which one he had pressed to activate the system. Presumably, the same button would deactivate it; but equally, she had no idea what pressing a wrong button might do, what other unpleasant surprises he might have had installed. As she hesitated, considering the matter, there were several knocks on the door. 'Sheikh Fahri...' What followed was a stream of Arabic, one of the few languages Anna did not speak. But the voice definitely belonged to Khouri.

She left the Browning where it was, to act as a bait, and unlocked the door, the Walther drooping from her fingers. 'Mr Khouri,' she said. 'Just the man I wanted to see.'

'What has happened? Why did Sheikh Fahri activate the system?'

'I think he had a rush of blood to the head. Probably caused by that bell. What was that?'

'Oh, someone at the outer gate. The boys downstairs will sort it out.'

The dogs were again barking.

'It was nothing to alarm the sheikh,' Khouri said.

'Well, then, a storm in a teacup. Would you like to deactivate the system? It's awfully stuffy with the shutters closed.'

'Only Sheikh Fahri has the power to deactivate the system. You must ask him to do so.'

'But just supposing he was incapable ... You know how it's done, don't you?'

'I cannot do it without orders from the sheikh. What do you mean, incapable?'

'But you *can* do it. I'm so glad. Because, you see, I don't think the sheikh is able to right now, and I would like to go home.'

'What? Let me speak to him.'

'Well,' Anna said, 'if you must. But I'd be very surprised if he replies.'

She stepped aside to let him into the room, moving behind him to close and lock the door.

The click went unnoticed. Khouri was staring at the bed.

'My God! He's...'

'Absolutely.'

'You...'

He turned back to her, and for the first time

216

noticed the pistol, which she had brought up. 'You...'

'Absolutely,' Anna said again.

'You have killed the sheikh? You came here with a gun? How could you do such a thing!'

'It's a habit of mine. Be prepared, as they say. I suddenly found that I had formed a violent dislike for him. And I must tell you that I formed a violent dislike for you the moment I saw you.'

His mouth was opening and shutting like a fish's. Anna could read his mind as if its contents had been displayed before her on a screen: total disbelief that this could be happening and a desperate urge to think of a solution to the immediate problem.'

'Now,' she said, 'all I want you to do is deactivate the system. And then, you see, I can leave.'

'You expect me to do that?' As she had hoped, his eyes were straying back to the dead man ... and the pistol. 'And if I refuse?'

'Then I will have to persuade you.'

'Ha!' he commented.

She had to concede that he did not lack courage, although she was also sure that he felt she had taken Fahri by surprise. Admittedly, she had to concede that Fahri had taken her by surprise, in the speed with which he had been able to move and the fact that he had had a weapon so handy. That she had not noticed it had been utter carelessness and overconfidence. Hubris!

But time was passing, and she was certainly

fully concentrated now. 'Very well,' she said, 'if you insist. Do you hang to the left or the right?'

For a moment he did not understand her, but as she levelled the pistol he realized what she intended. 'Wait! I will release the shutters.'

'Thank you.'

He had clearly taken the bait, but she could not kill him until she was free. She waited, as he turned away from her and knelt on the bed. His hand moved over the panel, and with a rumble the shutters went up. As he pressed the button, his other hand seized the Browning and turned back towards her, firing as he did so. But as he had not had time to aim, the bullet went wide, and Anna squeezed her trigger.

She surveyed the two bodies lying together in death, just as they appeared to have walked together in killing, for most of their lives. A hundred and thirty-seven. Would they be the last? She still had to get out of the house. She holstered the Walther, the little gun warm against her stomach, then knelt on the bed, removed the Browning from Khouri's hand, and checked the magazine. It had been fully loaded, and only the one shot had been fired. The heavier pistol had a much louder, sharper report than her own gun; but the door had been shut, as had the windows.

She moved to the door, opened it, and listened. Noise seeped up from below, but none of it suggested alarm. They had left it to Khouri to investigate the reason for the closing of the doors and shutters; and now these had been opened again so quickly, seemed to have accepted that it had been a mistake. Thus she was still ahead; but she still had to get past the front staff, and get the gates open. And if possible, obtain the car keys. Most important of all, however, she had to reclaim her coat.

She took the key from the lock, closed the door, and locked it again, putting the key in her purse, paused at the head of the private staircase, and listened to another bell ringing. But this one was much less resonant, and she reckoned it was the front door, as opposed to the gate – which might provide an easier way out.

She went down the stairs to the little lobby. In front of her was the door to the dining room, but she heard movement in there and deduced that the domestic staff were still clearing the dinner table. She did not wish to involve undoubtedly innocent people, and there was another door on the far side of the lobby. She opened this, and found herself in a very comfortable library-cum-study. She crossed this and emerged on to the upper gallery ... and stopped as if turned to stone. On the ground floor, immediately beneath her, two floors down, the front door had been opened, and a man was saying, 'That took you a hell of a long time!'

Shit! she thought. Shit, shit, shit, shit, shit, shit, shit! Clive!

What in the name of God, she thought, or, as God had no place in her professional life, of the

Devil, was Clive doing here?

'We have come to see Sheikh el Fahri,' he was explaining.

Which, clearly, meant he was mob-handed. The temptation to announce herself, and thus be able to relax in the warmth of his protection, was enormous. But it would also be catastrophic. She had just, in the eyes of British justice, committed a double murder. What is more, with Clive's long experience of her methods, he would need no more than a quick examination of the bodies to discover two single shots to the head and know who was responsible. Nor, as she now had Fahri's pistol, did she have much hope of claiming self-defence. In any event, it had been made perfectly clear that if she were ever to attempt to operate in England again she would be for the high jump – which would mean the long drop. And she could not face the situation of having to force him to choose between his wife and his duty; whichever he chose, it would destroy him.

But what was he doing here? Obviously that bastard Bally had gone to MI6 in preference to Scotland Yard, because he knew she had had links with the Secret Service before the War – even if he could not possibly know that she had worked for them since. And Billy Baxter, reasonably, had turned the problem over to Clive, who was not only her husband but was also supposed to be keeping her out of trouble in the Bahamas.

That all made sense, but how had he figured

out that she might be here? That was a question which would have to be answered later, but obviously he was here to try to prevent her getting to Fahri, either by warning him or by placing him under MI6 protection. Which would really have buggered things if she hadn't already completed the job.

But right now, her aim had to be to get out of the house, unseen, regain the Bahamas, and deny that she had ever left.

'I am sorry, sir,' the butler was saying, 'Mr Fahri is entertaining, and cannot be disturbed.'

'He can, you know,' Clive said. 'Do you know what this is?'

Anna did not dare look over the balustrade, but gathered from the sudden silence that he was presenting either a warrant or a badge.

'You are from the Secret Service?'

'That is correct. And it is vitally important that we see Sheikh el Fahri, now.'

'I will have to ask Mr Khouri, the sheikh's private secretary. If you will excuse me.'

Anna listened to a clicking noise, and understood that he was using a house telephone.

A few moments later he said, 'Mr Khouri does not appear to be in his room.'

'Won't he be with the sheikh, helping to entertain the guests?'

'That is unlikely, sir. Sheikh el Fahri is dining tête-à-tête.'

'Oh, my God!' Clive exclaimed.

'Sir?'

'Would his guest be a young lady?'

'Yes, sir.'

'With long golden hair?'

'Why, yes, sir. Do you know the lady?'

Shit! thought Anna, for the umpteenth time.

'I know who she is,' Clive said. 'Now, you listen to me. I have got to see Sheikh el Fahri, now. There is no time for you to locate Mr Khouri. Take me to the sheikh.'

'Well, sir...'

'I said, now! Or I will have my men tear this house apart.'

Another brief silence, then the butler said, 'If you will come with me, sir.'

Anna realized that they were about to mount the stairs, and as they would certainly come up to this floor, there was no way she could remain on the gallery without being seen. To return to the dining room was out, as that was where they would be going. But there remained the study. She ran to this, and waited, standing against the door in the faint hope that, not finding either Fahri or her in the dining room, Clive might go away again. But she knew the hope was faint; if he had been given a job to do, he would do it. And sure enough, a few moments later she heard voices in the lobby.

'I really do not think, sir, that we can go up,' the butler was saying. 'The top floor is reserved exclusively for the use of Sheikh el Fahri. And when he is entertaining, only Mr Khouri is permitted.'

'You mean they share the guest?' Clive's words were like drops of vitriol.

222

'Well ... sir!'

'I'll take responsibility,' Clive said, obviously starting up the steps. The carpet continued to deaden sound, but she was certain that there was at least one other man with him.

It was time to move. She reckoned she had about five minutes before all hell broke loose. Cautiously she opened the door on to the gallery. This was now deserted, so she advanced to the balustrade and looked down. There were two bodyguards standing together and muttering. She had no doubt that she could deal with them in short order. But waiting by the front door was another man, and she could have no doubt he was MI6. She knew that she could handle him as well, but it might mean having to kill him; and this she was not prepared to do.

At the end of the gallery there was a window. That was certainly a way out, but it would mean abandoning her coat and probably risking frostbite, not to mention possible injury getting down; she reckoned she would be dropping from about twenty-five feet. But if there was a window at the end of this gallery, there would surely be one on the lower level as well. She listened to a crashing sound from above her; they were breaking down the bedroom door. That cut her time to about three minutes. She returned to the gallery and looked down. The men were engaged in animated conversation. She took off her shoes, drew a deep breath, and went down the stairs. Still they did not look up. But as she gained the lower gallery, there was a shout from upstairs. Now she had only a few moments. She ran along the gallery to the window, opened it, and was greeted by an icy blast, while from downstairs there were shouts of alarm: the men had at last seen her. She dropped the Browning and her shoes, tucked her purse into her dress, wishing there was more of it, then clambered out and looked down, but could see nothing in the darkness. Now noise was spreading throughout the house, and there were heavy thumps as the men on the ground floor came up after her.

She turned, hung by her hands, and then dropped, doing a break-fall as soon as she struck. But she had landed in some bushes, which both broke the impact and prevented her from rolling very far. Panting, she extricated herself, and then had to look for her shoes. She located these easily enough, but could not find the gun; so she decided to abandon it, aware of a series of sharp pains running up and down her body, although she did not appear to have broken anything.

The men above her had reached the window. But as they did so, she heard a succession of thuds. Apparently, having decided that she still had to be inside, someone had pressed the panic button and all the doors and the shutters had dropped into place; the house was suddenly entirely dark. Which, she realized, could be a stroke of much-needed luck; she was gaining valuable time.

But the respite could only be temporary. And

she was still inside the grounds, and freezing cold. Now, as she crawled out of the bushes, she heard guttural growls, and two dark shapes came bounding towards her. She stood up, thrust her hand inside her gown, and drew her pistol. The dogs raced up to her, and she said, 'Listen, you! Shut up and go away. Or die!'

Taken aback by the fact that there was no fear in her voice or to be smelt on her sweat, only total menace, they stopped, panting. As they did so, a voice called, out of the darkness, 'Bruno? Balthazar? What have you found?'

Anna walked towards the man, the dogs escorting her, one on either side, but keeping their distance. And now she could make out the uniform. 'You,' she said, 'are just the man I wanted to see.'

He peered at her, but there was no mistaking the hair, even if it was somewhat tangled and had leaves sticking out of it. 'You!' he exclaimed. 'But you...'

'I'm Sheikh el Fahri's dinner guest, remember.'

'But...'

He looked her up and down.

'I know,' she agreed. 'I'm a little untidy. But that's your boss for you: a bundle of fun.'

'The dogs...'

'Don't worry,' Anna assured him, 'I haven't harmed them.'

'*You* have not harmed *them*?'

'They are my friends. Come along now, I haven't got all night. And it's bloody cold.'

She gestured towards the garage, and he noticed the pistol for the first time. 'You...'

'Yes,' she said. 'And I will use it if you do not do exactly as I say.'

He stumbled beside her to the garage. In it there were three cars, but Anna chose the Daimler in which she had arrived. 'Get behind the wheel,' she commanded, and sat beside him, the pistol pointing at his body. 'Let's go.' The dogs sat down, panting.

'I cannot leave without El Fahri's permission.'

'If that is going to be your attitude, I sincerely hope you do not have a wife and children. Refuse to drive and I will put a bullet in your gut, then one in your groin, and then one in your head. Obey me, and I give you my word that you will not be harmed.'

He started the engine. 'The gates are locked.'

'But you can open them. I saw you do it. Remember? And put the heater on.' Her teeth were beginning to chatter.

He obliged and drove out of the garage.

There was another car, clearly belonging to MI6, parked at the foot of the steps, with a man behind the wheel. But he did not appear to respond. Whatever orders he had received from Clive, they clearly had not included stopping El Fahri's car from leaving.

They gained the gate without mishap, the chauffeur signalled with his lights, and they drove through. As they did so, a man emerged

226

from beside the gate, waving them to stop. 'Keep going,' Anna said, as the car slowed, and they picked up speed again. 'Now drive me back to London.

'El Fahri is going to be very angry,' the chauffeur said. 'I may lose my job.'

'I'm afraid I can't guarantee your job,' Anna said, 'but I do promise you that El Fahri is not going to be very angry.'

He digested this silently. Enveloped in a gorgeous plume of hot air, she studied the road, recalling it from their drive out. The wood she wanted had been about twenty miles out of London. And there it was. 'Stop here,' she said.

It was just coming up to eleven and the road was deserted.

He glanced at her, anxiously. 'You promised...'

'That I would not harm you, if you obey me. I always keep my promises. Give me the keys.'

He obeyed.

'Now get out.' She followed him. 'Let's see what you have in the boot.'

He lifted the lid and she peered into the gloom. There was no rope; that was too much to hope for. But there was an assortment of tools, including a pair of jump leads with fairly long connections. 'Those will have to do. And is that a blanket? You're a lucky man. Take them out.'

He obeyed.

'Now let's a take a walk.'

She gestured at the trees; and after his usual hesitation, he obeyed. They had to slide down

227

into a shallow ditch and clamber out the other side, then they were on grass, and a few minutes later were in the darkness under the trees. 'Keep going,' Anna said.

They walked for another ten minutes, until the road was completely lost to view. 'Now spread the blanket and lie down with your back to me,' Anna commanded. 'And please do remember something very important. If you attempt to resist me, I will kill you. This is something I have been doing all my life, and I have no compunction about adding you to my list.'

He lay, half on his face. Anna placed the pistol on the ground, and took off his belt and then his tie. She used his tie to secure his wrists behind his back, and his belt to do the same with his ankles. She found a handkerchief in his pocket and stuffed it into his mouth. Then, having pulled him up and dragged him to a suitable tree trunk, she made him sit with his back to it and wrapped the leads – good strong, thick cable – round his body and the trunk, before securing the two terminals together, on the far side of the tree, and pulling them tight. She was both panting and sweating by the time she finished, but at least it had warmed her up.

She covered him with the blanket, tucking it into the now open neck of his shirt. 'I really don't want you to freeze,' she explained. 'But, of course, if you wriggle around too much, the blanket may come untucked. If that happens, and you catch pneumonia, I want you to remember that it was your decision.'

She made her way back through the trees to the car, and drove away. It was just eleven. She needed to ditch the car before she reached the hotel, as it would easily be traced. But even so, she'd be in her room by twelve, and even if she had a hot bath and changed her clothes, she'd be out again by one – which would surely be before the chauffeur could get loose, and then to a police station, and start telling them where she was staying.

She reflected that had she been the cold-blooded killer everyone supposed, she'd have put a bullet in his head. It would certainly have been the safest thing to do. Then his body might have lain in the woods for twenty-four hours; and in twenty-four hours she'd be back in the Bahamas. But the man had been English and she estimated that he was too young to have had any wartime links with Fahri, or even with his post-war activities, and she was not in the business of taking innocent lives. So, she thought, as the houses on either side began to multiply, informing her she was in the suburbs, she had condemned herself to spending the night on the street, or a bench at Heathrow. All without her fur. Damnation! But at least she would be more warmly dressed.

Fleurmann poured brandy, spilling some.

'I think you are nervous,' Pascall remarked. 'Because you encountered her?'

'You weren't there,' Fleurmann pointed out. 'She was not three feet away from me, gazing at me, for five minutes, while the elevator went down. It was an unforgettable experience.'

'Did she speak?' Hamilton asked.

'She merely said, "The lobby, please." I was closer to the control panel, you see. And it was not so much the voice, it was...'

He sighed.

'Was she as beautiful as Hamilton claims?' Pascall asked.

'More so. Far more so. There was not a flaw. The features might have been carved by a Greek god. The hair cried out to be stroked. And the body ... she was wearing a fur coat, but it was open, and her dinner gown was cut almost to her navel. Those breasts ... I shall dream about them for the rest of my life.'

'Did you see her tits?' This time Pascall's voice was eager.

'Well, no. She was not indecent, just provocative.'

'I have seen her naked,' Hamilton said, proudly.

The two men stared at him, and he flushed. 'We were swimming together, at night.'

'Did you have sex with her?' Pascall was more eager yet.

'No,' Hamilton said, brusquely. 'I do not think she is promiscuous, either.'

'That is not what they say of her,' Pascall argued. 'They say she fucks every man who comes close to her.' He grinned. 'Before killing them.'

'That is why Hamilton is still alive,' Fleurmann suggested. 'But you know, it was more than just her looks. It was her eyes. They were blue, so blue, and so large. And they looked at me ... they were soft. I remember going to a zoo, to the big cats' enclosure, and watching a female tiger waking up. Her eyes were soft, too...'

'You'll be telling us next they were blue,' Pascall scoffed.

'No, no. They were yellow. But as I said, they were soft, and they remained soft. But as she stood up and stretched, you could sense the immense power she possessed, that she had at her disposal whenever she required it. I experienced the same feeling when I was looking at the countess.'

'Pffft! Just remember what the boss told us. The one mistake any of us can make is to become fascinated by this woman. As you obviously are.'

'Well,' Hamilton looked at his watch. 'It's just coming up to twelve. We may have another two hours to wait.'

But at that moment the telephone rang.

Baxter wore striped pyjamas, and what was left of his hair was standing on end. 'For God's sake, Clive, do you know what time it is?'

'It's a quarter to twelve,' Clive said, 'and some of us are still working.'

'Well, come in. It's bloody freezing.' He led the way into his lounge. 'You look as if you could do with a drink. Brandy?'

'Unfortunately...' Clive removed his hat and coat. 'Some of us are still working.'

'My heart bleeds for you. May I remind you that the reason you are still working is the behaviour of your errant wife. However, I assume that you have regained conjugal possession.'

'Had I done that, Billy, I would happily accept your drink.'

Baxter lowered the balloon he was filling. 'You mean ... Where is she?'

'I haven't the foggiest idea. But I know where she's been.'

'Concentrate. The important thing is that you did not find her at Fahri's. So you managed to sort that out.'

Clive sat down. 'Billy, Kola el Fahri is dead.'

Baxter gulped at the brandy he had half poured, and then refilled the glass, ignoring the measure.

'So is his sidekick, Khouri.'

'But ... how?'

'The cause of death, in each case, was a bullet wound in the centre of the forehead.'

'Oh, Jesus Christ! Anna?'

'It is her trade mark.'

'But ... what were his people doing?'

'When I got there, they weren't doing anything. As far as they were aware, Fahri was upstairs entertaining a very handsome long-haired blonde, and was not to be interrupted.'

There was a sharp crack, and brandy dripped on to the floor. Baxter apparently didn't notice. He sat down in turn, still holding the broken

232

and dripping glass. 'But, if ... Are you saying she was still there?'

'Very definitely yes. In fact, the assassinations could only have happened minutes before I and my people arrived. We rang the outer bell and were allowed access, but by the time we reached the front door, a matter of perhaps two minutes, the house had been hermetically sealed. Fahri apparently had some kind of hi-tech protection system installed, so that at the touch of a button steel shutters come down over all the windows and all the doors. According to the staff, this extreme action could only be ordered or carried out by Fahri himself, or by this chap Khouri. I had no idea what was going on, so I banged on the door – which was, naturally, not opened because it was sealed. But after what couldn't have been more than a couple of minutes, the shutters went up again.'

'You mean Anna turned the system off. Why?'

'Well, obviously, Billy, to get out. She didn't know we were waiting on the doorstep. But here is the point. Anna couldn't have deactivated the system, because it is operated by a control panel the working of which was known only to Fahri and Khouri. And the butler, fortunately, or we'd still be there.'

'You've lost me. So what do you think happened?'

'As I said earlier, unless it's a matter of self-defence, in which case she's like a streak of greased lightning, Anna takes her time. An execution has to be meticulous; and most important of all, she has to be absolutely certain that her designated target is guilty.'

'Tell me another.'

'It's the way she operates. The way she has always operated. The way she has to operate, and still be Anna. If she ever felt she'd executed the wrong man, she would not be able to live with herself.'

Baxter cleared his throat, loudly.

'OK,' Clive conceded. 'But that happens to be a fact. So obviously what happened is that while she was establishing that Fahri was guilty of blowing up those planes, the penny dropped and he tried to take action. We have found a Browning automatic pistol, which is certainly not Anna's, with one cartridge fired. There is a bullet hole in the wall of Fahri's bedroom, immediately in line with the foot of the bed, where Anna would have been standing. So, when he realized he was for the high jump, Fahri must have produced the pistol. But at the same time he must have activated the alarm system. He also managed to get off one shot before Anna killed him.'

'All right. Let's suppose that scenario is accurate. She's killed her target, but she can't get out of the house. Why couldn't you pick her up on the spot?'

Clive sighed. 'Because we couldn't get in.'

'But you said that after a few minutes the door was opened?'

'Exactly. Clearly either Khouri was also

upstairs, and interrupted her, or she rounded him up. Either way, she made him release the shutters.'

'And then shot him. That doesn't sit too well with your conscience-satisfying theory.'

'Oh, come now, Billy. You know that Khouri was every bit as guilty as Fahri. The two men had been partners all their lives.'

'All right. You're now in the house. And so is Anna. How many exits were there?'

'Only two. Out the back through the kitchens, or out the front door.'

'And I assume you had them both covered?'

'I did. Anyway, to get out the back she would have had to pass through all of the staff, who were still clearing away after dinner.'

'And to get out the front, she would have had to pass you. But she got out. Don't tell me, she snapped her fingers and said Kazam, or whatever it is, and became invisible.'

'Billy,' Clive said severely, 'I have had an exhausting and traumatic evening, and I'm very tired. Don't press your luck. Anna got out because when necessary she can think with the speed and clarity of one of those computers which we are told are being developed. Having killed both Fahri and Khouri, and with the shutters opened, she must have headed downstairs to leave by the front door. But when she got to the gallery overlooking the entry hall, she saw me and my team. Those heavies who were on guard duty don't know just how lucky they were. If they had tried to stop her, they'd both have been dead.'

'You still haven't told me how she did it.'

'From the gallery, she would have been able to hear what we were saying, and knew we would be going upstairs to interview Fahri; at least, so we thought. So she opened a window and jumped out.'

'How high is this gallery?'

'The window is fifteen feet above the ground.'

'And you think she jumped out and walked away?'

'Someone did. The bushes beneath the window were broken and scattered. And we found the Browning there. She must have dropped it when she fell, and didn't waste time looking for it.'

'Now just a minute. She did all this while you were passing the gallery to go upstairs, and you didn't hear her? Or notice the open window?'

'No, because she obviously hid herself until we were past, and then we made a mistake. I had Wilkins with me, having left Osborne by the door. Wilkins is a very smart lad, unfortunately. When we got to the bedroom and saw the bodies, he immediately tested them and they were still warm. So he said the obvious thing, the killer must still be in the house. I reckoned he must be right; and as we had been shown the way by the butler, I pointed at the control panel and asked him if he could operate it. He could, and did, immediately. So we were sealed in.'

'Without realizing that Anna was already out. What a fuck-up! But wait a minute. Anna is now in the garden, apparently unhurt?'

'We don't know that.'

'Well, it doesn't appear that she was too much hampered. So she's in the garden. Are you saying that this so-called fortress doesn't have guard dogs?'

'There are two Rottweilers.'

'And what happened to them?'

'They're all right.'

'You've lost me again. The Rottweilers didn't attack her?'

'Billy, Anna doesn't have to kill dogs. When they get close enough to smell the hostility she can project, they are terrified.'

'So she then commandeered a car and drove out. While you and your henchmen were locked in. You have to either laugh or weep. But wait a minute. Didn't you have men outside the house?'

'Yes. And outside the gate. But Anna wasn't alone. She had a man with her wearing a chauffeur's uniform. The gates are controlled by a light signal, you see, which Anna could not have known. She needed the chauffeur to open them for her. My people on the gate tried to stop them and were nearly mown down. They then came to the house and banged on the door, which alerted us to raise the shutters again.'

'And your murderer got clear away. That is a most ingenious reconstruction, Clive, even if Anna's ice-cold thinking and decisive action contrast strongly with your utter incompetence. However, I cannot see that we are a lot worse off. She has disappeared, and there isn't a shred of evidence that will stand up in court that it was Anna. London is full of good-looking long-haired bimbos. And any competent defence lawyer would destroy in seconds any identification evidence offered by the bodyguards or the butler – who, as they were employed by Fahri, almost certainly have criminal records.'

'If she is caught, it could come to court, Billy.'

'My dear fellow...'

'Because we do have a positive identification.'

'Namely?'

'A sable coat hanging in the downstairs closet, worn by Fahri's dinner guest. Now, how many long-haired blonde bimbos who frequent sleazy nightclubs and allow themselves to be picked up by strange gentlemen also possess sable coats?'

'And you think Anna abandoned a coat like that?'

'I'm quite sure she regretted having to do it. But she didn't have much choice. Anyway, Anna's career is littered with abandoned sable coats. I know of two others at least.'

Baxter sighed. 'OK, so there's some circumstantial evidence that she was there. But to make that stick, she has to be arrested, and it has to be proved that she was in this country at all. She's probably already left, and will no

238

doubt produce evidence, supported by the CIA, that she never left the Bahamas. Wouldn't the best and safest option be just to let the police get on with it, if they can? Then we can hold up our hands and say that in visiting Fahri we were acting in good faith on information received, but don't have a clue as to who the assassin was.'

'I'm sorry, Billy. I don't think that's an option. Apart from the coat, though only I can testify that it's definitely hers, we have Bordman's positive identification.'

'That he saw her at a nightclub in London, and recognized her instantly after thirteen years. Even if he's believed, we can admit that she may have been breaking the rules by being in this country. But that doesn't prove that she had anything to do with Fahri's death.'

'Except that the maître d' at the club has identified her as being there on the night that Bordman claims to have seen her, thus confirming Bordman's story. And he saw her having a tête-à-tête with Khouri. Then the next night Khouri is murdered, by a long-haired blonde. Scotland Yard aren't too slow at adding two and two and making four.'

'Maybe. But they still don't know what name she is operating under, or where she has been staying, and probably still is. And as I said, there are an awful lot of long-haired blondes floating around London. Given Fahri's track record of luring them to his house with promises of a movie career and then throwing them out after having sex with them, there must be quite a few of these bimbos who would be very happy to put a bullet in his brain.'

'I'm sure you're right. Unfortunately, the police do, or shortly will have, a location where she can be found.'

'What? How?'

'According to the staff at the house, Anna was delivered there by Fahri's own car, a Daimler, driven by his personal chauffeur. Ergo, she was picked up by same car and chauffeur. And she left the grounds tonight in a Daimler with a uniformed man at the wheel. As I said, that had to be the chauffeur, probably with a gun in his ribs. When the police find the car and the chauffeur, he will be able to tell them where she is staying. They won't need to know her name. A description will do.'

'There is no chance of that,' Baxter argued. 'That fellow is dead by now.'

'Anna doesn't kill innocent people,' Clive said coldly.

'All right, all right. So the chauffeur is the key. What can you do about that?'

'Find him before the police do.'

'That's a bloody tall order. And supposing you do, are you going to put a bullet in his brain yourself?'

'I can put him under wraps for a couple of hours. The point is that at this moment Anna is confident that she has got away with it, as she has so often in the past. I don't know exactly what plans she may have, but I'm damned sure they involve flying back to the Bahamas and regaining the cay; then, as you said, she'll deny that she ever left it. Even if it is impossible to prove that she's working for the CIA, as she certainly is, they have always provided her in the past with every possible alibi, and they're likely to do so again. But the earliest flight to Nassau isn't until eleven tomorrow morning.' He looked at his watch. 'I beg your pardon, this morning. That means she will assume she has time to return to her hotel, maybe even have a sleep, and certainly change her clothes, before trotting along to the airport at about ten – blissfully unaware that well before that the police may be knocking on her door. Even if they're slow off the mark, they'll certainly get out an APB to all airports and ferry terminals. If I can get to her before that happens, I can get her out of there and keep her under wraps until it's safe for her to leave the country. To do that, I need to find that chauffeur before the police do.'

'Good luck,' Baxter said.

During her apparently insouciant shopping trips around London, Anna had carefully sized up and committed to memory all of the possible parking places within walking distance of the hotel, as from the beginning she had been trying to determine the best means of getting back after her assignment; the odds against finding a taxi in the middle of the night in rural Surrey were simply too long. But whatever means of transport she discovered, there was no way she

241

could risk being dropped at the Royal George, to which she could then easily be traced.

Of course all the parks would be closed, and there was no guarantee that she would be able to find a space on a street. But she had discovered that about eight blocks away there was another hotel, much smaller and less grandiose than the Royal George, that had a driveway where there were always parked cars.

She turned into this, stopped, and got out. The space was not really big enough and the rear of the car stuck out – which, sure enough, attracted the attention of the doorman, who at just before midnight was the only other person in the vicinity. He hurried down the steps and came towards her. 'I'm sorry, miss, but you can't park there. You're causing an obstruction.'

'Oh, gosh,' Anna said, and held out the keys and a folded £5 note. 'Do you think you could park it for me?'

He eyed the note, then took it and the keys. 'I can do that for you, miss. Guest in the hotel, are you?'

'Why else would I be here? Thank you so much.'

He peered at her, taking in the untidy hair, the torn dress, the scratches on her arms. 'Are you all right, miss?'

'I had an accident,' she explained.

'Oh, good lord! But...' He looked at the undamaged car.

'The car wasn't involved, thank God. I was

242

returning to it, and some beastly cyclist knocked me over, into some bushes. And the bastard
never even stopped.'

'These young people are terrible nowadays,'
he agreed. 'If you will give me your room number, I'll have the nurse come and take a look at
you to make sure you're all right.'

'That won't be necessary.' She set off down
the drive.

'Hold on, miss. Aren't you going in?'

'I just have to nip down to the chemists on the
corner. I'll be back in ten minutes.'

'Madam, there is no chemist on the corner.'

'Not that corner,' Anna said. 'The other one.'

That clearly needed working out. 'But you
don't have a coat,' he protested. 'You'll freeze.'

'Not in ten minutes.'

She hurried down the street, high heels clicking on the pavement. It was certainly necessary
to move quickly, to keep her blood circulating,
but when she was out of sight of the hotel she
paused beneath a street lamp to peer at herself
in her compact mirror. It was very small but she
could see that she looked a mess, and could
understand the doorman's concern. In addition
to her appearance, she was for the first time
aware of her cuts and bruises, which were becoming extremely painful. All things to be
attended to when she reached the hotel.

She hurried on. Her brain remained in tur-
moil. It was not that the assignment had turned
out to be any more traumatic than most of her
other assignments, nor had her escape been any

more enervating. But the appearance of Clive had been a considerable shock.

Obviously, as she had realized immediately, he had been there because of Bally's identification. But the rapidity with which he had deduced her target ... Of course, she knew that before he joined MI6 he had spent several years with Scotland Yard and had been considered one of their best detectives. But even so...

On the other hand, she reminded herself, while Clive, and no doubt Baxter, had been quite sure who they were after, no one else could possibly know who the mysterious woman had to have been; and she was equally certain neither of them would turn her in to be tried for murder. Of course there would be all hell to pay, and no doubt her certificate of immunity would be withdrawn, but once she got back to the Bahamas under the umbrella of Joe's certificate ... Besides, she had no doubt that he would step in and sort things out with the British Government. And then she would be done, done, done! Nothing else really mattered.

So all she had to do was get on that eleven o'clock plane before the police could trace her to the Royal George. She looked at her watch as the hotel came into sight. It was just coming up to twelve o'clock. She very much doubted that the driver would have managed to free himself yet. It was so tempting to have a hot bath and a lie-down before leaving again, but the lie-down would be too much of a risk. She could sleep the whole way back on the plane.

She went through the swing doors into the lobby, smiling at the man standing there, who looked askance at the sight of her. As she had now been a resident of the hotel for nearly two weeks, she was well known to the staff; and the doorman also did a double take as he took in her appearance. But he made no comment, only touched his cap; unlike the clerk on the reception desk, who peered at her as he handed her her key.

'Are you all right, Miss Kelly?'

'Apparently I am,' Anna said. 'The car I was in was involved in a smash.'

'Oh, good lord! The police...'

'Were at the scene, yes.'

'But are you all right? Shall I call the hotel doctor?'

'No, thank you. They called an ambulance, and the ambulance men checked me over and told me to go home to bed. But thank you, anyway.'

She went to the lift, rode up feeling the warmth seeping though her system. Her sole thought was of that hot bath she had promised herself. The lift halted at the fourth floor, and she stepped out. Halfway along the corridor she passed a man, without a sideways glance. But then he said, 'Anna? Mrs Bartley? I don't believe it!'

Anna turned, her right hand instinctively releasing the side vent in her dress to enable her to reach her pistol, then realized who it was. 'Mark? Good God! What are you doing here?'

245

'I'm staying here. Well, overnighting, actually. But you...'

Alarm bells were jangling, but she was still on her post-assignment high, and her mind was consumed with the thought of that bath. 'What a coincidence. And you say you're leaving tomorrow?'

'Well...'

His eyes flickered, and Anna heard movement behind her. She turned, her hand slipping inside her dress to grasp the pistol – but as she did so, Hamilton threw both arms round her, squeezing her tightly against him.

'For God's sake!' she snapped, and felt a sharp pain in her left shoulder.

WANTED BUT MISSING

Baxter opened the office door, and blinked at Amy Barstow. 'Good morning, Amy. I am assuming that it is, a good morning.'

'Well, sir...'

'Never mind, I have troubles of my own. Is there any word from Mr Bartley?'

'He is in your office, sir.'

'Thank God for that.' He opened the inner door. 'Where is she?'

Clive looked at him.

246

'Oh, shit! Don't tell me the police got there first?'

'Yes, Billy, the police got to the hotel before us.'

Baxter sat behind his desk, instinctively reaching for his pipe – which he was not allowed to take home. 'What a fuck-up! So she's under arrest?'

'No, Billy, she is not under arrest.'

'You mean she got out before they got there? You have to hand it to that girl, she's a quick mover. But hold on, if you reckon she's trying to get back to the Bahamas and there's no flight until eleven, they still have time to close the airports. Do you have any idea where she might be?'

'Billy,' Clive said, 'Anna was staying at the Royal George. But when the police got to the hotel, she wasn't there – because she'd been removed.'

'What do you mean, removed? You mean the CIA got her out? Well, bully for them. But that's going a bit far, on our patch.'

'Billy, Anna was removed from the hotel by ambulance.'

'Eh? You mean she did hurt herself, jumping from that window?'

'There is no evidence of that. She apparently returned to the hotel just before midnight – a bit dishevelled, according to the man on the desk. But she said nothing was the matter with her except she had been in an accident, then she went upstairs and collapsed in the corridor outside her room.'

'Good Lord! And...?'

'She was seen by a doctor, who announced that she had had a heart attack and should immediately be removed to hospital.'

'Well, I suppose it's fortunate he was so quickly available. But if she's in hospital ... we may have a problem. I suppose the police are waiting at her bedside?'

'Billy, you are right that we have a problem. Anna is not in hospital.'

'You've lost me. If she was removed by ambulance...'

'The police have checked every hospital in London. So have our people. The ambulance service received an emergency call-out to the Royal George Hotel; but apparently when their team got there, Anna had already been removed. By another ambulance.'

Baxter started to fill his pipe. 'It's a bit early in the morning to be faced with riddles. Anna was picked up by ambulance ... only you say she was not taken to any of the London hospitals?'

'That is correct. And there is no trace on the register of the ambulance that picked her up.'

'But didn't the hotel doctor supervise the whole thing?'

'Before the hotel doctor got there, she was examined by another doctor – who just happened to have been spending the night at the hotel and just happened to have taken a room on the same floor as Anna. He went with her in

248

the ambulance ... and never returned to the hotel. Neither did three other guests, who were present when she collapsed.'

Baxter had struck a match. Now he dropped it. 'Holy Jesus Christ! Are you saying...?'

'Yes, Billy. She's been snatched.'

'Anna? In broad daylight? From one of London's leading hotels?'

'Actually, it was the middle of the night. But it was under the eyes of quite a few people, yes.'

'But Anna? I would have said that of all the people in the world...'

'And you would be right. But she had just completed a pretty difficult assignment. The police only discovered where she was soon after dawn, when the driver staggered into a station. He'd been tied up and gagged and left in a wood, and it took him several hours to get free.'

'I'm surprised he didn't freeze to death.'

'Anna had covered him with a blanket.'

'She's all heart. But what the fuck are we going to do? Anna hasn't been in this country for seven years. She can't possibly still have any enemies here. Unless ... you don't think Bordman could have acted unilaterally?'

'Oh, don't be absurd, Billy. He has neither the guts nor the resources to pull a stunt like this. Anyway, he didn't know she was in London until he saw her at that club two nights ago. This was no spur of the moment business. It must have been planned days ago, if not weeks.

The kidnappers – including, apparently, the doctor – were all residents of the hotel. The ambulance appeared to be genuine to the hotel staff, as did the nurse who helped them get Anna into it.'

'But...' Baxter objected. 'To arrange all of that, the kidnappers must have known she was coming to England.'

'Yes,' Clive said, grimly.

'So...?'

'There is only one possible explanation – the identity of the people who sent her here.'

Baxter stared at him, while absently striking another match. Then he commented, 'You have to give the bastards credit for knowing how to do things.'

'You think so?'

'Well, hell, they must've figured out that there is no way she could get away with this, so they've simply taken her out of circulation.'

'How? In a trunk?'

'Well...'

'The several members of the staff at the Royal George who saw her, including their own doctor, have no doubt at all that she was very ill. The doctor said she was only just alive. She was breathing, but stertorously. He tried her pulse, and it was barely discernible.'

'So she was fed some kind of drug.'

'Which all but killed her? The CIA are supposed to be her employers, for Christ's sake.'

'They must know what they're doing. Unless ... Oh, my God!'

250

'Quite. They've written people off before. They tried to write Anna off once. Only they picked the wrong guy to do the job.'

'Shit!' Baxter muttered. 'In which case she is in a box. Oh, my God! I'm sorry, old man, that just slipped out. But ... what the hell can we do about it?'

'Plenty. I can, anyway. Anna is my wife. And if you say "was", I'm going to break your bloody neck and cheerfully swing for it!'

'Clive! Simmer down, for God's sake. I'm on your side. We all are, or will be, if this gets out. Trouble is, we can't let it get out, or all our necks are on the line.'

'Why?'

Baxter frowned at him. 'Well...'

'Billy, what have we been doing for the past twelve hours? Trying to protect Anna, right? If she returned to England, working for the CIA, that is not our fault. If she was caught, she'd be for the high jump. The worst that could happen to you would be a reprimand for being so innocent as to believe that her promise and your certificate of immunity would be sufficient to keep her toeing the line. But if Anna is reported as dead, that's it. You know and I know that the government will actually breathe a sigh of relief that Fahri is also dead, so long as they can hold up their hands and swear they had nothing to do with it. As for the unknown murderess ... well they can swear that if she is ever caught she will suffer the full rigour of the law.'

Baxter finally got his pipe going, and puffed

contentedly. 'That was a brilliant summing-up, Clive. I can't tell you what a relief it is to have you back on board and firing on all cylinders. Of course there is no way I can adequately convey my feelings about her death. I loved that girl as much as you do.' He paused, and had the grace to flush as Clive stared at him. 'All right. So we had our differences. But I tell you this. If I were ever in a tight spot, there is no one on this planet I would rather have standing beside me than Anna.'

'I'll believe you,' Clive said. 'Because I'm a sucker. The important thing is that our hands are now free.'

'Eh?'

'We can now go ahead and track her down and make sure she's all right. And get her back, in safety.'

Billy took his pipe from his lips; it had gone out. 'But ... Anna's dead! We just agreed on that.'

'Yes, we did. But it has just occurred to me that the timing doesn't add up. Anna entered the hotel just on twelve. She was carried out at twenty past, after collapsing completely and being examined by two doctors, having ridden up in the elevator, which takes a good five minutes. I checked that out. So her collapse, the obviously carefully staged panic by the three men with whom she was talking, then the appearance of this Dr Drimer, and then the hotel doctor, all took place in ten minutes; and it must have taken at least five minutes to get her down to the lobby. She left the hotel, remember, at twenty past.'

'Tight,' Baxter conceded. 'But it could have been done.'

'Certainly it could have been done. But where did they fit in the time for her to make her report?'

'You've lost me.'

'Billy, the CIA sent Anna to England to get Fahri. She checked into the Royal George twelve days ago. So it took her that long to set it up. But her employers couldn't have known exactly when she was going to complete the job. So if the plan was to eliminate her the moment she had carried out the assignment, they had to wait until they knew it was accomplished. She could just have been coming home from another night on the town, trying to make contact. Otherwise, if Fahri was still alive, the whole elaborate exercise becomes meaningless.'

'I'd forgotten you used to be a detective,' Baxter said. 'But if there's any truth in your theory ... Jesus Christ! It could have been the ... But *they* couldn't possibly have known that she was coming to England, certainly not that vital couple of weeks in advance.'

'Yes,' Clive said, again grimly.

'What are we going to do?'

'This buck began with Joe Andrews. It's bloody well going to stop with him, too.'

'Who the hell is this?' Joe Andrews barked into

the telephone.

'Clive Bartley.'

'Clive ... for Jesus' sake! Do you know what the time is?'

'Well, as it's nine fifteen here, I would say that it's four fifteen where you are.'

'Dammit! It's not even dawn.'

'You know what they say about early to bed and early to rise.'

'Look, what the hell do you want?'

'I have some information which I suspect may interest you.'

'Yes?' Suddenly the tone had changed, and become watchful.

'Which I will give to you in return for some information that I think you have, which will be of interest to me.'

'I have no idea what you're talking about.'

'Oh! Right. Then your government is no longer interested in Kola el Fahri?'

There was a brief silence. 'Are you saying that something has happened to the gentleman?'

'The gentleman is dead. Together with his sidekick, Alois Khouri.'

Another brief silence. Then Andrews said, 'Then I would have to say the world is a better place today than it was yesterday.'

'They each died,' Clive went on, 'as a result of a single bullet wound to the head, delivered by a beautiful long-haired blonde.'

'Well, in view of his reputation with women, I would say that was bound to happen eventually.'

254

'Joe!' Clive's voice suddenly stopped being pleasant. 'I want to know what has happened to my wife.'

'Anna? I imagine she's on her cay. Isn't she?'

'Joe, if you try to fuck us up, we are going to blow this thing wide open.'

'Don't try that one, old buddy.'

'I can see the headlines now,' Clive said. 'American CIA commits double murder in England. War hero falls victim to US hit man.'

'Except,' Joe pointed out. 'It happens to be a hit woman, and you'd be dishing your own wife.'

'I can't dish her if she's dead – or at least, she won't mind.'

'What?' He was clearly genuinely shocked. 'Are you saying that Anna ... Oh, my God!'

'You should be on the stage.'

'Look! What happened?'

'Are you saying you don't know? Are you denying that you sent Anna to England to carry out this job? Why the hell she agreed to that, I simply can't imagine.'

'She agreed to that,' Joe said, 'because we offered her the same terms that Baxter did three years ago. And our offer was considerably more valuable than yours. One last job, and she can retire to have your child or whatever other crazy scheme she has in mind, with lifelong immunity from prosecution anywhere in the States.'

Clive was silent for several seconds. 'She said she wanted to have my child?'

'You mean you didn't know? You should try spending more time at home.'

'Joe, I have got to find her, and make sure she's all right. So give.'

'You say she carried out the job? And got away? Then I would say she's on her way to Heathrow, to catch the eleven o'clock flight to Nassau. She'll be home this afternoon.'

'When Anna left Fahri, around ten o'clock last night, she returned to her hotel to change her clothes. She went up to her room, but never got there. In the corridor outside, she stopped to talk with three men and had a heart attack.'

Joe digested this, slowly. Then he said, 'Old buddy, you've been at the glue. Anna? A heart attack? She's the healthiest woman I have ever known. Or heard of. Come to think of it, she's healthier than any guy I've ever known, either.'

'I agree with you. But when she collapsed, around midnight last night, she was examined by two doctors. One may have been a fake, but the other was the hotel doctor, and he was of the opinion that she was seriously ill. An ambulance was sent for, and she was whisked off to hospital. Only she never got there.'

'What the shit do you mean, never got there?'

'Just that. Anna, the ambulance, the doctor, and the men who were with her when she collapsed, have all vanished into thin air.'

'And you thought ... Remind me to punch you on the nose next time I see you.'

'I may well punch you first! It is an inescapable conclusion. This has to have been set up

256

some time ago. Ergo, it had to be set up by someone who knew that Anna was going to be in England on a certain date. Who else but your lot could have known that? Anna hasn't been in England for seven years, and anyone studying her recent history would have to know the she is *persona non grata* here. So, if you didn't set this up, either to get her out of England or just to get rid of her, someone in the CIA is a very rotten egg.'

There was silence while Joe considered. 'In view of the seriousness of the situation, I will overlook your obscene suggestion. As for us having a traitor in this office, that is simply not on. No one knew of this deal save for a couple of very high-ranking officers.'

'Convince me. Anna has disappeared in a very elaborate snatch. Tell me who did it.'

Another pause for consideration, then Joe said, 'Holy Jesus Christ!'

'I don't think *he* had anything to do with it.'

'Hamilton!'

'Say again?'

'When Anna got back from her last assignment, three weeks ago, she spent a couple of days in Nassau. That was to meet me and put forward this retirement/mother-and-child bee she has in her bonnet. When we'd finished our chat, she mentioned this character. Seems this Hamilton, apparently an Englishman staying at the Royal Victoria, had been making advances to her. OK, at least half the men in the world would get around to making advances to Anna

257

if they found her apparently on her own staying at the same hotel. In most cases they get slapped down. But this guy bothered her. I'm not quite sure why, but I guess over the years she's developed an instinct about these things and he claimed to have met her at a cocktail party in England, when she was Mrs Bordman. He could remember her, but she couldn't remember him. So she asked me if we could find anything on him.'

'Don't tell me you could? 1939?'

'Yeah. Well, the FBI has a long memory. They had the name Mark Hamilton, under 1939, as a known Communist.'

'Oh, my God! But wait a minute. You told Anna this?'

'I had it conveyed to her.'

'And what was her reaction?'

'I don't know. I had it conveyed to her by one of my people, who was delivering the final bumf for this trip. Spence didn't mention that there was a reaction. But she definitely got the message.'

'And you seriously think Anna would have told this character that she was coming to London, and even given him the dates? That's ridiculous. Certainly after learning that he was a Red.'

'I have never been sure just what goes on in Anna's brain. I think that's one of her greatest strengths.'

Join the club, Clive thought.

'What I do know is that over the years of

unbroken success she has been becoming increasingly overconfident. And that can be a serious liability. I'm not suggesting that she would have confided anything to this man, but isn't it possible that she may have let something slip, in conversation?'

'You're suggesting that she may have spent quite a lot of time in his company,' Clive pointed out, coldly.

'Well, she had two days to kill in Nassau, waiting for me. And I gathered that you weren't around, and hadn't been around for some time. Anyway, old buddy, now is not the moment to indulge in husbandly pique. If I'm right, and there is no other logical solution to what has happened, well ... we may have lost her.'

'Which to you is just a case of ho hum, we'll have to find someone else to do our dirty work.'

'Look, if the Reds have got Anna, I'm going to head the list of mourners.'

'Mourners?'

'Beria has been trying to nail her for damn near thirteen years. At a cost of God knows how many lives; I've lost count.'

'You mean he's been trying to get her back to Russia to stand trial for that attempt on the life of Stalin in 1941. He wants, or his boss wants, a huge show trial with the cameras popping and the world's media hanging on every word. If the idea was just to kill her and they managed to catch her off guard, why make a huge charade of it? They could've done it, left the body lying on the floor of the hotel corridor and just taken off. It was just midnight. She wouldn't have been found until this morning.'

'Good point. But where's the difference, if she's on her way back to Russia? In Anna's case, that means the Lubianka. Nobody gets out of the Lubianka.'

'Anna did. With your help.'

'That was a one-off, Clive, and you know it. It was the day after Operation Barbarossa began. The whole country was in a flap. The only thing anyone was sure about was that the Red Army was falling apart; and that unless the Russians were given a massive injection of help in arms and material, the Nazis were going to be in Moscow in a couple of months. I was able to persuade Beria, who was in a bigger flap than most, that I could get that help rolling immediately if he would release Anna into my custody. I told him that she was wanted in the States for attempting the life of FDR. At that time he had no idea who and what Anna was; very few people other than Himmler and Heydrich did, apart from you and Baxter. Even I had no idea what I was getting myself into. I only knew that Anna was a beautiful girl I had met at a party in Moscow who had somehow got herself involved with the NKVD, even if I had a hunch she was connected to you lot. Beria had never even seen her. And he reckoned that the promise of US help was more important than the trial of one itinerant woman. Of course, his subordinates didn't see it that way, and that woman Tsherchenka, as well as Chaliapov – that chap who Anna had seduced – tried to stop us, with the inevitable result. That was the first time I had ever seen Anna in action, and frankly I was terrified. And that was the first time Beria realized just what he had let slip through his fingers. By then it was too late. We had got out, and in the confusion she was on her way to safety, one step ahead of his thugs. You must remember that; you took over her escape.'

'Of course I remember,' said Clive.

'But apparently he never forgot or forgave. And when he discovered that, instead of taking her back to the States to stand trial, I had turned her loose to go back to work for the Nazis, I became *persona non grata* in Russia. That's about it. My hands are tied.'

'You have people in Russia.'

'Of course we have. So have you. What are you thinking of? Some kind of raid on the Lubianka? Our people would wind up dead, and you'd probably be starting a war.'

Clive sighed. 'Well, if that's your attitude, then she's done. Anna! My God!'

'Hold on. I've an idea.'

'What?'

'If you're right, and Beria's ambition is a show trial, we have some time.'

'During which she will be tortured and brainwashed into confessing everything they want her to.'

'I think attempting to brainwash Anna would be rather counter-productive. As for being tortured ... she's survived that before. The same goes for sexual abuse.'

'You're a great comfort, Joe. When all of that happened, she wasn't my wife.'

'Now you're being juvenile. Anna is a bigger girl than most, in every respect. Just listen. If you're going to have a show trial, you have to have the world's media in attendance; and they don't turn up overnight. Therefore, the coming trial has to be publicized long before it takes place. Once they start doing that, they're declaring to the world that they hold the infamous Countess von Widerstand, the last of the great war criminals. And once they do that, you're not giving away any secrets if you react. I'm sure your people have someone, or even several people, locked up who they can offer to exchange for her.'

'They do,' Clive said sombrely. 'But that's a non-starter.'

'Why, in the name of God?'

'Since the end of the War, the British Government has not wanted to know about Anna. I suppose they feel guilty at having employed her in the first place. It took Billy and me three years to get them to agree to let her slide gently into oblivion in the Bahamas. And they required that to be entirely hushed up. As far as they are concerned, and have told the world, the Countess von Widerstand died in the ruins of Berlin in 1945.'

'Hold on. Didn't they employ her in 1949?'

'Yes, they did. But no one was supposed to know. And like you, they bought her with a guarantee of immunity. But as you know, it carried certain rules. Now she's broken those rules, firstly by returning here, and secondly, and more important, by committing a double murder, as the tabloids will see it, on British soil. They will probably refuse to admit that it could be Anna at all. They certainly are never going to admit that they have known about her and lied about her all along, and in real terms have been protecting her since the end of the War – as would certainly come out if they offered the Reds an exchange deal. Moscow would see to that.'

'Shit!' Joe commented. 'So where do we go from here?'

'It's where you go, Joe. You and your bosses put her in this position. So you and your bosses can bloody well get her out of it.'

He hung up, and brooded at the wall. Sounding off at Joe, although it made him feel better, had not really been very helpful. But it was just about impossible to accept that Anna could have gone. Over the all but fifteen years he had known her – ever since that SS ball in October 1938, when she had entered the room on the arm of an officer, in a pale-blue sheath gown which clung to her hips and seemed to have been created around that unforgettable décolletage – he had been fascinated, even though his instincts had warned him that here was trouble.

Everything about her had been compelling. The way she walked, the way she talked, even the way she stood still; and then the way she performed the sexual act. Looking back to March 1939, he was still amazed at himself, even after fourteen years. He had been thirty-eight years old, an experienced man of the world, in the middle of a long-standing affair with his fiery Anglo-Italian mistress, Belinda Hoskin. What is more, he had been a field agent for MI6 for several years and had regarded himself as fully capable of dealing with the worst that could be thrown at him by any enemy organization.

He had encountered Anna again five months after their first meeting. From the beginning, he had no doubt she was a German spy. That she had wormed her way into the very heart of British high society had been a continual irritant to his professional conscience. That he had been unable to prove his theory, or get any of his superiors, even Billy Baxter, to believe him, had been like a cancer, eating at his mind. And suddenly, there she was standing in front of him, on her own turf and therefore apparently invulnerable – and yet at that moment not the utterly, coldly, beautiful sophisticate of the ballroom or the cocktail party but a tormented, frightened, and thus indeed vulnerable eighteen-year-old girl.

How this situation had arisen, how it could have arisen, he had not then known. But the opportunity was there, and he would have been guilty of gross professional negligence had he not grasped it. That it would probably require grasping Anna as well had seemed purely an unexpected bonus. And from the moment he had accepted that invitation to have a cup of coffee in her Berlin apartment he had been utterly lost. To a girl less than half his age!

The memory of her dropping her knickers to show him the fresh weals on the so white flesh of her buttocks was implanted for ever in his brain, still as vivid as any photograph. But then so was the memory of holding all of that velvet flesh naked in his arms. And even that was overladen with the memory of what had happened when, while she was lying apparently sated – even exhausted – in his arms, the bedroom door had opened. Anna had left the bed, but whereas any ordinary woman might have screamed or attempted to cover herself, she had crossed the room in three long strides and dispatched the intruder with a single swinging blow to the neck.

He had been paralysed, by the most tumultuous variety of emotions he had ever experienced: amazement that anyone could act with such speed and unhesitating decision, consternation that for the past half-hour he had allowed himself to surrender, body and soul, to the caresses of what he now realized was a lethal machine, and self-pity that he should have assumed, with careless masculine egotism, that he was seducing an innocent girl! A girl who could think with the speed of light, act with the speed of light, and kill with the speed of light. My God, he had thought, what a weapon we would possess if we could possess Anna!

He had still not understood that of course he was going to possess Anna ... because from the moment of their meeting on the street Anna had intended to be possessed, professionally as well as physically. It had not been easy. Baxter had been aghast at the proposal, and considered that Clive had handed him a time bomb that was ticking loudly.

In many ways, Baxter had been right. Anna had never rejected any command and always carried out her missions with total integrity – but always using her own agenda. And however upset he may have been by some of the things she had done, even Baxter had warmed to her as much as Clive himself, even if Clive's warmth had taken a more positive course.

Even that had taken time, always aware that every time they shared a bed he was surrendering to a force that could destroy him before he could blink, a force that was governed by the most terrifying amoral pragmatism. How could he ever forget arriving at a hotel in Geneva, in 1943, for a rendezvous and on entering her bedroom finding himself standing between two dead bodies? They had been Gestapo agents who, suspicious of her activities, had tracked her to Switzerland and had made the mistake of attempting to arrest her. When, mind reeling, he had asked what they were going to do with the bodies, Anna had replied, 'Leave them there. They won't object.'

When, gathering that she still wanted to have

sex with him, he had tentatively suggested that they could at least move the dead men into the bathroom, she had said, 'We can't do that. I always have a bath first thing in the morning.'

It had not been until she had installed herself in the Bahamas that he had seen the loving, domesticated side of her character. The way she adored and cared for her parents, the love she bestowed on her pets, the affectionate loyalty she earned from her staff, had been a revelation – so much so that he had at last surrendered to his growing love and admiration and married her, as she had long wanted. Yet the reservation remained, because it was quite impossible to get inside Anna's head, to understand what she was thinking or discover any clues as to which was the real Anna. The Anna of the bedroom in Berlin and the bedroom in Geneva? Or the Anna of the cay, helming her boat with careless expertise? He sometimes wondered if she knew herself. Certainly he had no idea how she reconciled her two so separate personalities.

But to think of her in the hands of Beria's thugs ... it was unlikely that they would make any mistakes this time. There had been too many in the past twelve years, all of them catastrophic, beginning with that attempt by six NKVD agents to kidnap her in Washington in 1941. They had been successful, but in the two days they had had to wait before they could get her on a ship to Russia, had sought to amuse themselves by tying her to a bed and repeatedly having sex with her. All of which she had borne with her habitual fortitude, and the deadly patience that was one of her principal assets. And sure enough, eventually, on one of the occasions when, by then sure of her absolute subservience, they untied her to go to the toilet, they carelessly left a tommy-gun within her reach. When, in response to her telephone call, he and Joe reached the scene and were surveying the carnage, she had explained with her usual ingenuousness, 'Do you know, I had never fired a tommy-gun before? It was such fun!' Things like that were not likely to be forgotten.

He sighed, and watched his door opening, after a gentle tap. 'They've found the ambulance,' Amy said. 'Abandoned in the Pool of London.'

He snapped his fingers. 'I want to know every ship that cleared this morning.'

'I've done that.' She placed the list in front of him.

'Good girl.' He ran his fingers down it. There were six, and one of them...

'That one.'

She leaned over the desk. 'The *Vladimir Rostov*, bound for Sevastopol? That's a Russian ship, isn't it?'

'That's right.'

'You can't be sure she's on it.'

'I'd bet my last penny she is. What time did the *Rostov* clear?'

'Ah ... six o'clock.'

Clive looked at his watch. 'And it's only just ten! She won't even have left the Thames estuary yet. We can stop her.'

'Stop a Russian ship?'

'She's still in home waters.'

Amy continued to look doubtful, so Clive brushed past her and ran up the stairs to Baxter's office. 'We've found her.'

'What? Tremendous. I hope you're not talking about a body?'

'No, I am not talking about a body. We know where she is.'

'Right. Where?' Baxter was reaching for his telephone.

'On a ship called the *Vladimir Rostov* that cleared the Pool of London four hours ago.'

Baxter had picked up the phone. Now he replaced it.

'A Russian ship?'

'It is.'

'And you would like us to stop her on the high seas?'

'Billy, she cannot have got out of the river yet. Certainly not the estuary.'

'And you know for certain Anna's on board?'

'She has to be. The ambulance has been found abandoned at the London docks. The only Russian ship that has cleared this morning is this one.'

'But you don't *know*. You don't even know if the Russians were involved at all. I thought you were inclining towards the Americans?'

'It's not them. I spoke with Andrews just now,

and he was utterly horrified at what I told him.'

'And you believed him?'

'Yes, I did. He has as much going for Anna as you or I do.'

'So, did he admit that she was here working for them?'

'Yes,' Clive shouted. 'Yes, he did. But he didn't know it was going to be done last night. Billy, every moment we spend yammering that ship is getting further away. She's still well inside our territorial waters. We have the right to stop her and search her.'

'And if Anna's not on board?'

'Well ... Oh, for God's sake, Billy, she must be on it. It's the only place she can be.'

'To stop a foreign ship – especially a Russian ship at this moment – and demand the right of search, would require either cast-iron proof that she is carrying something she shouldn't be, or a Home Office order.'

'Then get it.'

'To get that order, the full facts of the case would have to be placed before the Home Secretary. What, precisely, are we going to tell him? That our tame wartime assassin, whose career was officially terminated in 1946, who is still on Scotland Yard's files in connection with the deaths of those four Russian agents in Scotland, and who we assured the government was going to disappear for ever and never be heard of again, is actually alive and well, and still operating in this country ... That she has committed a double murder, of two war heroes, and has now, we think, been kidnapped by the Russians ... And that it is for her sake that we wish him to start an international diplomatic incident. Have I got my facts right?'

'You are talking about a British citizen who also happens to be my wife.'

'And who, if we risk what relations we have left with Russia to get her back here, will go on trial for murder and almost certainly be convicted. Is there any point in prolonging her agony?'

Clive straightened slowly. 'You've written her off!'

Baxter sighed. 'I've had to write off agents before, when they have become liabilities. And so have you. Personal feelings cannot be allowed to interfere. So you married the girl. I felt at the time that it was a mistake, but you know I have always bent over backwards to protect her. I was even prepared to go the limit to get her out of this mess into which she has got herself, God alone knows why...'

'She got herself into this mess, Billy, because the CIA offered her the same terms as you did three years ago. One last job, which they reckoned only she could do, and she was out, no questions asked, with a lifelong immunity, not just in the Bahamas, but anywhere in the United States. And what is more, there were no restrictions on where she could go or, indeed, where she could live.'

'They have the ability to do things differently over there.'

271

'Can you blame her for seizing the opportunity?'

Another sigh. 'No, I can't. But it went wrong. Just as it would have gone wrong if Fahri or Khouri had managed to get a shot in before they died. You have got to accept that, Clive.'

Clive stared at him for several moments. Then he said, 'Well, bugger you, Billy. And the whole God-damned department.' He turned towards the door.

'Clive,' Baxter said. 'If you do something stupid, which might involve this country in a diplomatic bust-up with the Soviet Union, I cannot protect you.'

But Clive had already left the office.

Anna became aware of movement, although where it was coming from she couldn't be sure. She certainly wasn't moving herself.

She was feeling, in fact, strangely relaxed, and yet dreadfully drowsy, as if she had been awakened earlier than she should. But she was not aware of any discomfort, save for a dull throbbing in her left shoulder.

As for what had happened ... she remembered entering the hotel and taking the elevator up to her floor, her mind soaring at the thought that her career as an assassin was finished. Also, as always, her mind had been focused on what came next, in this instance the hot bath she would have before leaving for the airport; she had been absolutely freezing.

She was not freezing now; she felt as warm as

toast. She moved, slowly, uncertainly; her arms and legs seemed curiously disjointed. But she was lying beneath a blanket, in a heated room ... Her eyes flickered across the walls and the porthole ... She was on a ship! And the slight movement was because the ship was under way. But ... the movement had changed. Instead of a forward feeling, it was a slight roll, from side to side. The ship had stopped.

But how...? Slowly her brain was clearing. She had been speaking with Hamilton ... in the corridor of the Royal George Hotel, close to her room. Hamilton! And there had been movement behind her. And then...? Instinctively she moved her hand to feel her shoulder, and realized that she was naked beneath the blanket.

It didn't feel as if anything else had been done to her. As if it mattered, against the fact that she was on a ship, at sea, and that she was here because of that meeting with Hamilton. Hamilton ... she thought, her brain slowly hardening.

Voices! In the distance, shouting. And one of them ... Clive! My God, she thought, he's come to my rescue. Oh. Clive! She put her arms down to push herself up and discovered to her horror that she had not the strength even to raise her own weight.

She fell back, panting, and the cabin door opened. Hamilton! And two more men, dressed as sailors. 'Hurry,' he said. He spoke Russian, but it was a language in which Anna had become fluent during the War.

The two sailors stood above her, bent to lift

273

her, and one said, 'She's awake!'

'What? Holy Jesus Christ! Get ropes, quickly.'

'You are nervous, comrade. She is only a woman.'

'More than fifty of your comrades have made that mistake,' he said, 'and they are all dead. Fetch the ropes, quickly.'

'Anna, can you hear me?' Hamilton stood above her, a pistol presented to her head.

Anna just stared at him. She was completely enveloped in the blanket, with only one arm free; and in any event, at that moment she lacked the strength to move. So, patience! Indeed, she had long ago learned that nothing upsets an adversary so much and so quickly as an utter failure to respond. Besides, Clive was coming ever closer.

'I think you can hear me,' Hamilton said. 'So listen. Attempt to move and I will blow your brains out.'

Anna listened again, to the voices; not yet on board, she thought, but coming closer. And now the sailors were back, hurrying. A length of rope was wrapped round her, and round her blanket. One of them, nervously, held her arm and pushed it down. Then the rope was drawn tight and secured, leaving her helpless, even had she regained her strength. Having made sure she was immobile, Hamilton laid down the pistol and forced her jaws apart to insert a roll of cloth, and this was secured by a cord round her head.

Still the voices drifted to her ... Now Clive was definitely on board and, judging by the raised tones, was engaged in a dispute with the ship's captain – Clive insisting that he intended to search the ship, and the captain equally insistent that he had no right to do so. But he was there, and he would not go away until he had found her. Surely.

'Careful, now,' Hamilton said. 'She must not be harmed.' He did not seem to be aware that he was contradicting himself. Then he looked around the cabin and, from a table against the bulkhead, collected her knickers and her gun belt – which, she saw, still contained her pistol and the spare magazine. What had happened to her torn gown and her purse, she had no idea.

Next, the cabin door was opened and the two men carried her into a small lobby. There was a door on her right, and beyond this the voices were still shouting. On her left, a ladder went down. 'You take her, Oscar,' Hamilton commanded.

She was set on her feet. Her knees gave way and she would have fallen, but the larger of the two sailors, presumably the one named Oscar, caught her and heaved her across his shoulder – like a sack of potatoes, she thought.

'Mind she doesn't bang her head,' said Hamilton.

Anna's head bumped on the man's back, while strands of golden hair drifted past her face; most of her hair had been caught in the enveloping rope, and bound against her back. Oscar's left hand was gripping her thighs to hold her in place, the fingers biting through the blanket into her flesh, while his right hand grasped the rail. She could not raise her head without extreme discomfort, but she could see immediately below her. Hamilton was following.

She was carried down to another deck and then down another ladder, and now the sound of the voices was lost in the increasing noise from below. The engines had not been shut down, but even idling in neutral they were loud; and grew louder still as they descended. A last landing, a last ladder, and they were actually in the world of machinery, with the noise now all around them. Here there were several men, their overalls stained with sweat, who stared at Oscar and his burden and then at Hamilton.

'This the woman?' asked one, who wore a battered peaked cap.

'This is her, Chief,' Hamilton said.

'The bridge said we've stopped because of a police boat. Looking for her?'

'That's right. And they could be down here at any moment. They mustn't find her.'

The engineer nodded. 'Stick her in the bilge.'

'You sure? She mustn't be harmed, or marked in any way. That's an order from the top.'

'She won't be harmed. She may get a little wet. This way.'

Anna was carried past various pieces of machinery, all rumbling away, to the aft end of the room, where the noise was loudest (this, she gathered, was due to the generator). The engineer signalled his men, and one of them produced a pair of earmuffs – similar to the ones she wore in her firing range – and fitted them into place. 'We don't want you going deaf,' the engineer bellowed. 'But it shouldn't be for too long.'

Two of his men unscrewed the steel plates that comprised the deck, revealing an odoriferous darkness, in which water slurped to and fro.

'It's only a couple of inches deep,' the engineer shouted reassuringly.

'But if you put those plates back, how is she going to breathe?' Hamilton bawled.

'There's always a current of air down there,' the engineer claimed. 'The plates have to be in place, or those bastards may notice.'

Anna was already holding her breath as two of the men inserted her, feet first. She anticipated being frozen all over again, but the water was surprisingly warm. She was laid on her back, and water surrounded her earmuffs. For the first time, she was assailed by panic. Clive was only a few feet away, but she couldn't tell him where she was! She kept reminding herself that she had been in stickier positions than this and survived – by patiently accepting whatever happened to her, and waiting for her opportunity.

Then the steel plates were clapped into place, and screwed down. She was in an utterly dark, very wet, and very noisy world; the generator seemed to be grinding away next to her ears. Then she heard another sound: feet clunking on the steel immediately above her. Clive! It had to be Clive. Immediately above her head, now. She had a desperate urge to scream and kick, but she could do nothing. The deck was only inches above her, but in her weakened condition even lifting her legs was an effort; and to raise them out of the water while wrapped in a waterlogged blanket, in such a confined space and with sufficient force to penetrate the steel, was quite impossible.

The footsteps receded. The police were going. A few minutes later, the engine noise grew in volume as the ship got under way. After thirteen years, she thought, they have got me in the end.

IN TRANSIT

Although it seemed an eternity, it could only have been a few minutes later that the plates were unscrewed and a welcome gush of fresh air surrounded her. Carefully she was lifted out and laid on the deck, now aware of being very cold again. Hamilton and the engineer were peering at her and speaking, but she couldn't hear what they were saying, although she could tell that Hamilton was very anxious.

278

Then another face appeared, this one bearded and reassuringly friendly. He knelt beside her, rested two fingers on her neck for several seconds, then gave some instructions, at the same time untying the cord round her head and removing the cloth from her mouth. She gasped in relief, and he actually smiled.

Oscar was waiting, and he picked her up, slung her over his shoulder, and climbed back up the ladders. Anna no longer cared about the manhandling she was receiving. She could breathe freely again, she could work her tongue, and she had the reassuring knowledge that she was in the hands of the ship's doctor. More importantly, she was apparently not to be harmed, at least until they had got her to Moscow. As to whether she would be able to do anything about her situation before then, she would have to play it by ear, as she had had to do so often in the past.

Not that the immediate outlook was very promising. They regained the cabin, where she was placed on a waterproof sheet that had been laid on the bunk. To reach the cabin they had passed an open door, and she got a glimpse of sea and sky; the absence of any sight of land and the obviously increased speed of the ship told her that they were now out of the estuary and on the open sea.

The cold February air flooding through the door made her shiver, which the doctor observed. 'Quickly,' he said, 'get that blanket off.

Tatiana, draw a hot bath. She must be warmed up.' As she could hear him, she realized that her earmuffs had been removed.

Oscar fumbled at the ropes, watched by Hamilton. 'There is no need for you to stay, comrades,' the doctor said.

'I have to stay,' Hamilton said.

The doctor snorted. 'So that you can play the voyeur?'

'It is my duty to deliver the countess, personally, to Commissar Beria. Besides, you may need my protection.'

'From a barely conscious half-frozen woman?'

The rope was pulled away, and he was about to unfold the blanket.

'Wait!' Hamilton said. 'I do not think you know who this woman is.'

'I know what I have been told.' But he hesitated. 'That she is, or was, a German countess, who ranked highly in the Nazi Party and is a wanted war criminal.'

'She is the Countess von Widerstand, Himmler's private assassin. Were you to be alone with her, she could destroy you in a matter of seconds.'

'With her bare hands? This woman?'

'This woman, with her bare hands. I have seen her do it.'

The doctor looked at him, then bent over Anna, staring at her. Anna stared back. 'I am not sure that she is fully conscious, or has any idea where she is.'

280

'Dr Strassky, take my word for it, she is fully conscious and she knows where she is.' There was a click, followed by another. The two other men in the room had drawn automatic pistols, and Hamilton pressed his to Anna's temple as he bent over her in turn. 'You can stop playing games now, Anna. We know too much about you. Now listen to me. There is a hot bath waiting for you, which you will no doubt enjoy. But remember that we will be present at all times, with our guns pointed at you. I know that you have heard what we have been saying, and noted that we are to deliver you to Commissar Beria unharmed. However, there is a supplementary order of which you are probably unaware. It is that if there is the slightest risk of your escaping, Commissar Beria is prepared to forego the pleasure of watching you die himself and wishes you shot dead. Please remember this.'

Anna stared at him.

'It is my professional opinion,' Dr Strassky said, 'that at this moment the woman is not *compos mentis*. She is clearly in a state of shock.'

'You may do your duty, doctor, as you see fit. Kindly allow me to do mine.'

'It is very irregular,' Strassky grumbled. 'And improper. However...'

'The bath is ready, Comrade Doctor,' the woman Tatiana said, coming closer to stare at Anna. Anna stared back, and recalled her face. The woman from the airport! They had been on to her from the moment of her arrival.

'Very good.' Carefully, as if she was a piece of priceless porcelain, Strassky unwrapped the sodden blanket. And caught his breath.

'Yes,' Hamilton agreed, 'she is a goddess. But a goddess of death.' He still found it difficult to believe that he had once held her naked in his arms.

Strassky cleared his throat. 'Countess,' he said, as if he were addressing a small child, 'you are very chilled. And your blood pressure is down, I suppose because of the drug you were given. It is very necessary for you to be kept warm and dry for the next few days, or you may catch pneumonia. The first step must be to restore your bodily functions as rapidly as possible, which can best be accomplished by a hot bath. This is now waiting for you. Do you understand me?'

Anna continued to stare at him while she considered. But she knew he was right. Apart from the fact that she was shivering with cold, she had absolutely no chance of getting out of this mess if she became ill with pneumonia. She sat up, and a rustle went round the room. Then she swung her legs to the deck and eased herself off the bunk. There was another rustle, and Hamilton and his two aides all levelled their pistols.

She stood up, and staggered from a combination of her own weakness and the motion of the ship. Strassky made to catch her, and she stared at him. Hastily he stepped back, and she moved,

282

uncertainly, towards the inner doorway. Here the red-headed woman had positioned herself, but she also hastily stepped back as Anna came up to her.

'You have tested the water?' Strassky asked, anxiously. 'She must not be scalded.'

'The temperature is acceptable, Comrade Doctor,' Tatiana protested.

Anna gained the tub, held on to the rim, stepped into the bath, and turned to lower herself, one hand on each rim. But her arms gave way, so that she sat down with an enormous splash, scattering water everywhere. Everyone exclaimed, Tatiana – who was nearest – giving a shriek as she was soaked. But Anna ignored them, as she leaned back, closing her eyes, and allowed the delicious heat to seep through her flesh.

'Do you think she should be soaped, Comrade Doctor?' Tatiana asked.

'Why?'

'Well, that bilge water was not very clean, and there are scratches on her body...'

'I noticed those,' Strassky agreed. 'Do you have any idea where she got them?'

'The hotel staff said something about her being involved in an accident before she returned last night,' Hamilton said. 'Do you think they should be attended to?'

'I will do that, as soon as she has had her bath.'

'Then definitely she should be soaped. And her hair must be washed.'

'Why?'

'Because it too is filthy with bilge water, and it is such lovely hair.'

'I think, Comrade Terpolov, that you are too fond of this woman.'

'Terpolov,' Anna thought. Well, well.

'It is my duty,' Hamilton said, 'to present this woman to Commissar Beria in perfect condition, if it is at all possible. This I intend to do. Soap the countess, Tatiana. And wash her hair.' He knelt beside the tub, and put the muzzle of his pistol to her ear. 'Do not forget, Anna,' he said, 'there are three pistols pointed at you. And if necessary, Tatiana is expendable.'

Anna opened her eyes and he flushed. Then she turned her head to look at Tatiana, also kneeling, a cake of soap in her hands. She closed her eyes again and leaned back.

Fair Girl nosed alongside the dock, and Tommy gave a short burst astern to check her, then slid down the ladder to step ashore with the stern warp and make it fast, before returning to attend to the bow. 'You go on up to the house, Mr Bartley,' he said. 'I'll bring your gear.'

'Thank you, Tommy.' Clive stepped ashore. He had changed his shoes alongside in Nassau, and as he was no sailor had left the handling of the boat entirely to Tommy, who watched him walk up the path with sombre eyes.

There was nothing unusual in Mr Bartley arriving by himself. He and Miss Anna never travelled together save when going to Nassau or

Miami for the weekend, and on those occasions they never took him. But he had never known Mr Bartley in such a mood. Always in the past he had been unfailingly good-humoured; and the more so when returning to the cay from one of his business trips abroad. Today he had neither smiled nor spoken throughout the three-hour journey, and he had three suitcases instead of just the usual valise.

And as Tommy watched the two dogs come bounding down the path to greet them, to his amazement he saw that, instead of giving their heads the usual ruffle, Mr Bartley dropped to his knees to hug them both for several seconds, while they licked his face in appreciation of this unusual affection.

Something was wrong. He could only hope that it wasn't a case of Mr Bartley and Miss Anna falling out.

Clive continued his walk up the hill to the house, where Jane waited on the veranda. 'Clive!' She embraced him. 'Welcome home. I'm afraid Anna isn't here.'

'I know.'

He held her hand as they entered the lounge, while she frowned, surprised both by his demeanour and his apparent pre-knowledge of Anna's movements.

'Clive!' Johann shook hands. 'Good trip?'

'I think we should all sit down,' Clive said.

'But you'll take a glass of champagne? It's open.'

'Later, perhaps.' Clive sat on the settee, Jane beside him. Now also frowning, Johann sat opposite.

'Something's happened,' Jane said.

'I'm afraid it has.'

'Oh, my God! Anna?'

He sighed. 'Did you know where she was going on this trip?'

'She never tells us, and we never ask.'

'But it was a big one,' Johann said. 'There's a cheque for a hundred thousand dollars in her desk, which we are to deposit if she's not back by the fourth of March. That's in three days' time.'

'A hundred thousand,' Clive said quietly. 'As you say, Johann, a big one.'

'And the very last,' Jane said. 'Andrews has agreed to that.'

'Yes.' Clive nodded.

'You mean you knew about it?'

'Had I known of it, Jane, I would not have allowed it to happen. But I have found out about it, too late. It involved returning to England, and carrying out an assignment there.'

'But...'

'Yes. Anna is not allowed into England, much less to do a job there.'

'And you think she's been caught? By the police?' Johann asked. 'What will happen to her? I mean did she complete the job?'

'Anna always completes her job. Which makes her, in the eyes of English law, guilty of murder.'

Jane clasped both hands round her neck.

'Yes,' Clive agreed. 'However, if she was in the hands of Scotland Yard, there would still be a possibility that we could negotiate some kind of a deal, in view of her past services. Unfortunately, she has disappeared.'

'Thank God for that!' Jane cried.

'But she has not returned here,' Johann pointed out.

'She's obviously lying low, until it's safe to return. That's why...' She bit her lip.

'Why what?' Clive asked.

'A week ago.' Johann said, 'we had a call, from Nassau, from a man named Smitten. He described himself as a colleague's of Anna.' He paused at Clive's expression. 'Do you know this man?'

'I know of him,' Clive said. 'Did he come to the cay?'

'No. He said he had something for us, from Anna. So Tommy went across and met him at the Royal Victoria. He brought back a large suitcase.'

'It contained a whole lot of Anna's stuff,' Jane explained. 'Including some clothes we had never seen before, and her passport.'

'And just about all her jewellery,' Johann put in. 'We reckoned she knew that she was going to have to hide out after this job.'

'But Smitten brought no message from Anna?' Clive asked.

'No. So ... do you have any idea where she is?'

'I'm afraid I do. Anna was kidnapped from her hotel room just after midnight Wednesday before last.'

'Kidnapped?' Johann was aghast. 'Anna?'

'I know it sounds impossible. But as far as we have been able to work out, she had just completed her job and was returning to the hotel to change her clothes before catching a plane back here. What we know indicates that she had had a difficult time, and that when she returned to the hotel she was both dishevelled and coatless. It was February, and the temperature was not much above freezing. But she also appeared to be completely in the clear. My bet, knowing Anna, is that she was thinking of a hot bath before she did anything else, and that her guard had slipped, just a little. These people were waiting for her, and seem to have been able to fake a heart attack.'

'Anna?' Jane cried. 'That's not possible.'

'I said faked. We think they used some drug or other that produced the same symptoms.'

'You say this happened Wednesday before last?' Johann said. 'That is more than a week ago. There must have been a ransom demand by now.'

'There has been no ransom demand. Nor is there going to be one. We are pretty sure she's been taken by the Russians.'

'What?!!' Both Fehrbachs shouted together. 'But ... after that hurricane ... It's been three years.'

'Yes,' Clive agreed. 'I imagine Anna felt the

same way, that they'd given up. Which is probably the root cause of what happened. Did she ever mention the name Hamilton to you?'

'Hamilton?' Johann shook his head. 'Not that I recall. You think this man knows where she is?'

'We think he's probably with her. He obviously wormed his way into her confidence. How, I have no idea.'

'But if we know the Russians have her,' Jane said, 'can't we do something? The government...'

'The British government is not prepared to do anything. As far as they are concerned, Anna has not only broken her agreement with them, she has now committed murder on British soil. In short, she has become an embarrassment. And so have I.'

'What?' Johann cried. 'You? But were you connected with this job?'

'Only by being her husband. But we traced the kidnappers' movements to Tilbury Docks, and it so happens that a Russian vessel had left Tilbury at six o'clock on Thursday morning. But that was only a few hours earlier. So I commandeered a police launch and caught her up, still within the Thames Estuary, then forced her to stop and boarded her.'

'Tremendous!' Johann shouted.

'But you didn't find her?' Jane said.

'Not in the time available. I'm damned sure she was on board, and I would have placed the entire ship under arrest and forced her to return

289

to port for a proper search. But we were recalled before I could do so. At least, the police were.'

'But why, if you were certain...?'

'Because,' Clive said grimly, 'I acted without authority. I had, in fact, been officially warned not to interfere. So I was required to resign.'

'Oh, Clive.' She squeezed his hand. 'This is your home, now and always. You know that.'

He squeezed back. 'I hoped you'd say that.'

'And Anna...?' Johann said.

'I watched that ship sail away,' Clive said bitterly. 'I just could not believe it was happening.'

'What will happen to her?'

He sighed. 'They have spent twelve years, and God alone knows how many lives, trying to capture her. As far as they are concerned, she is the last of the great war criminals still at large. At the very least there will be an elaborate show trial. But the outcome will be predetermined.'

Johann got up, poured the champagne and handed out the glasses. 'Anna would have wanted it.'

'There is one ray of hope,' Clive said. 'The Americans know what is happening, and Anna was working for them. Therefore she is their responsibility. I have spoken with Joe Andrews, and he has promised to do everything he can.'

'But what can they do?' Jane asked.

'They hold several Russian spies. They could offer to exchange one, or even two or three of them, for Anna.'

'Do you think they will?'

'Like I said, she got into this mess while carrying out an assignment for them. I've told Joe that I would be returning here, and I expect to hear from him at any moment.'

In fact the HF set was crackling when he checked the radio room the next morning, after a very long and almost sleepless night. It was the first time he had ever slept in Anna's bed without Anna, with only a restless Isis for company; and the cat obviously wondered what he was doing there without her mistress.

He sat down in front of the radio. 'Fair Cay.'

'Where have you been, old buddy? I've been calling half the goddamn'd night.'

'I was early to bed,' Clive confessed. But his heart lurched. Despite the greeting, there was no *joie de vivre* in his friend's voice. 'What have you got?'

'Nothing,' Joe said. 'Damn all. I've gone as high as I could, and the answer was the same: that's the way the cookie crumbles.'

'She was acting on your orders!' Clive shouted.

'Easy,' Joe said. 'Easy. You've put your finger on the problem. You know as well as I do that the Soviets have been after her since she got out of the Lubianka. They know I played a part in her escape, but they couldn't really connect me with the State Department. However, they've always had their suspicions about how she got out of this country after that shoot-out in 1941. We always denied we had anything to do with

291

that, but they kept pressing it until the big boys decided that, for the sake of relations, she would have to be sacrificed. Well, that didn't work out, and the Reds accepted the fact that from then on she was a British problem. If we now try to negotiate her release, it will involve revealing the fact that she has been working for us and has been protected by us, not the Brits, all these years. And to the world at large, Anna remains a war criminal.'

'So you're prepared to write her off? A girl whose only crime is that she has spent most of her adult life doing your dirty work for you.'

'Hold on, old buddy. Quite a lot of that dirty work was done for you guys. And it was your government that wrote her off first.'

'I know. And I've quit.'

'Yeah. Well, as Anna's husband, I guess you're entitled to do that – and also in a position to do so. I'm not so lucky. I don't suppose it would do any good to say what a shit I feel about this whole thing.'

'No,' Clive said. 'It wouldn't do any good at all. Fair Cay out. For the last time.'

'Time to get up,' Hamilton said, jerking the blanket away to stare at the naked body on the bunk.

He had done this every morning of the six they had been at sea. Anna had gathered that the shorter route, via the Baltic to Leningrad, had been blocked by ice, and so they had headed south, for the Mediterranean. And as she was

292

allowed on deck for an hour's exercise every day, she had been able to watch their progress. They had stayed well out at sea after crossing Biscay, and the Portuguese coast had been nothing more than a cloud on the horizon (the weather had been bad on that part of the voyage). But land had been very close as they passed through the Straits of Gibraltar.

She had gazed with glowing, but not very hopeful, eyes at the mountain indicating the British colony. She had in fact just been recovering from twin shocks. First of having allowed herself to lower her guard just a few minutes too soon, from the sheer relief of feeling that it was all at last over; and then of having had Clive within touching distance without being able to let him know she was there.

But by Gibraltar she had regained control of herself. It was time to consider her position. What she might be going to did not bear con-templation. But until she actually faced the firing squad or felt the noose being placed round her neck, she must, as she had always done in tight situations, count her assets and wait, always ready to take the fullest advantage of whatever chance might be given her.

Besides, even though Clive had been unable to find her during the search, it meant that he, and therefore MI6, had worked out into whose hands she had fallen. Thus they would already be working round the clock to get her back, as would the CIA, who would also by now know what had happened. Obviously they could do nothing about it while she was at sea. But once she was in Russia, unless she was destined for immediate execution (and she did not believe that Beria would be satisfied with anything so quick), they would bring pressure to bear. All she had to do was stay alive and as healthy as possible until then.

With that comforting thought in mind, it was even possible to be amused by her immediate situation. Whether it was their idea of soul-destroying humiliation she did not know, but she had been given no clothes to wear. As being naked in front of glowing eyes did not concern her in the least, certainly as the ship was well heated throughout, they had quite failed in that objective; and she had to smile as she exercised on deck, where the wind, though getting steadily warmer as they moved south, was still chilly enough to bring her out in vast goose pimples. It was amusing to see the enormous precautions that were taken to prevent her from either throwing herself overboard or attacking one of them. She was surrounded by men, and a rope was made fast round her waist and controlled by two men standing in opposite directions, so that they could bring her back if she attempted to stray.

But it was even more amusing to observe the manner in which, during her exercise period, every member of the crew, even the engine room staff, managed to find some reason to visit the boat deck; the sight of the infamous

Countess von Widerstand standing naked in the wind with her golden hair flowing behind her was apparently something to be committed to memory, no doubt for the solace of their old age.

But best of all was the pleasure of watching their frustration grow. Especially Hamilton's. He could look at her for as long as he wished, but he could not touch her, at least in any way that might leave a mark, while even stroking her involved, as far as he was concerned, the memory of the blow with which she had destroyed the man on Love Beach. All the guards in the world would be unable to help him if she were allowed the split second to deliver such a blow, certainly as her guards were under the same orders as he was: that she must be delivered to the Lubianka unharmed and unmarked.

In Lavrenty Beria's apparent lust lay her greatest hope of salvation – at least until she was actually delivered. In the meantime, she was being fed three perfectly palatable meals a day, although the only alcohol on offer was vodka, a drink she remembered disliking during her sojourn in Russia thirteen years ago. And all the while, for six days now, she had refused to say a word. From time to time, she could see Hamilton's frustration coming close to fury. He had tried everything, from threats and blandishments to outlining, in as graphic a manner as he could, every last thing that she was going to suffer before oblivion – quite unaware that, as he had a limited imagination, he was suggesting nothing that she had not already experienced during her long and tumultuous career.

And her only response, over the past six days, had been to stare at him. She wondered what nightmares that stare was inducing into his midnight hours.

But now the voyage was nearly over. Two days after sighting Gibraltar there had been land again as they passed between Sicily and Malta, and the following day they had found themselves cruising through the Aegean Islands before turning north for the Dardanelles. And yesterday she had watched the graceful minarets of Istanbul rising above Seraglio Point as they slipped by to port.

They had entered the Black Sea. And now...

'Today we reach Sevastopol,' Hamilton told her. 'So it is time for your bath.'

This was another daily routine, and one with which she certainly had no quarrel. She could soak in a hot tub, watched by both Hamilton and Tatiana, and torment them even more by washing herself with sensuous luxury, even giving little sighs of pleasure as she soaped between her legs.

'I'll be damned glad when we are rid of the bitch,' Tatiana remarked.

'It'll be a day or two yet,' Hamilton reminded her. 'Time to get out, Countess.'

Anna got up, stepped from the bath, and he handed her a towel. She dried herself, took a second towel from Tatiana, and worked on her hair for five minutes, by no mean drying it completely but leaving it merely damp.

'Now,' Hamilton said. 'I have some things for you.' They had returned to the cabin, and he indicated the bed.

Anna gazed at the clothes lying there, and then looked at him.

He grinned. 'I know. They are not your usual chic. No silk and satin, eh? No furs. But they are what you must wear.'

Anna dressed herself. There was no underwear, the trousers were baggy and completely obscured her legs. The blouse, of an equally rough material, hung straight from her shoulders in a shapeless mass and was heavy enough to obscure her breasts, while the boots were the heaviest things she had ever had on her feet, huge, thick-leather monstrosities that required lacing up.

'Now this.' He handed her a very large bandanna. 'Your hair must be entirely obscured.'

Anna pinned her hair into a bun, then tied the kerchief under her chin.

'There,' he said. 'Now you look exactly like a Russian peasant woman. A very handsome peasant woman, to be sure. But nonetheless a peasant.'

Anna frowned, mentally. She had assumed that her return to Russia would be a publicized triumph for the Soviet Union, the capture of the last remaining major war criminal, after twelve years of determined pursuit, which would also

297

be a means of severely embarrassing Great Britain and the United States. There should be cameras and reporters by the score, and a crowd of carefully orchestrated onlookers, booing and hissing. But this made it appear as if she was being smuggled into the country, incognito.

'Do not fear,' Hamilton said. 'I am sure that you will be supplied with proper clothing in which to be hanged.'

Then it was a last meal, by the end of which the ship was entering Sevastopol Harbour; and shortly afterwards Anna was setting foot on Russian soil, for the first time since 23 June 1941.

For the trip ashore she was handcuffed, and then shrouded in a cloak that effectively concealed her from neck to ankles, making a nonsense of anything she might be wearing.

This was the first time that she had been in Sevastopol, or indeed anywhere in the south of the vast country, but she had no time to admire the architecture or the landscape, as she was placed in the back of a closed car, sitting between Hamilton and Tatiana, and driven directly to the airport, where a military aircraft was waiting for her.

Still handcuffed, she was at least given a window seat. 'Take a good look at it,' Hamilton suggested. 'It is the last time you will ever see it.'

As usual, Anna ignored him, though in fact there was not a great deal to look at, as they were flying quite high and, when the clouds cleared sufficiently to reveal the ground, there seemed to be nothing beneath her but an endless sheet of snow, occasionally punctuated by wisps of smoke rising from what she supposed were factories. And as it was after lunch when they landed, it was dark long before they approached Moscow.

As they had taken away her watch, she had no idea what time it was when they touched down, but as it had been dark for several hours, even allowing for an early sunset at the beginning of March, she reckoned it was about midnight. Not that she would have recognized anything even had it been broad daylight, as she had never flown into or out of Russia before. In the autumn of 1940 she had entered Russia by train on her way to take up her official position as a secretary at the German embassy; and when the British and Americans got her out of the country the following June, they had smuggled her north to Murmansk to board a British ship.

But she could remember the city itself well enough to realize, during the drive in from the airport, that Moscow had changed out of all recognition. She knew that it had been heavily bombed during the War, with widespread destruction, but it seemed that no attempt had been made to restore any of the ancient character of the place. Instead, she was surrounded by high-rise apartment blocks in every direction, all apparently built to identical designs, creating a monolithic similarity entirely lacking in distinction, and soul.

However, the centre of the city was largely as she remembered it, dominated by the immense fortress of the Kremlin, from the wall of which Lenin's tomb protruded into Red Square, and at the top end by St Basil's Cathedral (a show-piece even though Christianity had been offici-ally abolished) and at the other by the State Historical Museum – while opposite the Krem-lin, on the other side of the square, was the GUM department store, barred to the ordinary Muscovite as only 'hard' foreign currency could be used there.

It was in this square, Anna recalled, that the infamous photograph had been taken of her when she was on a tour of the city in September 1940. At that time she had been too young (just twenty) and inexperienced to regard it as more than an impertinence on the part of the photo-grapher, who had apologized profusely. But when she had become the Soviet Union's most wanted criminal, that photo had found its way into the hands of the NKVD; and thence, eight years later, into the hands of the Mafia hit squad hired by Beria to kill her. She had retrieved it from the first of the boats sent to deal with her, before sinking the craft and its crew, and it was now in the hands of the CIA – although so far, she reflected, that had not done her a lot of good.

Now, the Kremlin was behind them and they were in the heart of the city. In front of them were the lights in the windows of another huge building, also a relic of a bygone age – in the Tsarist days it had been the home of Russia's leading insurance company. It was entered by a gated archway in the surrounding walls. The car rolled through, and the gates clanged shut behind it.

After twelve years, she was back in the Lubianka.

How familiar it all seemed. Her last visit could have been yesterday. But there was a difference. Twelve years ago, in the eyes of the arresting officers she had simply been a criminal, undoubtedly deranged, who had been caught breaking into the Kremlin; as she had been unarmed, they had not even considered her to be dangerous. Now they were regarding her as if she were a keg of dynamite with a burning fuse. Then they had pushed her and kicked her with the careless brutality they inflicted upon all their prisoners. Now they were afraid to touch her. When she got out of the car, although she was handcuffed, she was surrounded by men with drawn pistols pointing at her. It would have been amusing, had she not been growing increasingly conscious that she was running out of time and, therefore, of room to manoeuvre.

Hamilton indicated the open door. 'I believe you know the way, Countess.'

Anna went into the lighted hallway, which she remembered so clearly. There were stairs leading up, and doors opening to either side. She turned automatically to her left, where a door was guarded by an armed sentry.

'You do know the way!' Hamilton commented. 'Inform Colonel Berisova,' he told the guard. 'She is expecting us.'

The sentry took the phone from its wall bracket. 'There is a prisoner for you, Comrade Colonel.'

Anna could not hear the reply, but a few moments later the door swung inwards.

The woman standing there was surprisingly small, in contrast to the last commandant of the Women's Section she had encountered. This one was almost attractive, with her neat features and soft black hair, worn short. In her perfectly tailored green uniform and brown boots, she was almost chic.

'The Countess von Widerstand.' Hamilton introduced her.

Colonel Berisova merely nodded.

'You understand...'

'I have read the file, Comrade Terpolov. Besides, I remember her.'

Anna raised her eyebrows in mystification.

'We must say goodbye, Countess,' Hamilton said. 'But I hope to see you again. At least once.'

Anna merely looked at him.

'Come,' Colonel Berisova said, indicating the doorway.

Anna stepped inside, her memory now stimulated by the smells and sounds. Even in the middle of the night, she could hear sighs and groans, even the occasional shriek.

'They never cease,' Colonel Berisova remarked. 'But one gets used to it. The office is the door on the right – but you no doubt remember that.'

Anna went into the office. The last time she had been in here she had killed two people.

Berisova went behind the desk and sat down. 'You may sit,' she invited.

Anna lowered herself into the chair before the desk.

'I do not suppose you remember me,' the colonel suggested.

Anna was under no illusions that the apparent pleasantness was meaningless; it cost nothing to be pleasant to people who were absolutely in your power and to be treated entirely as you chose. But she also knew that her chances of survival, at least until she could be extricated, would not be enhanced by continued antagonism on her part. On the other hand, she sensed, and indeed remembered, that these people would treat her best if she met them on their own ground; to cringe, or reveal fear of any sort, would be fatal. So she spoke, for the first time in seven days. 'I must apologize, Comrade Colonel, but I do not remember ever having seen you before.'

'There is no reason why you should,' Berisova agreed. 'I was very junior in 1941, but I did see you – and as I remember, you were very chic. But now of course...'

She got up and came round the desk. Anna braced herself for whatever was coming, but the colonel merely jerked the bandanna from her head, allowing her hair to flood past her shoulders. 'That is better. Now you look more like the beautiful woman I remember. And I am sure that beneath those rags you are even more beautiful. Sadly, in 1941, Colonel Tsherchenka considered you her private property. I am sure that you remember her, Countess. Dear Ludmilla.'

'I remember her very well,' Anna conceded.

'Well, you should, of course. Did you not break her neck in the act of escaping, with your American accomplice, Andrews?'

'It seemed a good idea at the time,' Anna agreed. 'She was trying to prevent my departure.'

'I was not on duty that day,' Berisova remarked.

'Which may have been fortunate for you.'

'Or you would have broken my neck as well?'

'If it had been necessary, yes.'

'Then I assume you also remember Olga Morosawa.'

'I remember her.'

'You shot and killed her in Germany in 1945.'

'I did not.'

The colonel raised her eyebrows. 'You deny killing her?'

'I have never denied killing anyone, Comrade Colonel. And I would certainly have killed Olga Morosawa, had I been given the opportunity: she tortured me, when I was last here. But an associate of mine beat me to it.'

304

Berisova gazed at her. 'Olga Morosawa was my best friend.'

'I can understand that,' Anna agreed.

'So, if I now torture you, would you then kill me?'

'If you ever gave me the opportunity, yes.'

'You do not lack courage. But that fits with what I have been told of you. Sadly, I am forbidden to torture you at the moment. But perhaps, when he is finished with you, Commissar Beria will give you back to me. He will see you in the morning. Until then...'

She pressed a button on her desk, and a moment later the door behind Anna opened.

'I want four of you.'

Anna did not turn her head, but from the sounds of movement behind her she gathered that the colonel was being obeyed.

'Now,' Berisova said, 'place this prisoner in Number 47.'

'I need to go to the toilet,' Anna said.

'Up to your tricks already?'

'I genuinely need to go. It has been several hours. I have also not eaten for that time.'

'There is a bucket in your cell, and you will be fed tomorrow morning ... Now listen to me very carefully, comrades. When you have conducted the prisoner to her cell, you may remove her handcuffs. Here is the key. However, before you do that, you will draw your pistols and be prepared to use them. And for the remainder of her time with us, whenever it is necessary to open the cell door it must be in the presence of

305

four of you, and you will always have your pistols drawn.'

'Is this woman really that dangerous, Comrade Colonel?'

'This woman,' Berisova said, 'is the most dangerous creature in the world.'

'You do,' said Anna, 'say the sweetest things.'

THE PRISONER

Anna was desperately tired, even more so than she was hungry. She had been travelling all day and half the night, in some discomfort; and if the narrow bunk on which she found herself was equally uncomfortable, she was too exhausted to care. As for what tomorrow would bring, there was no point in concerning herself with that at the moment. The thought that it might be her last day on earth was unacceptable. This was not because she was afraid of death – she had faced it so often in the past – but because in the past she had always managed to survive, by using all of her assets and all of her skills, and by being ready to take advantage of the slightest window of opportunity, the slightest lapse in concentration on the part of her enemies.

But, for all her refusal to surrender, she had always known deep within herself that, as the

Good Book had it, those that live by the sword also die by the sword. That her death might, in her present circumstances, be preceded by a prolonged agony was no longer an issue. If it happened, it would be because of her own carelessness. Her hubris. And because of a perverse desire to experience everything that life had to offer before taking leave of it. From her very first assignment for the SD, she had been provided with a cyanide capsule, with the assurance that it would act in ten seconds; but however dire the situation, it had never once occurred to her to use it. Nor, she knew, would she have done so now.

She woke when her door opened. 'Breakfast,' said the guard, who was, as commanded, backed up by three other powerful young women, each equipped with a drawn pistol. In view of what had been let slip on board the boat, Anna felt quite sure that they would not actually kill her; and she equally had no doubt that if she could get hold of just one of their guns, she could do for all of them. But she could see no way further. She knew that every cell and each corridor was overseen by constantly monitored CCTV, and she would be surrounded and overwhelmed long before she could reach the door, while the door itself could only be opened by instructions from the commandant or orders from the commissar.

So, more patience. Besides, she was so very hungry, and the thick soup and bread were by no means unpalatable, even though she would have preferred coffee rather than unsweetened tea. And after the meal, she would have liked a hot bath; but she knew that was not on. She knew from her previous experience here that there were no baths, only showers; and that these were used as instruments of torture, powerful wafer-thin jets of water being directed at the victim's naked body. The jets could kill if concentrated on the face for more than a few seconds, and they could ruin the victim for life if inserted into either of the two private orifices of the body.

She had undergone this treatment, briefly, during her previous incarceration, and that had been June. What it might be like at the beginning of March did not bear contemplation.

In any event, no sooner had she finished her meal than Berisova arrived.

'Stand up.'

Anna obeyed, and was immediately surrounded by guards.

'Handcuff her.'

Her arms were pulled behind her back, and the steel bracelets clipped on to her wrists.

Satisfied, Berisova tied Anna's hair up in the bandanna. 'Come along. Two of you will accompany us.'

The guards fell into place at her shoulders. They proceeded along the corridors, then the outer door was opened for them and they were in the lobby, being stared at by the curious guards. Berisova indicated the stairs, and they climbed up to the next floor, on which all the doors were closed. Then there was another flight of stairs, to the second floor, where there were only two doors. Berisova knocked on one of these and then opened it. They were in an outer office, containing several men and women. All wore uniform, and all were hard at work typing or on the telephone, or studying papers. But all of them stopped work to look at the colonel and her prisoner.

'For the commissar,' Berisova announced.

One of the secretaries got up, went to an inner door, and knocked. 'Colonel Berisova is here, Comrade Commissar, with a prisoner.'

'Ah, Vera. Come in, Vera.'

Berisova went into the inner room. 'Good morning, Commissar Beria! May I present the Countess von Widerstand.'

Anna was for a moment blinded. In contrast to the gloomy interior of the prison, and even to the lighted but still dull outer office, this large room was illuminated by several windows, through which the winter sunlight streamed. Then she got her eyes into focus and gazed at the big, heavy man standing before her, his huge pale face seeming to glow as the light reflected off his hairless head. He wore a pince-nez, which was the only positive feature between his chin and his forehead; even his eyebrows seemed non-existent, and his eyes themselves were no more than pinpricks in their pale surroundings. Like Berisova, he wore a perfectly cut green uniform, and highly polished brown boots.

Beria was studying her with equal interest. 'Countess!' he said. 'Countess, what on earth are you wearing?'

'What I was given to wear, Your Excellency.'

'Cretins! Colonel Berisova, I wish a dressmaker here within the hour. And send to GUM for a selection of underwear and clothes, both casual and formal.'

'Sir?'

'Clothes, Vera, clothes. The countess must be properly dressed.'

'Yes, sir.' Berisova was in a fog. So was Anna. She could only suppose that this man liked dressing up his victims before destroying them.

'And why is she handcuffed? Get rid of them.'

'Your Excellency! This woman is highly dangerous.'

'This I know. But she is not going to be dangerous to me. Are you, Countess?'

For one of the very few occasions in her life, Anna was speechless without meaning to be.

'Well, come on,' said Beria, 'remove those cuffs.'

Fingers stroked Anna's wrists, and she heard the click of the key. She brought her arms round in front to massage her hands and get her circulation going.

'Now leave us,' Beria commanded.

'But ... Your Excellency...'

'Leave us. And carry out your instructions.

Close the door.'

A last hesitation, then Berisova waved her people from the room and left. The door closed.

'I am surrounded by cretins,' Beria grumbled, and indicated the chair before his desk. 'Sit down.'

Cautiously, Anna obeyed. She was still trying to determine exactly what was going on.

'And take off that terrible kerchief.'

Anna freed her hair.

'Now, that is better. Your crowning glory, eh? Although I am sure that beneath those rags there are other glories still to be revealed.' Beria sat down behind the desk. 'I can see that you are a little confused. Let me clarify the situation. There are two reasons why I know that you are too intelligent to wish to attack me. One is this...' He moved a document on his desk to reveal an automatic pistol. 'I would not dare to claim that I am as proficient as you are, but I am perfectly capable of shooting straight; and if you attempt to leave that chair until I invite you to do so, I will shoot you, much as I would hate to destroy so much beauty. The other reason is that, while you may consider that to attack me and die from a bullet wound is preferable to suffering hours of torture with execution at the end of it, it is even more preferable to live, without being tortured at all. And I am the only person who is in a position to grant you that preferable ending.'

Anna could keep quiet no longer; she could not believe what she was hearing, unless it was some ghastly mental torture. 'You are offering me my life, Your Excellency? After...'

'I know. After nearly twelve years of trying to lay my hands on you. At a cost of ... Do you know, I have quite lost track of how many lives you have cost.'

'So have I,' Anna admitted.

'You mean you do not carve notches on the butt of your pistol?' With his left hand he picked up the Walther, which was also lying on his desk. 'There would scarcely be sufficient room, would there? And this intriguing belt...' He held it to his nose. 'Do you know, it still carries your scent. You must show me how you wear it.'

'I wear it round my waist, under my clothes, Comrade Commissar.'

'You mean, next to your skin? What a fortunate piece of leather. However, the point is that throughout those twelve years I have been acting under orders. Oh, I wanted you here in my office. Make no mistake about that. But I have always felt that killing you would be a sad waste of some very valuable material.'

Anna had a sudden surge of mixed emotions as she began to understand what he was driving at.

'With respect, Comrade Commissar,' she commented, 'you have tried to have that done often enough to convince me.'

Beria chuckled. 'And the fact that all of those men and women failed has even more convinced me that my original judgement was correct. Tell me what happened three years ago. You know, employing the Mafia, after so many failures on the part of our people, was Premier Stalin's idea. He felt it could not fail. While our people have always stood out like sore thumbs in the West – you could see us coming a mile off – the Mafia, being an American organization, would simply meld into the background until they were ready to reveal themselves.'

He paused, and Anna gave a slight shrug. 'It's a valid point.'

'And we understood that they were attending to the matter, that it was all settled and was about to be completed ... and then heard nothing more. Not even from our agent who had organized the matter.'

'May I ask, sir, who this agent was?'

'A man called Botten.'

'I have never heard of him.'

'But how did you cope? I know you shot up a lot of our people in Germany in 1946, but then I understood that you were backed up by both the American and the British Secret Services. Botten told us he had ascertained that you lived alone on your island, with just your aged parents and a couple of black servants. And the Mafia, Botten assured us, were sending twenty men to complete the job.'

'Well, you see,' Anna explained, 'they did rather broadcast the fact that they were coming, by sending an advance party that was totally incompetent to reconnoitre the cay.'

'Of whom, I assume, you disposed?'

'Yes, I did. But I also received a great deal of help from the weather. The idiots tried to land on the cay in a hurricane. Maybe they thought this was a good idea because the storm would obliterate the fact that they had ever been there. But unluckily for them, their plan backfired. The storm certainly obliterated their presence on the cay – but by then I had already sunk their boat.'

'You sank a boat carrying twenty men, with that little pistol?'

'Oh, good lord, no, Comrade Commissar. I used a bazooka.'

Beria looked as if he was about to scratch his head, then changed his mind. 'You, have a bazooka?'

'Doesn't everyone? But as you must have gathered, I didn't bring it with me on this trip.'

He stared at her for several seconds, then returned to the subject that was of greatest interest to him. 'And no one got ashore?'

'Several did, but only one survived.'

'And?'

'I shot him. After all, he was trying to kill me.'

This time Beria produced a handkerchief to wipe his neck. 'And you think that was Botten?'

'No. He told me he was a Mafia bigwig. I think he was trying to frighten me.'

'What a silly fellow. So what happened to Botten?'

'I have no idea. If he was on that boat, he

314

must have gone down with it. But if you knew what he was planning to do, then you knew where I lived.'

'The fool never told us where you lived,' Beria said. 'Only that he had tracked you to the Bahamas. Then he disappeared.'

'And you never followed that up? For three years?'

'That also was Marshal Stalin's decision; I think he felt that in some way you had become immortal. And for all those years I have been, as regards you, in a subordinate position. You must understand that what enraged Premier Stalin was not merely the fact that your mission was to kill him, but that you so bewitched him with your looks and personality that he was falling in love with you ... then you were un-covered as an assassin. And he was old enough to be your grandfather! But then, as they say, there is no fool like an old fool – which is very true when it comes to matters such as sex and desire, which tend to fade as time goes by and become difficult to inspire. Thus when he discovered that every time you took tea with him in the Kremlin – and fluttered those long eyelashes at him and told him what a great man you thought he was – you were actually plan-ning how best to go about murdering him, the humiliation caused him to hate you more than any other living creature in the world.'

'And you are saying that he has changed his mind?'

'Oh, no. He still dreams of having you

stretched in front of him, naked and helpless. You could describe him as the original dirty old man. But he has come to recognize that it can only ever be a dream now.'

'Then, sir, I do not understand what I am doing here. If Marshal Stalin is still your commander and he is still out for my blood ... Or have you merely been amusing yourself in the most unpleasant possible manner, and do still intend to deliver me to him, naked and helpless?'

'You are so forthright, Anna. You do not mind if I call you Anna? I feel that we are going to get to know each other very well.'

'You mean you intend to have me, naked and helpless, for yourself?'

'What an entrancing thought. But I would hope that if – or should I say when? – we get to know each other, coercion will not be an issue.'

'Forgive me, Comrade Commissar, but I have lost the point. You have spent twelve years, and a great deal of time, money and human life, just to get to know me better?'

'I have explained, Anna, that for those years I was constrained, and required to follow the instructions of my master.'

'And you no longer have to do that? Marshal Stalin *is* still alive, and ruling Russia?'

'Marshal Stalin is still alive,' Beria agreed. 'Just. And he continues to assume – and it is accepted by a great many people – that he is the absolute ruler of Russia. However, his grip on affairs is becoming increasingly tenuous. I thus find myself in a position where I can employ whoever I choose to do whatever I choose.'

Anna stared at him in total consternation. Even if she had suspected that he might be heading in this direction, she had not expected him to state it so bluntly. 'You want me, to work for you?' she asked. 'What as?'

'My dear Anna,' he said. 'I had never thought you would be naïve As far as I am aware, you have only one talent. Well, perhaps two. But I have always understood that you used the one to achieve the other.'

'You wish me to become a member of the MGB? I'm not sure I could ever be popular with my colleagues.'

'Have you ever had any colleagues? My understanding is that you have always worked alone – except perhaps for that occasion in Germany in 1946. But we are not here to talk about the past. And in any event, I do not wish you to join the MGB. You will work for me, personally. As you once worked for Himmler, personally.'

'And may I assume that you have a specific target in mind?'

'We will discuss targets later. Do you accept my offer?'

Her brain was spinning. But throughout her life, survival had been the key. 'Do I have a choice?'

'Everyone has a choice, Anna. Although I agree that some choices are more easily made than others.'

'And can you be sure that I will carry out your orders?'

'I can be quite sure. As you will realize when I give them to you.' His voice, hitherto quiet, suddenly hardened. 'Your answer?'

'I accept.' Whatever reservations she was already considering, she could do nothing until she had discovered just what he had in mind, and how closely she was going to be supervised.

'Excellent. Now, we have talked business for long enough. What, at this moment, and given your circumstances, would you like most in the world?'

'I would like to get rid of these clothes, and have a hot bath and a square meal.'

'Of course.' He got up and came round the desk. 'And I hope that, at some stage, you will demonstrate to me some of your skills. I have had to exist far too long on hearsay. Come.'

He gestured her to her feet, ostentatiously leaving both guns on the desk. He knew she was not going to attempt to break out, with no hope of success other than perhaps the satisfaction of killing him, while he held out the carrot of a far better opportunity later on. She had to be content with that.

He opened the door for her, and she went into the outer office, where it seemed that his entire staff were waiting, as well as Berisova – all looking extremely anxious, and retreating from

318

her as they saw that she was unrestrained in any way.

'Well?' Beria demanded.

'The clothes are on their way over now, Comrade Commissar,' Berisova said, 'as well as the dressmakers.'

'Very good. We shall be in the apartment.'

'You, and you,' he said to two of the female members of his staff, 'will come with us.' He indicated the corridor, and then the second door on this level. 'In there.'

Anna opened the door, and found herself in a bright, airy and comfortably furnished lounge. To her left there was an open-plan kitchen; on her right an open door revealed a bedroom.

'Draw a hot bath for the Countess,' Beria commanded, and the two girls hurried through the bedroom.

'Is this where you live?' Anna asked, genuinely curious.

'Oh, no. I have a dacha, well, several, in fact, scattered about the country. This is where *you* will live during your stay in Moscow. At least until we can make other arrangements, eh? Vodka?'

'At nine o'clock in the morning?'

'It is as good a time as any. Or perhaps you would prefer tea?'

'I would actually prefer coffee. Preferably strong.'

'Our coffee is dreadful stuff. Vodka would be better for you.'

Anna shrugged. He was determined to

illustrate his control of the situation, and she was content to go along with that, for the time being, because he did of course hold all the high cards, at this moment. The important thing from her point of view was that she was alive, and unharmed, and seemed to have some prospect of remaining that way for the immediate future. And all the while, the wheels would be turning in Washington and London. But he was unaware of that.

Beria poured two small glasses and gave her one.

'To your continued good health.'

'And to yours, Comrade Commissar,' Anna replied. At least, she thought, until I have an opportunity to alter the situation. The fiery liquid was certainly warming.

'Now tell me, when did you last eat?'

Anna grimaced. 'I had what passes for breakfast in your cells.'

'Ha. But our business is simply to keep our prisoners alive, not to fatten them.'

'But before that...' She shrugged again. 'I had no dinner last night.'

'That is inhuman. You must indeed be starving.'

'I am hungry, yes.'

'Then you shall have a proper breakfast, eh? As soon as you have bathed. I would not like your figure to be in any way diminished. Not,' he added, 'that I have seen it yet.'

One of the young women appeared in the doorway. 'The bath is ready, Your Excellency.'

'Thank you. Anna?'

Anna drained her glass, the glow spreading from her largely empty stomach to every part of her body, and followed the girl through the bedroom, aware that Beria was behind her. Well, he had made it perfectly clear that he intended to enjoy her as well as employ her, and she was in no position to resent it.

She went into the bathroom, where the other girl waited, sleeves pushed up to her elbows.

'She would like to wash you,' Beria explained, unnecessarily. 'But I imagine you are perfectly capable of washing yourself.'

'I am, yes.' Anna sat in the one chair to remove her boots, then stood up to lift her blouse over her head and drop her pants. The girls stared at her like starving dogs.

'Get rid of those rags,' Beria commanded. 'And those disgusting boots.'

They gathered up the discarded clothing and left the room. Anna cautiously dipped her hand in the water, but it was just the right temperature. She stepped in and lowered herself with a sigh.

'You are exquisite,' Beria commented, sitting in the vacated chair. 'But I imagine you have been told that often enough.'

'Men like to pay me compliments,' Anna acknowledged, soaping herself with sensuous contentment.

'And some women, I believe.'

'Those too.'

'But that crucifix ... Are you a Roman

321

Catholic?'

'I was once. I was educated at a convent.'

'How remarkable. And...?'

'Yes, Comrade Commissar, I would like to be one again, one day.'

He watched her for several seconds, then said, 'My man Terpolov ... or I suppose you know him better as Hamilton...'

'Hamilton,' said Anna, controlling the venom.

'A detestable fellow, but good at his job. He had an English mother, you know, and was thus able to fit into the English background.'

'Except that you gave him a Scottish name.'

'Did we? That was careless. No one told me, until now. But you were not suspicious of him?'

'Not sufficiently,' Anna said, sadly.

'He claims that he saw you kill a man with a single blow to the neck.'

'I was trained by the SD,' Anna said, modestly.

'So it was not a lucky blow.'

'It was not a lucky blow. Although I will admit that I hit him harder than I had intended.' She turned her head to look at him. 'He was trying to rape me, you see, and I suppose I lost my temper.'

'You do not like being raped?'

'Do you, Comrade Commissar?'

'Ha ha. Do you know, I have never had that experience. What I am trying to establish is that you are confident that you can destroy a man – any man – with a single blow.'

There was a bottle of shampoo; it was a long

322

way from her favourite scent, but it was better than nothing. Anna washed her hair. 'I am a confident person.'

'I can see that.'

'Would I be right in assuming that you wish me to kill someone for you without using a weapon?'

'You would be right.'

'And for this purpose you have spent all this time and money to have me kidnapped?'

'It is a task only you can perform.'

'If you knew the number of times, Comrade Commissar, that I have been told that.'

'Well, are you not unique?'

'You say the sweetest things.' Anna rinsed her hair, then stood up. This was no time for thinking, only absorbing. Beria handed her a towel, and she stepped from the bath. 'Would it not have been simpler merely to approach me with a proposition?'

'Would you have accepted a proposition from me? Would you have allowed my emissary the time to make it?'

'You never know your luck. But as I'm here, am I allowed to ask what brought you to this decision, after spending twelve years trying to have me killed?'

'I have explained, that I was acting under orders. I have always had my doubts so to whether destroying so valuable an asset as a woman like yourself was not a mistake.'

Anna dried herself. 'And now your orders have been changed, is that it? By Marshal

Stalin? Who you say has hated me more than any other living creature for all of those twelve years?'

'Marshal Stalin,' Beria said, 'does not even know that you are in Russia. Yet.'

Slowly Anna wrapped her hair in a fresh towel, while her brain spun round in circles. 'I hope, Comrade Commissar, that you are not telling me what I suspect you are telling me.'

'They said you were a genius,' Beria declared, and sniffed. 'I think breakfast has been served. Shall we eat?'

There was no dressing gown, but that was obviously how he wished her to be. Besides, her brain was still spinning with the implications of what he had just suggested. Now she could only wait to find out exactly what he had in mind.

The two girls stood beside the table in the lounge, together with Berisova, whose eyes were no less hungry than theirs as they looked at her. But, for the moment, Anna was preoccupied with the plates of steaming eggs, tubs of yogurts, thin slices of bread, and, of course, a bubbling samovar of tea. She would have enjoyed some bacon, but that was irrelevant compared with the effect the sight of food was having on her empty stomach.

Beria gestured her to a chair, and she sat down. He sat beside her.

'The clothes are here, Comrade Commissar.' Berisova indicated the various boxes piled on the floor, and the half-dozen dresses draped across the settee; there were also several pairs of shoes.

'Thank you, Comrade Colonel.'

'And the dressmakers are standing by, to make whatever alterations are required.'

'Tell them to wait until after the countess has had her breakfast.'

'Yes, sir.' Berisova looked at Anna again, this time less in lust than increased astonishment at the way she was being treated.

'Now leave us,' Beria commanded. 'Leave this door open, but close the outer one.'

'Yes, sir.' She gestured the girls from the room, and followed.

Beria waited for the outer door to close, then said, 'Poor Berisova is very confused. I wouldn't put it past her to try to overhear what we say to each other. I would hate her to do that, as I would then have to shoot her. I would not like to have to do that; she is very efficient.'

There was a huge cruet in the centre of the table; Anna added salt and pepper from the two outsize containers, and ate the eggs. 'And what are we going to say to each other, Comrade Commissar? Or, perhaps, do?'

'Do. Later, perhaps. As for what we have to say, you understand why you are here?'

'I'm hoping you will explain more fully, sir. Otherwise I will find it impossible to believe.'

Beria drank tea. 'I think you know that I have served Marshal Stalin faithfully and well for some fifteen years. To the extent that he has trusted me with enormous powers. I have the power of life and death over every man, woman, and child in this country. However, that power has always been subject to his ultimate endorsement, or veto.'

Anna buttered some bread.

'Unfortunately, men who wield unlimited power tend to become megalomaniac.'

She understood that he was not referring to himself.

'And when that megalomania is added to an already existing paranoia, it comes close to madness. Marshal Stalin has always been prone to a paranoid mistrust of those around him. You remember the show trials of 1937? Those men were all old comrades in arms who he had come to believe were plotting to dethrone him.'

Anna swallowed the bread. 'Should you be telling me this, Comrade Commissar?'

Beria chuckled. 'Should I not, as you are now working for me?'

'Ah!' Anna commented.

'There is one fact that you need to keep constantly in mind,' he continued. 'Should anything happen to me, when I mount the scaffold you will be standing beside me – whether you have betrayed me, or attempted to betray me, or not.'

'I quite understand that that's something I shall need to remember.'

'Quite so. Now, the marshal is an old man. Older, perhaps, mentally than in years. In fact, he is only seventy-three. But although he knows his powers are fading, he cannot bring himself to hand over the reins to anyone else; to someone younger and more capable, perhaps. Indeed, I suspect he dare not do so. He has made too many enemies within the senior ranks of the Party to be certain of his own survival, should he relinquish supreme power.'

Anna drank some more tea. She understood exactly what he was telling her.

'And that paranoia of which I spoke is now leading him to believe that certain of those younger men are plotting against him, plotting his deposition. He is thus becoming too danger-ous to be allowed to continue.'

'In other words,' Anna said, 'his suspicions are more correct than paranoid.'

Beria regarded her for several seconds. Then picked up his knife, dug it into the butter, and smeared the pat on to her left nipple. Anna's head jerked, but she immediately realized that this was merely another, somewhat childish, way of demonstrating his mastery.

'That sharp brain of yours could get you into serious trouble,' he said.

She resisted the temptation to remove the butter. 'I was merely saying, Comrade Com-missar, that I understood your problem. But I don't see why you need me. Doesn't the posi-tion of premier require the support of the Politburo? And if the premier loses their support, can he not be legally deposed?'

'That is the theory. But the reality is some-what different. For two reasons. Firstly, the members of the Politburo are all afraid of him. And secondly, and more importantly, not one of them trusts the others; and they are all ambitious men. Every one of them sees himself as a possible successor. Even that total moron Kruschev ... Did you ever meet him?'

'If I did, I don't remember the name.'

'Well, actually, he was never in Moscow during your sojourn here. He was down in the sticks, where he belongs, in total obscurity. But he earned himself a reputation for ruthlessness in carrying out orders; and when in 1942 it looked as if Stalingrad was going to fall, Stalin hooked him out of obscurity and gave him *carte blanche* as long as he held the city. I thought the marshal was mad. At such a moment! But Kruschev did it, you have to give him credit for that. He shot people left right and centre, cashiered generals, and drove the defenders on and on. God alone knows how many lives it cost. But it cost the Nazis more: an entire army. And so he became famous overnight, and since then has steadily climbed in the Party hierarchy. Now he is a member of the Politburo. And his ambitions roam even higher.'

'And for that you hate him,' Anna suggested.

'I hate him,' Beria agreed. 'I hate them all. Because they all hate me. Because they fear me. We only ever hate the things we fear. Those we do not fear we simply hold in contempt. They fear me because I am Stalin's right-hand man. As long as I am that, they are at my mercy.'

'But if, for any reason, you cease to be

Stalin's right-hand man...' Anna said, thought-fully.

'I do like women who do not have to have everything explained to them. We will defeat them all, Anna. Together.'

The most unholy partnership in all history, Anna thought. But...

'You must forgive me, Comrade Commissar. After all, I am just a woman. I understand your problem and what you intend to do about it, but why have you imported me to help you? Do you not have an armed force of several thousand men and women here in Moscow, sworn to do your bidding without question?'

He was looking at her with a most peculiar expression, but it was one that she had seen before on the faces of other men. Oh, my God! she thought, he's getting worked up.

'Anna,' he said, 'may I remove that butter? It is starting to melt.'

'Of course, Comrade Commissar.'

She turned towards him and held out her napkin, but to her consternation he dropped to his knees and began licking the nipple. I am in the hands of a superannuated schoolboy, she thought ... who seeks to rule a country!

He raised his head. 'Anna...'

She sighed. But he had to be humoured, until she could discover some way of getting out of this mess. 'What would you like, sir?' She was pretty sure that it was not straightforward sex.

He licked his lip. 'You mean...'

'Your wish is my command, Comrade Commissar.'

'Would you ... ah ... lick him?'

'You mean suck him?' Her tone was redolent of relief; she had feared something far worse. 'Then you had better sit, and I will kneel.'

'Anna ... you are a treasure.'

Anna's brain squirmed. Every man who had called her a treasure, and there had been quite a few, beginning with Adolf Hitler, was now dead. But then, she reflected, is that not what I have in mind for this man, the moment it can be safely accomplished?

'But,' he said. 'I would like to fondle you, while...'

'Ah,' she said. 'In that case, I think you should take some of these clothes off and lie on the bed, and then I can kneel beside you.'

For all his fervour, he was by no means ready; but she soon rectified that, after which it was very quick. Then he lay back, sighing, while she used the bathroom to wash her hands and face, before returning. 'Now, sir,' she said. 'May we return to business?'

'Business,' he said, dreamily. 'Business!' He sat up and began to dress. 'You understand what is required of you?'

'I understand what is required, sir. I still do not understand why it is required of *me*. Are you saying that among all your staff there is no one who will obey you without question?'

'Sit down, Anna.'

Anna obeyed.

'Every member of my staff will obey me without question,' Beria said, 'as long as they believe that I am carrying out the wishes of Marshal Stalin. To them, he is the man who led them to victory over the Nazi hordes and saved the country from the abyss of slavery. That point of view pervades the entire country; it is taught in the schools. But there is a further consideration. If Stalin were to die at the hands of a Russian, there would immediately be a witch hunt for the assassin's employer – and no one can say how it would end.'

'Whereas if he was killed by an obviously demented itinerant Irishwoman, rather as nearly happened to Mussolini thirty years ago...'

'You have a profound knowledge of history.'

'It is one of my hobbies. As I was saying, the culprit would simply be turned over to you for torture and execution. And anything I might attempt to say in my defence, would be dismissed as the ravings of a mad woman.'

'That will not happen to you, Anna. You will never be brought to trial.'

'You mean you intend to kill me the moment the deed is done?'

'I mean, Anna, that once the marshal is dead, but not by my hand or that of any member of the MGB, my people *will* obey me – and only me – without question. I have ten thousand men and women in and around Moscow. A couple of telephone calls will summon them to action. They will take over every important position in the city, especially the Kremlin. This will be to prevent any *coups d'état*, you understand. I will then take supreme power, at which time I will make the laws. Which will include protecting those who work for me.'

Anna was left speechless. He might have the sexual tastes of a schoolboy, but there could be no doubting the breadth and scope of his ambition. A case of those whom the gods would destroy they first drive mad?

Once his immediate needs had been satisfied, he was all bustle and efficiency. 'Now,' he said, buttoning his tunic, 'I have work to do, and so have you. Choose whatever you wish from the garments on offer; the dressmakers will make whatever alterations are necessary. You must look your very best when you visit the premier.'

Anna could not resist the temptation to put him to the test. 'In view of the weather out there, I will need a coat.'

'Then order one.'

'I always wear sable.'

He turned to look at her. 'Then a sable you shall have.'

'With a matching hat.'

'As you wish.' He bent over her and planted an almost husbandly kiss on her forehead. 'I will see you this evening. Have a nice day, but do not leave this apartment.'

He hurried off, and a few minutes later the dressmakers hurried in, pausing in consternation at discovering her in the nude. But they fell to with a will, and in fact it was an enjoyable session, even if the clothes on offer bore very little resemblance to anything that might have interested her on Bond Street or the Champs Elysées, or Fifth Avenue. But they were all brand new and reasonably well cut, although the Russian idea of knickers were voluminous drawers; and she had the pleasure of shocking them all over again by declining their equally voluminous and even more all-embracing nightgowns. But the sable, with its matching hat, immediately delivered from GUM, was as good as any of those she had previously owned ... and lost. She wondered if she would be able to keep this one.

Spending the day on her own gave her time to think. Obviously to trust Beria would be the equivalent of taking a crocodile to bed; and yet to refuse his proposal was the shortest possible route to a bullet in the back of the head.

So it was a time for the absolute pragmatism that she had practised all her life and which, as much as any of her skills, had been responsible for her survival. Killing Stalin was not a matter for concern. Had she been allowed to complete her mission, he would have been dead twelve years ago, which might have saved a lot of people a lot of grief.

Equally, gaining access to him had obviously been carefully worked out, and would no doubt be told to her that evening. It was what happened after that that mattered. From a coldly logical point of view, Beria's obvious course was to have her commit the murder and then be killed by the guards on her way out. Then he could deny any knowledge of her; and thus who she was and where she had come from would remain a mystery, and he could calmly proceed with his plan.

If that was what he planned, she was already dead. But she suspected that, in his overweening ambition, he wanted more from her. In the first place, given her track record, he could not be sure that she would be killed, even by several armed guards. Secondly, she also felt that he was planning some more work for her, regarding his various rivals for power, who would all have to be eliminated. And thirdly, she had no doubt at all that over the years of hunting her he had contrived to fall in love, if not with her, then with her image; and that he was now infatuated with both her beauty and her expertise. That would not last, of course; but however distasteful the prospect, she needed to make it last until either Clive or Joe, or both, arranged her rescue, or until she could organize her escape. As long as she was alive, she had a future.

'Well,' Beria said, 'I hope you have had a good day. I must say, you look absolutely stupendous. But then, you always do. You looked stupendous even in those ghastly clothes you were wearing this morning.'

'Thank you, sir.' Indeed, physically she was feeling stupendous. She had had an utterly restful day, punctuated only by a splendid lunch and another bath. And she was wearing one of her new dresses. Now she allowed him to take her in his arms and kiss her on the mouth.

'I think,' he said, 'that we are going to have a very fruitful relationship.'

'I would like to think so, sir.'

He released her to pour two glasses of vodka, then sat on the settee, gesturing her to sit beside him. 'I imagine that you have spent most of the day considering what lies ahead.'

'No, sir.'

He raised his eyebrows. 'You regard it as that simple?'

'No, sir. But I make it a rule never to anticipate until I am in possession of all the facts. Then I can plan both my strategy and my tactics. In any event, I suspect that you have already planned the strategy,'

'You are an amazingly calm young woman. Is that born of experience?'

'Successful experience, sir. Or I would not be here now.'

'Quite. And you are not afraid that one day you may be set a task you, even you, cannot accomplish?'

'It has not happened yet.'

He gazed at her for several seconds, still uncertain whether or not she was making fun of him. Then he nodded. 'Well, it so happens that, compared with some of your previous exploits ... By the way, have you any idea how many men you have killed? I mean, in total. I remember that you said you had lost count, at least of the Russians, but I suspect that was a preliminary act of defiance, coming at the beginning of our relationship.'

'It was, sir. I have endeavoured to keep count. The tally would appear to be one hundred and thirty-seven. That is to say, as far as I know, I have been responsible for one hundred and thirty-seven deaths, although I did not kill all of them personally.'

'Good God! Are you serious?'

'I'm afraid so, sir. Of course, there have been one or two women included in the list.'

'Including two of my most trusted aides,' he reminded her. 'However, with that record, you will find this one – how do you English put it? – a piece of fruit.'

'I happen to be Irish,' Anna pointed out, 'and the correct phrase is a piece of cake.'

'A piece of cake. I will remember that. Now listen very carefully. Premier Stalin spends very little time nowadays in the Kremlin. As I have told you, he is in poor health and has developed a paranoid suspicion of his old associates. He therefore only comes into town for special occasions when it is necessary for him to make a public appearance. The rest of the time he lives and works at his dacha, just north of the city.'

'And that is safer than in the Kremlin?'

'He regards it as so, and he is actually right. In the Kremlin there are people coming and going all the time, and many of them are of course armed. The dacha is small and easily monitored. It is guarded twenty-four hours a day, by a detachment of my people.'

'And he trusts them?'

'He trusts me,' Beria said proudly. He did not seem to realize that he was contradicting what he had said earlier, but then she had never really had any doubt that he was acting less from fear than out of personal ambition.

'Now,' Beria said, 'there are no guards within the house. But he is looked after by a most formidable housekeeper. Her name is Valentina, and she is absolutely devoted to the marshal. No one is allowed to see him, not even members of the Politburo on official business, without her say so.'

'You are saying that she will have to be disposed of?'

'That is certainly possible, but it would be best if you could avoid doing this, as it will make your escape easier if she remains alive. In any event, she must remain alive until you have been admitted to the premier. He is surrounded by alarm buttons, and if he presses one you will not get out alive.'

'I see,' said Anna, remembering Fahri. 'But you think this Valentina will allow me to see him alone?'

'Certainly. Despite his age, he does like to entertain young women from time to time. I shouldn't think any actual sex is involved. In fact, I very much doubt that he can still get an erection. But he likes to look, and even to feel.' He paused to stare at her.

Anna kept her face expressionless.

'Your appointment will be arranged by telephone. However,' he went on, still studying her as he spoke, 'you will have to submit to a search, a very thorough search, before Valentina will allow you into his presence.'

Anna recalled the search she had had to undergo – by a man – before she had been allowed into Hitler's bedroom in his bunker at Rastenberg. She had been engaged on an identical mission, only then she had been carrying a bomb in her bag. It had been very carefully concealed, and was composed of several different components that appeared innocent in themselves. But the man searching her had been more interested in exploring her body than her belongings. The bomb, connected to an elaborate timing system operated by acid eating through glass, had been intended to give her time to escape before the explosion. The scheme had worked very well, even though she had had to share the Fuehrer's bed and wait for him to fall asleep before she was able to assemble the bomb, then set the fuse and leave.

And then the damned thing had failed to explode! Her bag had even been returned to her with it still inside. One of the most traumatic moments of her life. This time she could not fail, because she would be escaping not to friends but to enemies.

'This does not disturb you?'

'It will be an experience,' Anna said bravely.

'Hmm. But this is why you cannot carry a

weapon ... why I had to make sure that you can complete the mission without one.'

Anna nodded.

'Now, when you are alone with the premier, you will, I imagine, wish to complete your task as rapidly as possible; but you must remain with him for some time, otherwise Valentina may be suspicious. Then you will leave the bedroom, close the door, and inform her that the marshal is sleeping and does not wish to be disturbed.'

'You think she will accept that?'

'I see no reason why not. But if you have any doubts, you may, as I have said, dispose of her as well. You will have to use your own judgement, but it will be best if she can see you out, as that would entirely reassure the guards. Then you simply get into your car, which will be waiting for you, and drive away. I shall also be waiting for you; and the moment you return with the information that Marshal Stalin is dead, I will take over. If we are fortunate, his body will not be discovered for some hours, by which time all my people will be in position. They will not, of course, at that time know the reason for the action I am taking – and when the news breaks, they will continue to obey me, because their future will be inextricably bound up with mine.'

'And my future?'

'In the short term, you will simply disappear.'

'I can see that would be most convenient for everyone.'

'My dear Anna, I simply meant that the mysterious woman who visited Premier Stalin on the night he died will disappear. He has carelessly executed so many fathers, husbands, sons and lovers, it has long been inevitable that one day some injured relict would seek revenge. Oh, they will seek his assassin everywhere. But they will never look, they will never be allowed to look, inside this prison, much less this apartment. And once I am in complete command of the country, you will emerge as my right-hand woman. Is that not an exciting prospect?'

'Dazzling!'

'So, are there any questions?'

'Two.'

Beria raised his eyebrows.

'The first is have you considered the possibility that Premier Stalin may take one look at me and recognize me before I can even get close to him?'

'After almost twelve years?'

'I have not actually changed that much. Your man Hamilton, or whatever his name actually is, claimed to do so. And that was after fourteen years.'

'Oh, come now, Anna. Terpolov had never seen you before encountering you in the Bahamas. He was acting entirely on the description given him by my office. By me, in fact.'

'Just checking.'

'In any event,' Beria went on, 'Premier Stalin, as I have explained to you, is showing every
340

sign of senile decay. Not only is his memory going, but he has become extremely short-sighted. The risk is negligible. You said there were two questions?'

'Yes. The other one is when exactly does this operation take place?'

'Why, tonight. The sooner it's done the better, don't you think?'

INCIDENT IN MOSCOW

The car slithered to and fro on the hard-packed snow. 'How soon does the first thaw set in?' Anna asked, innocently, as if she hadn't previously experienced a Russian winter.

'It is only the third of March,' the driver said. 'There will be no thaw until the middle of April, at the very earliest. You are nervous, comrade?'

'Would you not be? I have never met the Premier.'

'Neither have I.' He stopped before ornamental gates, where there waited two fur-clad, green-uniformed men, stamping up and down. He rolled down his window and held out his pass. 'A guest for Premier Stalin. I understand that we are expected.'

The MGB agent peered into the back of the car and shone his torch on Anna's face, which was exposed, as she was wearing her hair up beneath her sable hat. She smiled at him. 'Your name, comrade?'

'Anna Terpolova,' Anna said, as instructed. Presumably this was Beria's idea of a joke; but it suited her well enough, as it meant that if by any chance she went down, her 'brother' would go with her.

He checked his list, then nodded. 'Do you know Comrade Terpolov?'

'I am his sister,' Anna said, proudly.

'Ah.' He signalled his colleague and the gates were opened.

The car rolled through and passed along a short tree-lined drive before reaching the house, which was certainly modest. Here three more MGB men were waiting, one wearing the insignia of an officer. He opened Anna's door for her. 'Comrade Terpolova!'

Anna got out. 'Comrade Captain. The car is to wait.'

'Of course.' He gestured at the short flight of steps and she went up, aware that he was following. 'You understand,' he said, 'that you must be searched.'

'I have never experienced that. Is it very unpleasant?'

He gave a brief knock, then opened the door for her. 'It is ... an experience. Your guest, Valentina.'

Anna stepped into a softly lit, comfortably furnished sitting room, of which the best thing was that it was deliciously warm. And found herself facing just about the biggest woman she had ever seen. Valentina was at least her own height, and had to be about four times her weight. Her face, surrounded by straggly brown hair, might have been handsome once, but had become shrouded by jowls and puffy cheeks. Equally, any pretence she might once have had to a figure had disappeared into a mountain of flesh – and Anna had a feeling that this was muscle rather than fat. Her voice was, nevertheless, surprisingly soft. 'Comrade Terpolova,' she said. 'Welcome.'

'Thank you,' Anna said. 'It is a privilege.'

'Of course. His Excellency is awaiting you. But first, please undress.'

Anna glanced at the captain.

'I am required to be present,' he explained. 'At least until it is established that you are not carrying a weapon.'

'A weapon?' Anna's voice was redolent of alarm.

'I understand,' he said sympathetically. 'But it is a requirement.'

'What he means,' Valentina said, 'is that it is his perquisite. And not all of our guests are as handsome as you. However, it is never a good thing to keep His Excellency waiting.'

As the captain continued to stand beside her, Anna handed him her hat and allowed her hair to tumble down.

'What beautiful hair!' Valentina observed.

'You say the sweetest things.' Anna handed the captain her coat as well.

'And such a lovely coat,' he remarked, stroking the fur.

'It was a gift.' Anna undressed, leaving her boots until last, so that when she bent over to unlace them the effect would be devastating.

'Exquisite,' Valentina said. 'His Excellency will be pleased. Thank you, Comrade Captain.'

'Ah ... yes.' The captain laid the hat and coat on a chair, while never taking his eyes from Anna's body. Then he saluted, and left the room.

'Lecher,' Valentina commented. 'But all men are lechers.' She indicated an inner door, and went towards it.

'Shouldn't I put something on?' Anna asked.

'Why? He will want to look at you.' She gave a little sigh. 'Most of the time that is all he can do.'

'Will you stay? When ... I mean...'

'You are so innocent, my child. Do not be afraid. He will not harm you. I shall wait for you out here. If I fall asleep, wake me up when you are ready to leave.'

Anna reckoned she would make a decision about that afterwards. Valentina escorted her to the door, then knocked and opened it. 'Comrade Anna Terpolova, Your Excellency.'

She glanced at Anna and nodded. Anna took a deep breath and stepped through. Valentina closed the door behind her.

She was in a rather small bedroom, furnished with what looked like a single bed, a couple of armchairs, and a bureau. Stalin stood in front of the bed, wearing a dressing gown over pyjamas.

344

At first glance, he did not look very different to how she remembered him, from the last time she had seen him, in June 1941. There was the same shaggy hair, the same enormous moustache. But both hair and moustache were now quite white. His cheeks, once a trifle florid, were also colourless; and his hands, although still suggesting great strength, trembled. His eyes, once so apparently somnolent, but constantly changing the direction of his gaze as he took in every movement of whoever was facing him, were now dull and devoid of any interest.

Until he saw her. His first gaze was indeed somnolent. Then his eyes suddenly came alive, and his face became suffused with blood. 'You,' he said, 'you...'

'Anna,' she reminded him. 'Twelve years, Josef.'

His arm came up, extended, the hand pointing. 'You...' he said again, and took a step towards her. But as he did so, and she prepared to deliver the fatal blow and then catch him before he could hit the floor, he made a peculiar, quite ghastly, choking sound. His hips seemed to give way and he fell to his knees. But these gave way as well, and the entire house reverberated to the crash.

For just about the first time in her life, Anna could not move. His collapse had been so sudden and so unexpected that she was temporarily incapable of thought. But then she realized that, as Stalin was certainly dead, that could be her salvation.

The door behind her burst open, and she recovered, giving a shriek of horror. Valentina virtually pushed her over as she passed her. 'What happened ... My God, what has happened?'

The crash could well have been heard by the guards. 'I don't know!' Anna wailed, clearly on the verge of a hysterical fit. 'I don't know! He came towards me, and then ... he just fell.'

Valentina peered at the inert figure. Then she said, 'Don't move,' and left the room, closing the door behind her.

Anna had to trust her judgement that letting her live and play the innocent was, for Valentina, the best way out of this totally unexpected development. Now she heard her calling, 'Captain Kharrov! Captain Kharrov! Something terrible has happened. Hurry!'

The captain was there in a few seconds, and when the bedroom door was opened, Anna saw two of his men in the outer doorway. Unarmed as she was, she realized that her choice had been the right one. So she gasped, again, 'He came towards me, and just collapsed.' She allowed her voice to rise an octave. 'He just collapsed!'

Kharrov dropped to his knees beside Stalin, rested two fingers on his neck.

'He must have had a seizure,' Valentina said, her voice shaking. 'We must get a doctor. Quickly.'

'The Premier is dead,' Kharrov pronounced.

'What!' Valentina shrieked. 'Dead? How can that be?'

'Dead!' screamed Anna.

'Dead,' Kharrov repeated, and carefully turned the body over. There was no movement on the front of the dressing gown. The last vestige of colour had faded from Stalin's face, and his eyes stared sightlessly at the ceiling.

'Oh, my God!' Anna fell to her knees, while her brain continued to race. Her assignment was completed ... but *she* had not completed it! She had no idea how Beria would react. She, and therefore he, were absolutely innocent of any crime. But as he was waiting to hear from her that the job was done before going into action, he stood a very good chance of being caught with his pants down, perhaps literally.

Valentina rested her hand on Anna's head. 'It was not your fault.'

'What happened?' Kharrov asked.

'I opened the door and showed Comrade Terpolova in, and...' she looked at Anna.

'Valentina closed the door. The Premier looked at me ... I think he liked me because he smiled, and came towards me...'

'Did he speak?' Kharrov asked.

'He said something, but I'm not sure what. But he was smiling. And then ... he just collapsed.'

'He had a seizure,' Kharrov said. 'The sight of a beautiful woman...'

Anna decided to resume wailing. 'They will say I was responsible. I must go. I must...'

'You are going nowhere, comrade,' Kharrov said.

'But...'

'No one is going to blame you for what has happened, but you are the only witness as to exactly what and how it did happen. Put some clothes on, and sit in that chair and wait.'

'But...'

'What are we to do?' Valentina asked.

'We are going to call Commissar Beria,' Kharrov said. 'He will know what to do.'

Beria arrived within half an hour. He stamped into the room and looked around the frightened faces. 'What is happening? I was told there has been an accident. The Premier...'

'The Premier is dead, Comrade Commissar,' Kharrov said.

Beria stared at him, then stepped past him, and stood in the bedroom doorway. 'Who did this?' He turned back. 'That woman? Who is she? Why is she not under arrest?'

Anna caught her breath. If she had prepared herself for a betrayal at some stage, she had not anticipated it so immediately and so publicly ... or when she was so helpless.

'No, no, Comrade Commissar,' Kharrov protested. 'This is Comrade Terpolova, the sister of Comrade Terpolov, of our department. She came here tonight as the Premier's guest, and was present when he collapsed. She was devastated. Can you not see that she is suffering from shock?'

348

Beria looked at Anna again, then at Valentina.

'That is what happened, Comrade Commissar,' Valentina said. 'I showed Comrade Terpolova into the Premier's bedroom, and he was about to embrace her when he simply collapsed.'

'He must have died instantly,' Kharrov said.

Beria looked at Anna again, his face still sternly impassive. 'Who knows about this?'

'Only us, Comrade Commissar,' Kharrov said. 'And the guards outside.'

'No one must know of it until the Politburo has been summoned. I will do that immediately. Until they are assembled, no one must leave here.'

'What about the woman, sir?'

Again Anna held her breath.

'What about her?'

'The Politburo will wish to see the body,' Kharrov pointed out. 'If they find her here ... well...'

'Do you not think the Politburo are aware of the Premier's habits? But you are right. She should not be here. At the same time, we cannot turn her loose to spread what has happened all over Moscow.' He turned back to Anna. 'You will go to the Lubianka.'

'The Lubianka?' Anna cried. 'What? Me? I have done nothing. They know that. I was just standing there...'

'Stop being hysterical,' Beria snapped. 'You will remain in the Lubianka until you are required as a witness to what happened. But...'

He pinched his lip as a thought apparently occurred to him. 'We do not wish this spread all over the Lubianka, either. Kharrov!'

'Sir.'

'You will take Comrade Terpolova in my car. When you get to the Lubianka, you will take her up to my private apartment and place her there. You will speak to no one, and she will speak to no one. You will lock her in, and return here. And you, young lady, will behave yourself and remain where you are put until I either come for you or send for you.' He stared at her. 'Is that understood?'

Anna allowed herself a little shiver. 'Yes, Comrade Commissar.'

'You will be comfortable here, comrade,' Captain Kharrov assured Anna. 'It is the Commissar's private apartment when he is in Moscow.'

He obviously had no idea that she had spent the entire day there; but in any event, it was her business to continue to present a picture of innocent anxiety, at least until she could again be alone with Beria. So she said, 'What is gong to happen to us, to me, Comrade Captain?'

'Put your trust in the Commissar,' he recommended, and closed the door. She heard the key click in the lock.

So, it appeared, she had to do just that. She had not regained possession of her watch, but there was a clock on the mantelpiece that showed nine forty-five. They had passed quite a few people on their way through the prison, but

350

none of them had revealed any curiosity as to her reason for being there; wearing her sable coat and hat, and not being restrained in any way, she was clearly not a prisoner. The staff in the outer office on the second floor had all gone home.

But, as the captain had said, she was now entirely dependent on Beria's use for her. She could see that he needed her alive to testify as to the exact events of Stalin's death, and thus prove beyond a shadow of a doubt his own innocence of any conspiracy. The question was, did he still have employment for her? Because if not, her situation was grim ... And there was damn all she could do about it. Events had moved far too quickly for there to be any chance of the CIA or MI6 mounting a rescue operation in time. All that was left to her was to go out in a blaze of glory. But even that would be impossible without a weapon.

It had not occurred to her earlier that this might be necessary. Now she hunted through the apartment, looking in every drawer and every cupboard, but the only thing remotely resembling a weapon was one of the knives in the kitchen. This had a six-inch blade and a point; but it was not terribly well balanced and would, in any event, be futile against a man armed with a gun unless she could take him entirely by surprise.

But she took it from its rack anyway, went to the bedroom, which was about fifteen feet square, and used the lipstick provided with her other toiletries – she had no idea what had happened to her purse – to draw a six-inch circle on the wall. Then she stood against the opposite wall and commenced throwing. She had only ever used a knife in combat on half a dozen occasions in her life, but because of her constant practice she was still very proficient. Unfortunately, as she had feared, the knife's lack of balance made it almost useless. But she persevered for an hour – it kept her mind occupied – making a sorry mess of the wall, but eventually landing five out of six throws in the circle.

By then it was nearly eleven, and she was exhausted. She returned to the living room, poured herself a vodka, and sat down to wait, tucking the knife into the left-hand sleeve of her dress. However useless it might be, it at least enabled her to feel that she was not going to be led helplessly to a firing squad.

She finished her drink and actually dozed off – to be awakened by the sound of the door opening.

Beria came in, carefully locking the door behind himself. She observed that he was wearing a pistol holster on his belt. 'Anna? I thought you would be in bed, asleep.'

'I thought I should stay up, Your Excellency, until I had some idea what is happening. May I ask, what is happening? Or going to happen?'

He took the glass from the table beside her chair, went to the bar, and refilled it, pouring one for himself. Then he sat opposite her. 'First, you tell me. What did happen between you and the Premier? How did you do it? The doctors could find not a mark on his body, save those made when he struck the floor.'

'As I told you, sir, I did not do it. I never touched him. I did not have to.'

'You are not telling me that you can kill by remote control?'

'Would that I could. But as I warned you might happen, Marshal Stalin recognized me on sight. I don't know whether he thought I was a ghost come from hell, or whether he just thought I had returned to complete the assignment I had been given in 1941. But he sort of gaped at me, took a step towards me, and just collapsed.'

'What a remarkable thing! And he must have died instantly. Now we must wait for the results of the post-mortem. That will be carried out this morning.'

'What are you going to do?'

'I have already done it. At least, I have set the wheels in motion.'

'But ... the Politburo...?'

'I had them summoned immediately, took them to the dacha and showed them the body. The doctors were already there. As I supposed would be the case, they were all profoundly shocked, and there is to be a meeting later on today to determine a successor. Then they went off, presumably to make plots and deals amongst themselves. So I returned here and instructed my people to surround the Kremlin, place the entire Politburo under arrest, and confine the army to barracks. That is happening now. By dawn the city, and then the country, will be in my hands, and I will be premier.'

'Will the Politburo confirm that?'

His smile was sinister. 'They are hardly likely to do otherwise with my people guarding every door.'

'Then I congratulate you, sir.' She tensed her muscles, as she realized that the crisis, her crisis, might be about to recede. But his pistol was still holstered, and she had the knife. 'And...?'

'Ah, yes. You. You did not complete your assignment.' This time his smile was friendly as he watched her expression. 'But then, you did not have to. And things have worked out better than I could have hoped. I had nothing to do with the premier's death, and now I am saving the nation from anarchy and perhaps even civil war. I think you have brought me luck, and may continue to do so. So we will continue with our original plan. You will remain here until I am firmly in control. That should be by this evening. Then you will remain in the background, serving as my personal assistant. There are a great number of things you may be able to do for me.' He squeezed her arm. 'Now, you have had an exhausting night. Go to bed and get some sleep.'

Anna slowly released her breath. Could it really be all over, with just her escape to be organized at a later date? She almost felt some affection for him. 'And you, sir?'

'I must remain here. I am expecting progress reports. I will see you later, Anna.'

'As you wish, sir.' Enveloped in a sense of unreality, she went into the bedroom, closed the door, and undressed, laying the knife on the bedside table. She used the bathroom, and then was asleep in seconds; there were no more decisions that had immediately to be made.

She slept heavily, although vaguely disturbed from time to time by the jangling of the telephone in the next room. And then was awakened, very suddenly, by the sound of gunfire near at hand.

She scrambled out of bed, ran to the door, and pulled it open. Beria was shouting into the telephone, almost incoherently. He turned at her entry, lips drawn back in a wolfish snarl. 'Bitch!' he shouted. 'Foul thing from the pit of hell!'

'What are you saying?' she cried.

'You have betrayed me! You have betrayed Russia!'

'How am I supposed to have done that?'

'Fool that I was to trust you, to leave you alone in this apartment. To call Kruschev and tell him my plans.'

'Comrade Commissar, I have no idea what you are talking about.'

'You did not know that the army was alerted? That my men who went to confine the army to barracks would be overwhelmed? That they are surrounding this building now? Well, you will not live to enjoy your treachery.' He reached for his holster. But Anna, anticipating things reaching this stage, had moved closer to the table, and now hurled the large pot of pepper into his face.

He gasped, stepped backwards, and tripped over a chair, hitting the floor heavily. Before he could recover, she had crossed the room in two strides. She could have killed him then – but her lightning reactions were already warning her that she might need him in order to get out of the Lubianka, so she merely grasped the wrist that was scrabbling for the gun, twisted it so that he gave a squeal of pain, and drew the pistol herself before standing away from him.

His pince-nez had come off, and he blinked at her, his face ashen with terror. 'Anna!' he gasped. 'I saved your life.'

'Not my life, Comrade Commissar. You preserved something you felt might be of use to you.'

Then there was a banging on the outer door.

'Now,' he said, 'if you kill me...'

'Get up,' she commanded. 'And go in there.'

He scrambled to his feet, glanced at her face and the gun, and went into the bedroom.

'In there.' She gestured at the wardrobe.

Another glance, then he obeyed. 'I can save your life, again, Anna!' he said. 'I will save your life.'

The banging on the door was becoming more

insistent. 'We can talk about that later,' Anna said, and stepped up to him, hitting him on the head with the butt of the pistol. He collapsed without a sound, half into the cupboard. His legs were still outside, so she bundled these in as well, and closed and locked the door. Then she turned towards her clothes, and heard a splintering sound as the outer door was forced.

There was no time to dress. As she looked at the bedroom door, this in turn was thrown open. It was Vera Berisova, accompanied by two women and two men. All were armed, but also terrified.

'The army are in the building,' Vera gasped. 'They are shooting everybody. They are...' She realized that she was addressing not her commander but a naked Anna, and Anna was already firing.

The five people went down in a welter of blood, the echoes reverberating around the apartment; not one of them had got off a shot in reply. Anna stepped over them and went to the outer door, listened to the growing noise seeping up the stairs: gun shots, most of it automatic fire, shouts, screams, curses ... It was time for another quick decision. Several, in fact, governed by the single overwhelming fact that not even she could take on the Red Army, but also by the realization that if this was, as it had to be, a counter-coup, Beria would be their ultimate target ... and she had Beria!

Continuing to use her nudity as a weapon, she

left the apartment and went next door. The outer office was empty, presumably because four of the people she had just shot had been members of the staff. She went through to Beria's office, riffled through the drawers of his desk, and found her purse. From this she took her passport, but discarded everything else; she could see no profit from trying to use the Walther against a sub-machine-gun.

She returned to the apartment and closed the door. Obviously it would be unwise for her to be armed in any way when the soldiers came in, or they might shoot her on sight, so she dropped the pistol in the midst of the dead bodies. Equally obviously, she needed to seem as ordinary and vulnerable as any woman would be in her position, and that meant being as modest as possible. She pulled on her knickers, and the door opened.

Hamilton stared at the five dead bodies, then at her. 'You did this?'

'It seemed like a good idea, Comrade Terpolov.' He was carrying a pistol, and was a good ten feet away. She could not possibly reach him before being shot. She backed against the bedside table.

'Where is Commissar Beria?'

'In a safe place.'

He glanced around the room, then came back to her. 'You have played your last trick, Countess. Tell me where the commissar is hiding, or I will shoot you in the stomach. I do not think even you will enjoy that.'

Anna stared at him, and the gun came up. But she had closed her fingers on the blade of the knife, and now she swung her arm to hurl it with all her force, at the same time stepping to one side. The bullet smashed into the wall behind where she had been standing; the knife thudded into Hamilton's chest. He fell backwards with a shriek, hitting the floor heavily.

Anna watched him while she put on her dress, but he was clearly dying; blood was frothing from his lips. Now he gasped, 'A knife?'

'That too,' Anna agreed, and sat on the bed to pull on her boots.

She had just finished lacing them when the door opened again, and she faced six soldiers, armed with tommy-guns. 'Oooh!' she screamed, rising like a startled pheasant.

The men stared at her, totally taken aback, then parted to allow another man through. This man was short and heavily built, with a bald head and pugnacious features. He was also, to her surprise, in a lounge suit, rather than uniform, and was unarmed. He regarded her for several seconds, then asked, 'Who the fuck are you?'

'Me?' Anna kept her voice high. 'My name is Anna Kelly.'

'Kelly? You are English?'

'I am American. My parents are Irish.'

He gazed at her, and she gestured at the table. 'My passport is there.'

He went to the table, picked it up and looked at it, and laid it down again. 'What happened to

359

these people?'

'They burst in here, shouting and screaming, then one seemed to hit another and they started shooting and knifing each other ... It was terrifying, I thought they were going to kill me. But you came in the nick of time.'

Another long stare, while Anna assumed her most innocent expression. 'Where is Commissar Beria?'

Anna pointed at the wardrobe, from where there were coming vague sounds.

'What is he doing in there?'

'I put him there.'

'You...' He looked at his aides for an explanation, and got none. 'Who are you?'

'Anna Kelly.'

'You said that. But what are you doing here?'

'I was kidnapped.'

He sat down, continuing to gaze at her. 'You were kidnapped. By whom?'

'By Commissar Beria.'

'Why?'

'Well...' Anna licked her lips. 'To have sex with me.'

'What?'

'I came here a couple of years ago, with a trade delegation. I met the commissar at a party. Apparently he fell in love ... well, he wanted to have sex with me, from the moment he saw me. So he organized that I should be kidnapped while on a visit to London a couple of weeks ago, and I was brought here bound and gagged.'

'And?'

'Yes, sir. He forced me.'

The man looked at his aides, who by now had been joined by several others. 'This man, this lecherous creature, would rule Russia! So you put him in that cupboard? How did you do that?'

'I hit him on the head.'

'In the middle of the Lubianka. How did you hope to get away with that?'

'Well, sir, he came back in the small hours of this morning, boasting that Marshal Stalin was dead and that he intended to take over the state. I asked if he didn't need the authority of the Politburo to do that, and he laughed and said he intended to arrest and execute the lot of them. I realized that he was about to commit a great crime, but there was nothing I could do about it here, surrounded by his people. And then this morning there was the sound of gunfire, and he burst in and said a counter-coup was being attempted. I realized that I had the chance to help Russia, to help the world; so when he turned his back on me, I hit him and put him in the cupboard. Did I do the right thing, sir?'

'You certainly did the right thing, comrade. But you took a terrible risk. If we had not come ... You would have done better to kill him.'

'Kill him?' Anna gasped. 'Oh, sir, I couldn't have done that. I have never killed anyone in my life. I prayed for you to come, and you did.'

'Prayed,' he said thoughtfully. 'And I came. Let us see what we have here. Open that wardrobe.'

'He will be very angry,' Anna suggested.

'Ha ha. He is going to be angrier yet.'

The door was opened, and Beria, who had been trying to get up, fell out. He turned on his knees, glared at them, his face suffused, and identified Anna. 'That bitch,' he shouted. 'Arrest her.'

'No, no,' Anna's new friend said. 'It is you who are under arrest, comrade.'

'You fool,' Beria snarled. 'Do you not know who that is? That is the Countess von Widerstand.'

'The Countess ... who is this person? Are you a countess, comrade?'

'Do I look like a countess?' Anna asked.

'I have never met a countess,' he confessed. 'Who is he talking about?'

'I have no idea.'

He looked at his people, and they shrugged.

'She is a war criminal,' Beria shouted. 'A mass murderess. She is the most wanted woman in the world. Premier Stalin...'

'Premier Stalin is dead. And the only criminal here is you. Take him downstairs. Lock him in one of his cells.'

The soldiers dragged Beria from the room, still shouting.

'What will happen to him?' Anna asked.

'He will be tried, convicted, and executed.'

'Gosh! And what will happen to me?'

'Ah! Technically, I should hold you here as a witness to his crimes. But that is not really necessary. His treason is self-evident. To add

362

charges of kidnap and rape would merely muddy the water. Nor do I feel that it would be in the best interests of the state. You have just done the Soviet Union a great service. You may even have saved us from the horrors of civil war. But you are not Russian, and it would be bad publicity to have to admit to the world that our state was saved by a foreigner. I am assuming that you will not rush off to a newspaper and sell your story?'

'I would not dream of it,' Anna said. 'Do you think I wish to confess to the world that I have been raped?'

He smiled. 'And we would, in any event, dismiss your story as the ravings of a mad Irishwoman. But we do owe you a great deal, and the least we can do is repatriate you as quickly and quietly as possible. Where would you like to go?'

'Miami.'

He nodded. 'I will arrange a flight.'

'Without, if possible, touching down in England.'

He raised his eyebrows.

'I am Irish, you see.'

'Ah! I think there is more to you than meets the eye, young lady. But we will arrange it through a French airline. How soon will you be ready to leave?'

'Just give me the time to pack my suitcase.'

He nodded. 'One of my aides will wait for you.' He got up and went to the door. 'It has been a privilege to meet you.'

'And for me, Your Excellency. May I ask your name?'

'My name is Nikita Kruschev.'

'Kruschev ... I will remember it.'

'You will hear of it again, I promise. When I am ruler of Russia.'

Donald Petersen looked up from the newspaper he was reading, seated behind the desk in his bookstore, and did a double take as he surveyed the tall, soberly dressed woman with the sable coat slung over her shoulders. 'Anna? Good God!'

'Shouldn't I be Anna?'

He cast a glance around the shop. There were half a dozen potential customers browsing, but none was very close. 'It's just that I was told...'

'That I am retiring. That is correct. I am on my way home from my last assignment now. But it so happens that I have been robbed of my purse and all my money. So I need your assistance, for the last time.'

'*You* have been robbed?'

'I was careless, I relaxed too soon. Will you help me?'

'Of course we'll help you, Anna. What do you need?'

'Well, first, there's the taxi that brought me from the airport. The driver needs paying.'

'I'll take care of it.'

'Thank you. Then, I don't know what time it is, but I imagine I've missed the last flight to Nassau.'

Petersen had worked with her for six years. 'You, Anna, don't know what time it is?'

She showed him her naked wrist.

'Shit! Not that lovely German thing?'

'I'm afraid so.'

'It was solid gold, wasn't it?'

'Yes, it was.'

'What a goddamn'd shame. Well, yes, I guess you've missed the last flight to Nassau. You'd have made it if you'd checked in right away instead of coming down here.'

'Donald,' Anna said, 'I don't have any money.'

'Ah! You want...'

'A flight out tomorrow morning.'

'I guess we can manage that.'

'That means I'll need a hotel for tonight.'

He sighed. 'OK, you got it. I'd better see to the taxi.'

'There's just one more thing.'

'What?'

'We were talking about the watch I no longer have.'

'Anna, there is no way you are going to be able to replace a Junghans in Miami.'

'I know that. I'll settle for a Rolex.'

'You want a Rolex!'

'A gold Rolex.'

'You have to be kidding.'

'I always wear gold,' Anna pointed out.

'Anna,' he almost wailed, 'you're talking about five thousand dollars.'

'So take it out of your emergency account.

Listen, if Joe doesn't authorize it, send me the bill and I'll send you a cheque. Now, there's just one thing more...'

'Oh, my God! What now?'

'I need a passport.'

'How did you get here without a passport?'

'I have one, in the name of Anna Kelly. But I can't use that to get into the Bahamas. I'm too well known.'

'So where is your real passport?'

'On the cay, I hope. Come on, Donald, I know you keep a stack of spare passports, including British ones. It doesn't have to be perfect, just something to wave at Immigration as I go through.'

He sighed. 'I'll need a photo.'

'Then let's do it. As soon as you've paid the taxi.'

'Mrs Bartley!' Charles beamed. 'You had a good trip?'

'It had it's moments,' Anna said. She had been to the bank before coming on to the hotel, made sure that the certified cheque had been paid in, cashed a counter cheque for herself, and then bought herself a new purse as well as a summer dress with a matching sun hat and a pair of dark glasses. Incongruously, in the Nassau heat, her sable was draped across her arm; the hat was in her suitcase. 'Can you squeeze me in for lunch?'

'Of course, ma'am. You staying the night?'

'I'm afraid not. I think I should be getting

back, I've been away rather a long time.'

'Yes, ma'am. You want me to call Mr Bartley?'

'Mr Bartley is back?'

'Oh, yes, ma'am. He been back over a week.'

'That's good. But I think I'll surprise him. Can you charter me a boat for this afternoon?'

'No problem, ma'am. And lunch?'

'Why, Charles, I'll have avocado, fillet – medium, with carrots and beans – and a bottle of Batailley. I'll eat on the terrace.'

'Yes, *ma'am*. Welcome home, ma'am.'

'It's good to be home, Charles.'

'You sure you know the way through here, ma'am?' Hawkins the charter skipper was anxious as he surveyed the ripples of white to either side.

'Of course I do.' Anna stood beside him at the helm. 'I live here. Port a point.'

He obeyed, and a few minutes later they were nosing along the outside of the dock; with *Fair Girl* moored inside, there was no room for another boat. 'Thank you,' she said, and paid him the agreed fare.

'You sure you going be all right, ma'am? This place got big dogs, maneaters they say.'

'I know. They're my dogs. Now, you sure you can find your way back out?'

He lifted her suitcase on to the dock. 'Well, ma'am, I reckon I going along a bit on the inside. They got a better passage lower down.'

'Good thinking. Well, thank you again and

have a good trip.'

She left the suitcase on the dock to be picked up by Tommy, put on her sun hat, and carried her coat on her arm as she walked slowly up the path, listening to the ever-present rustle of the casuarinas and the faint rumble of surf from the north beach. Then there was a ferocious barking, as the dogs raced down the path, teeth bared, and came to a sudden halt as she approached them; then advanced again, tails wagging, gurgling their pleasure.

Anna hugged and kissed them both. 'You darlings! Have you been good?'

More gurglings. Anna looked up the slope and saw Tommy coming towards her. 'Miss Anna? Is really you?' Slowly he came towards her.

'Did you think I was a ghost, Tommy?'

'Well, Mr Bartley was saying...'

'He was always a pessimist.' She embraced him. 'All well?'

'Oh, yes, ma'am. Save, well, nothing ain't well if you ain't here.'

'I'm here now. And I'm not going anywhere again, ever. Do you think you could bring my bag up to the house?'

'You got it, ma'am.'

She looked past him at Clive, standing at the top of the slope. 'Anna? My God, Anna!' He ran almost as fast as the dogs, took her in his arms, and kissed her again and again. 'My darling, darling girl ... we thought...'

'That I was done for? So many people have thought that, so often, throughout my life.'

'But how...?'

'It's a long story. I'll tell you all about it.'

He held her hand as they walked up the slope, the dogs padding behind them. 'But ... your coat? We took it from Fahri's hall.'

'I was there, remember. This is a new one.'

'In addition to getting out of Russia, you managed to pick up a new sable?'

'I had a friend,' Anna said modestly.

'And that watch? It looks like...'

'It is, a Rolex.'

'A gold Rolex?'

'Another friend.'

'Oh, Anna ... if you knew...'

'I know you stopped that ship.'

'You mean you *were* there?'

'I was in the engine-room bilge.'

'My God! But...?'

'It wasn't so bad. Save when I could hear you standing immediately above me, and couldn't get to you. I was bound and gagged, you see.'

'The bastards! I wanted to impound the ship and take it apart. But the police received a radio call informing them that I was acting without authority, and insisted on calling off the search.'

'Baxter?'

'I think Billy was almost as upset as I was. It was a government decision. Those bastards can't think beyond their parliamentary majority, and by killing Fahri you had become too much of a liability. As far as they're concerned, you're dead or in a gulag, not to be thought of again.'

'That can't be bad. So my immunity is gone?'

'No. They wanted to revoke it, but I pointed out that if you were dead there was no point. I also told them that if they did, I was going to the newspapers with the full story of your life and your employment by the government.'

'That couldn't have made you very popular.'

'It didn't. I was sacked.'

'What!'

'Well, I was invited to resign.'

'Oh, Clive. I'm so terribly sorry. But if you thought I was dead...'

'That was logic. My heart told me that one day I'd see you stepping ashore on to that dock.'

'Oh, my darling! But your career...'

'The only career I want for the rest of my life is caring for you.'

'And fathering my children.'

'I would love that. If you want it.'

'More than anything else in the world. Clive ... do you know why I took on the Fahri job?'

'Joe explained.'

'And he wouldn't help?'

'He was in the same position I was. The State Department couldn't risk the diplomatic fall-out of trying to get you out of Russia, which would have meant admitting that you had been working for them all these years, and also that you committed a murder for them in England. But you still have your immunity.'

'Well, then...' She ran up the steps to embrace

370

her mother.

'Oh, Anna!' Jane held her close. 'Is it really you?'

'Really and truly. Papa!'

He hugged her, then released her so that she could embrace Desirée. 'What have we got for dinner?'

'I got grouper steaks, Miss Anna.'

'Oh, splendid. May we have it a little early?'

'You got it, ma'am.'

'Isis! Sweetheart!' She scooped the cat from the floor. 'Now, Papa, what have you got?'

'I have a bottle of Veuve Clicquot on ice.'

'Then let's have it.'

Jane sat beside her on the settee. 'Anna ... are you really home?'

'I'm home, Mama,' Anna said. 'For ever and ever and ever.'

EPILOGUE

Anna drank champagne. We had moved up-stairs to be in the cool of the naya. 'The trouble with for ever,' she said, 'is that for ever is such a very long time. Happiness is a very transient business, even in the most perfect circum-stances, because it depends on so many factors.'

'Such as Fair Cay?' I ventured.

'Such as Fair Cay. It was Paradise, for twenty-five years. In that time Clive and I had two lovely children, and grew to know and love each other more and more. But of course, in twenty-five years...' She sighed. 'Papa died first. I think those years in prison took more out of him than he would ever admit. But Mama soon followed. Then the dogs. They were sixteen. Isis lived to be twenty.'

'You never replaced them?'

'They were my friends. One doesn't go into a shop and buy new friends. One remembers them as they were. Then Desirée. Then, in 1978, Clive went. He had been ill for some years. Elias had long gone, so that left Tommy and me. Tommy was by then well into his sixties, and I was getting towards that figure. Oh, my family

372

visited me as often as they could, but they had their own lives to live, their own way to make. There was nothing for them in the Bahamas, certainly after independence. And by then, too, everyone who knew anything about me was dead. Billy Baxter, Joe Andrews ... I don't know for certain about Jerry, but as he was a couple of years older than me, I imagine he's gone by now.' She smiled. 'Even Kruschev is dead.'

'And Beria got the chop.'

'Yes, in July 1953. It must have been a very long four months for him before he finally faced the firing squad. Even Charles was dead. Anyway, Tommy used to come up to the house every night for a drink before dinner, and we were sitting there one night and suddenly we looked at each other. I don't think we said anything: we just knew our time was up. I gave him a golden handshake, a few instructions as to selling the chickens, and left.'

'Just like that? What happened to the cay? Did you sell it?'

'No, I still own it. But I've never been back. Although I intend to, when I'm dead, to be buried with Mama and Papa and Clive, and the animals. The kids know that. But until then ... after thirty years there'd be too many ghosts. I imagine by now it's a real Sleeping Beauty island. I like to think that some day someone will visit it and say, Hell, I could turn this into paradise.' She sighed. 'So I settled most of my money on my children, keeping only enough capital to provide me with a comfortable old

age, and looked around and found this place.'

'What made you choose Spain?'

'Two reasons. My family is all settled in Europe. Mainly in England, and as you know I can never return there. But travel nowadays is so easy they can drop in whenever they feel like it, or when they feel I might feel like it. The other is that Spain is full of ex-pats, quite a few of whom have pasts they'd rather keep to themselves. So I could lose myself in the crowd, and live with my books and my memories. Anyway, there you have it. Will you tell my story, Christopher?'

'I certainly will.'

'Without comment, criticism or prejudice?'

'Yes.'

'But I'm so sorry to have reached the end. It's been such fun remembering it all again.' She squeezed my hand. *'But of course you are going to see me again, Christopher. You have become my principal link with my past. I expect you to come and visit me at least once a year from now on. And now, do you know, I feel like anther bottle of champagne. Encarna,'* she called.

There was no reply.

She went to the door into the lounge. 'Encarna,' she called again. *And then her voice changed, and became the crack of a whip. 'Down! Flat!'*

She had never spoken to me like that before, although I suspected that she had used that tone often enough during her career. I obeyed without hesitation. As I fell to the floor, I heard

374

several sharp cracks, and the sound of shattering glass, accompanied by a dull thud. I looked up and saw Anna, also on the floor, a crumpled heap. There was no blood to be seen, but... 'Anna?' I whispered. 'Oh, my God, Anna!'

I heard a soft footfall, and turned my head, still lying flat on the floor. I felt the hair on the back of my head begin to prickle; then the prickle seemed to spread to my entire body. I was looking at an exquisite pair of bare feet, thrust into sandals. And as I raised my head, my gaze followed a pair of the longest and most perfectly shaped legs I had ever seen, before reaching a pair of shorts enclosing narrow hips and thighs. Above, a loose shirt fluttered slightly in the breeze, which flattened the material against full breasts; and above them there was a classically beautiful face, framed in a long skein of golden hair. It was as if I had, magically, been transported back to Berlin in 1945: this girl was certainly no older than twenty-five, and she was carrying a Walther PPK in her right hand. Now, in a soft voice that was like liquid silver, she exclaimed, 'Damnation!'

I could not stop myself looking from her to the body on the floor.

'No,' she said, 'I am not a reincarnation, Mr Nicole, although I have been told that I take after my grandmother.' She knelt, rested two fingers on Anna's neck, and sighed.

'I don't understand,' I said. 'You know my name?'

'Of course I know your name. I have kept you under surveillance every moment you have been in this house.'

Slowly I pushed myself up. 'But...'

'I think by now you know enough of Grandma's methods, and indeed, her approach to life, to understand that she never took an unnecessary risk. Do you think she would have allowed you, or any man, into this house without adequate support?'

'You mean you live here? And I never saw you?'

'I do not live here, Mr Nicole. I live in London. But I happened to be spending the summer with my grandmother when you first telephoned, and she told me to keep an eye on you. But never to let you see me.' She gave a smile that was absolutely a copy of Anna's. 'Grandma was a very feminine person, as you may have observed. I suspect that she felt my presence might distract you from her.'

'But when we went out together...?'

She nodded. 'I was against it. But by then she had come to trust you.'

'And now she is dead. While...'

'While I was in the garden. Because I, too, had come to trust you. I felt she was quite safe while in here with you. And anyway, I was sure Encarna would call me if I was needed. But those thugs must have surprised her. So I didn't even know they were in the house until she managed to get the back door open and call.'

'Those men!' I looked through the door at the

376

two bodies lying on the floor, surrounded by spreading blood. Both had pistols in their hands, and both had bullet wounds in the head. I turned to her, my mouth open.

'Grandma taught me everything she knew,' she said. 'Do you know these men?'

'No. But if they followed me here ... that means I am responsible for Anna's death!'

'I do not think so. You have been here for three hours. If they followed you, they took a very long time to come in. In any event, Grandma died of a heart attack.'

'How can you be sure?'

'Because her heart has been weak for a long time. After the sort of life she led, I suppose that's not surprising. We had been warned that it could happen at any moment. That is why Mother insisted one of us always be here.'

'But the shock...'

'The slightest shock would have done it. It had nothing to do with you. I would say that these men, like you, have been tracking her for years, but not to interview her.' She stooped and turned one of the men over, felt in his breast pocket, found his wallet, and looked at the driving licence. 'Edel.'

'My God!'

She looked up. 'You know the name?'

'Edel was the name of the atomic scientist turned traitor who Anna executed for MI6 in Argentina, in 1949.'

'Did he have children?'

'There was a wife and son. Anna actually paid

for their passages back to their home in Den-
mark. This must be the son.'

'I don't think so. How old was the son when
his father died?'

'I think she told me he was six.'

'This man isn't sixty-six. I would say he is not
more than thirty-five. He must be the grandson.
Two generations, living in hate. That is very
sad. Sad for all of us.' She stood up. 'Now, I
think you had better leave.'

'But ... what about...?'

'Encarna and I will dispose of these two
bodies. Then arrange for Grandma to be em-
balmed, before she is taken to ... well, the place
where she wishes to be buried. Please don't ask
me where that is, because I'm not going to tell
you.'

I didn't have to, because I knew. 'But may I
ask you one thing more?'

'Yes?'

'You said that Anna taught you everything she
knew. Does that mean that, well, you...'

'Yes, Mr Nicole. That is what it means. Now
let me ask you something. Did you know my
grandmother when she was a girl?'

'Unfortunately, no. But I feel, after meeting
you, that I know her now. As she was.'

'You say the sweetest things. Now go and tell
her story. I wish we could have met in happier
circumstances.'

'So do I.' I looked down at Anna, for the last
time. 'To think of Anna dead...'

'But Anna is not dead, Mr Nicole. Anna can

never die. Is she not a reincarnation of Eury-
nome, the Goddess of All Things, who spends
eternity dancing across the heavens in a glow of
light, creating and destroying as she thinks fit?
She is up there now, smiling at us. And do you
know, I would say her smile is warmest when
she looks at you. Goodbye, Mr Nicole. We shall
not meet again.'

I turned to the door, but stopped to ask her
one last question. 'Won't you at least tell me
your name?'

'Why,' she said, smiling, 'my name is Anna.'